SHADOWMASTER

SUSAN KRINARD

Published in Great Britain 2014
by Mills & Boon, an imprint of Harlequin (UK) Limited,
Eton House, 18-24 Paradise Road, Richmond, Surrey, TW9 1SR

© 2014 Susan Krinard

ISBN: 978 0 263 91388 0

89-0314

Harlequin (UK) Limited's policy is to use papers that are natural, renewable and recyclable products and made from wood grown in sustainable forests. The logging and manufacturing processes conform to the legal environmental regulations of the country of origin.

Printed and bound in Spain
by Blackprint CPI, Barcelona

Susan Krinard has been writing paranormal romance for nearly twenty years. With *Daysider* she began a series of vampire paranormal romances, the Nightsiders series, for the Mills & Boon® Nocturne™ line.

Sue lives in Albuquerque, New Mexico, with her husband, Serge, her dogs, Freya, Nahla and Cagney, and her cats, Agatha and Rocky. She loves her garden, nature, painting and chocolate…not necessarily in that order.

With thanks to Lucienne and Leslie,
who have never given up.

Chapter 1

"We don't know who he is," the director said. "We know it's a he, and we believe he goes by the name *'Drakon.'* There are certain unconfirmed reports that he has connections in the Fringe, here in the city. We don't know where he's hiding, if he's working alone or if he has contacts within this very agency."

Aegis Director of Operatives Julia Chan swept the table with her gaze, pausing to search each pair of eyes locked on hers. Phoenix was only one of many, but she felt as if Director Chan were looking into her soul. Weighing strengths and weaknesses. Going over a mental checklist of successes and failures in Phoenix's relatively brief and undemanding career—mentally studying her psych eval, deciding if the agent's abilities and qualifications were up to the task.

No doubt the director was wondering if an agent who was only half-dhampir like herself—only a quarter Opir and three-quarters human—and had never had a major mission in the field, could possibly be capable enough for a job that could mean life or death for the largest Enclave of humans on the West Coast of the former United States of America.

Then the director's gaze moved on, and she nodded brusquely. "You'll have full, detailed reports on your tabs. Study them thoroughly. We're sending only one agent during the initial stage of the search. We're betting that the assassin is heterosexual, and like most Opiri, he'll naturally be attracted to dhampir blood." She swept the audience with a cold stare. "Let me be very frank—you may have to use sex as a way of getting to him, not to mention your blood. As always, if you feel or believe you're not up to the task of using every personal asset to find this killer before he brings down our government, tell me now. You'll receive no black mark on your record for declining, under the circumstances. And, as always, every word spoken in this room is strictly confidential. Any leaks will be investigated and the traitor will face the harshest possible penalties."

She closed her tab, gathered up a few printed notes and left the room.

"Well, that was clear enough," Yoko said close to Phoenix's ear as they rose from their seats at the table. "We always knew what we were getting into when we joined Aegis."

"Joined?" Phoenix said, shaking her head. "Since when did you dhampires have any choice in the matter? You can't be left to run loose in society, half-vampires that you are."

Yoko took Phoenix's arm, her catlike pupils dilating. "You talk as if you don't think you're one of us. Just because you *look* fully human…"

"I inherited my looks from my mother, eyes and all. And she didn't go through what most of yours did. She wasn't taken during the War by some bloodsucker against her will."

"No. But she married one of the first dhampires ever to be identified," Yoko said, her round face suddenly serious. "Even the people who adopted him as a kid before the Awakening had no idea where he came from. At least most of us knew our real mothers."

"But not the Nightsiders who made them pregnant," Phoenix said, brutally blunt. "Who abandoned them as soon as they were done with them. I had a complete family to begin with, even though no one outside a few in the old government knew my dad was working against the bloodsuckers during the War."

"And kept on working for us after," Yoko said, "even when he could have retired with honor."

"Do you really believe that?" Phoenix asked, unable to hide the bitterness that never quite went away. "In the end, he left us like any true dhampir's *'father.'*"

"He died on a mission. He was a hero, and everyone knows it."

A hero, Phoenix thought. The kind she could never be. And all her anger, all her hurt couldn't change that fact.

"Aegis was everything to him, more important than his own wife and child. I'd rather have a live father than a dead hero."

For once, her voluble friend had nothing to say. It wasn't as if this were the first time the subject had come up between them, but sometimes—when Phoenix least expected it—the anger came boiling up again.

Oh, Aegis had provided well for the widowed wife and fatherless child. And once Mother died, the agency had become Phoenix's only family: deciding, after much evaluation, that the half-dhampir child was worth training, though her abilities were constantly tested and weighed against those of every full dhampir, the agents sworn to maintain the Armistice between humans and Nightsiders by every means possible. Unauthorized combat, ambush, deceit, submission, sex. Whatever it took.

Because only dhampires, with their almost catlike eyes, could see by night like full-blooded Opiri, could move nearly as fast and were nearly as strong, could meet Opir operatives in the Zone with some hope of survival.

But this wasn't the Zone. An Opir assassin was inside the walls of San Francisco Enclave, ready to kill the mayor and foment chaos in the city at a time when the volatile politic situation could be set off by the smallest spark. The forthcoming election had the two factions—the mayor's and Senator Patterson's—at daggers drawn. And every report confirmed that the bloodsuckers were preparing for a major offensive.

And yet the mayor insisted that peace could be maintained and renewed. Mayor Aaron Shepherd. The man Phoenix had once loved. And had thought loved her.

Yoko seemed to read her mind. "I know," she said. "This is kind of personal for you."

Phoenix didn't encourage further conversation on the subject, so Yoko moved on. "'Contacts within this agency,'" she quoted Chan. "If they think that's even possible, it's bad. Could make this job a suicide mission."

"So what's new?" Phoenix asked as she and Yoko stopped by the mess hall for coffee and sandwiches. "I'd go in a heartbeat if I thought they'd pick me."

Yoko grabbed a steaming mug and chose a table. The room was nearly deserted. Once they were seated, Yoko looked around and leaned close to Phoenix again.

"Maybe you didn't notice how long Chan stared at you," she said. "Maybe they haven't sent you on any really dangerous missions. They haven't been able to look past their prejudice. But you're still Titus's daughter."

Titus's daughter, Phoenix thought. That was the thing, wasn't it?

"I don't want any lives in my hands," Phoenix said, sipping the nearly scalding coffee and welcoming the almost painful burning on her tongue.

"But you don't have to cut yourself off from everyone," Yoko said, laying her hand on Phoenix's wrist. "I worry about you. You don't go anywhere or see anyone. Except me, of course."

Phoenix smiled. "Stop worrying, Yoko. I keep busy. I don't feel deprived."

"Look, Shepherd was one guy. There *are* guys who don't care what we are, whether it shows or not. They won't try to keep you hidden. Like Abdul...we're happy together. Might not last forever, but almost nothing does."

No, Phoenix thought. *Nothing does. Not even life.*

"Not interested," she said. "I don't like having those kinds of ties to weigh me down."

"Because no matter how much you may complain about our being forced to join Aegis because of what we are," Yoko said, "you live for the work, like your father. That's another reason why Chan didn't leave you off the list."

"Or they just think it would be safer to send in someone who doesn't have dhampir eyes. A lot easier than performing surgery on one of you."

Yoko bit her lower lip. "It all depends on their tactics. A full dhampir could really tempt the assassin, and the Agency doesn't seem to think your blood would be addictive. But if Aegis wants to keep a low profile..."

"I guess we'll have to wait and see," Phoenix said.

Uncharacteristically quiet, Yoko gazed into the depths of her cooling coffee. "Phoenix...can you be objective if they assign you to this mission?"

"Whatever my past relationship with Shepherd," Phoenix said, drawing herself up very straight, "I know what he means to the Enclave. He's holding everything together, giving the people courage and hope. He wants to end the mandatory deportation of minor lawbreakers to Erebus."

"Which the bloodsuckers will never agree to," Yoko said. "They have to have serfs, after all."

"But he's against it, and that's a very popular position now that the Enforcers are scraping the bottom of the barrel to find citizens to deport," Phoenix said. "I respect him for that."

"And the alternative is Senator Patterson, who wants to crack down on so-called 'offenders' even more."

"What else can you expect from a guy who used to be commissioner of the Enforcement Bureau?" Phoenix asked.

"The elections are going to be ugly this year, no matter how civil they try to be."

"That's why they have to choose just the right operative," Phoenix said.

"You may not think you can do it, Nix, but I have faith in you." Yoko covered Phoenix's hand again. "I hope you're the one."

Yoko got her wish.

Chan called Phoenix into her office the next day. The spring morning was sunny but cold, with a brisk wind off San Francisco Bay.

"You read the report?" Chan said as Phoenix took the seat on the other side of the wide and very valuable cherrywood desk.

"I did," Phoenix said.

"What were your thoughts?"

"I assume you chose me because I look human."

"That was indeed a major factor, Agent Stryker. It was

not the only one. You also have no need for blood or a patch to help you digest human food like all full dhampires, though your protein requirements must be met to the best of your ability. Any further thoughts about this mission?"

"I can get him," Phoenix said, half-afraid of appearing so much more confident than she felt.

The director looked at Phoenix as if she were peering over the tops of old-fashioned reading glasses. "You will have a great deal of personal discretion in this, but your job is not to *'get him.'* It is to watch and listen, try to make contact with someone in the Fringe who knows Drakon, locate his headquarters if possible and report back without being caught. That is more than sufficient."

But not for me, Phoenix thought. *Dad died for this city. If I have any way to bring this assassin down myself…*

"The question is whether or not your former relationship with the mayor could in any way compromise the mission," Chan said, shaking Phoenix out of her thoughts. "Do you believe there is any chance it might in any way affect your performance?"

Phoenix knew she couldn't avoid the issue now, as she had with Yoko. The affair was supposed to have been secret. Aaron had convinced Phoenix that it would be a good idea if the then vice mayor kept his personal relationships private. He didn't want to be seen as having possibly influenced her acceptance as an operative for the Agency.

"It's different with us," Aaron had said. And Phoenix had accepted, because she'd been hungry for love, for acceptance by those who couldn't decide where she fit in.

They'd parted *"friends."* At least from Aaron's side of the equation. It was easy enough for him. He didn't have to think of her at all. She saw his photo on her tab nearly every day. Mayor Shepherd, one of the most successful and beloved leaders in Enclave history.

Phoenix sat very straight and held the director's gaze. "No, ma'am," she said.

"No resentment of this Agency for sending your father off to die?" Chan asked bluntly. "No undue hatred of the Opiri for killing him?"

"No, ma'am. No more than any dhampir operative would have."

The director cocked her head. "Honest, at least. Is there anything else you wish to say?"

"I know the mayor must be protected at all costs for the sake of our survival."

"All costs," Chan said, looking down at her tab. "Including the possible seduction of whomever seems likely to assist in your locating Drakon. There are several known Bosses in the Fringe you might approach in your search for him. You'll find a list on your tab, but our preferred candidate is a Boss called The Preacher." She paused. "Are you up to that, Agent Stryker?"

"You don't forget how to ride a bicycle," Phoenix said.

For the first time, the director smiled in apparently genuine amusement. "You're beautiful, Agent Stryker. Most men would consider you very desirable, regardless of species. You wouldn't have been considered if you didn't have most of the advantages dhampires possess. And your blood shouldn't be addictive to Nightsiders, either…which could be a mixed blessing."

"But it'll still attract them," Phoenix said. "And I can use that."

"It'll be at your discretion whether or not you wish to reveal your dhampir heritage at any point during the mission," Chan said, "but remember that you are not to engage Drakon or his followers unless you have no other choice. If the enemy recognizes what you are and fails to believe any of your cover stories, there won't be anyone to get you out."

"Understood, ma'am."

"And you have to remember that though you're still stronger and faster than humans, you're at a disadvantage in a head-to-head with most other dhampires and certainly all Opiri, with very few exceptions."

"Yes, ma'am. I'm grateful for your confidence in me."

"Frankly," Chan said, chewing on her stylus, "I was against it. I think you still have something to prove. You were an orphan, mother dead by suicide, no other living relations. Your father's legacy is all you have to define yourself. During this mission, you have to put all that behind you."

"Ma'am, I've always—"

"You're not out there to be a hero, Stryker, only to complete the mission as outlined in the briefing."

"I understand completely, Director Chan."

"I hope you do." Chan sighed. "The committee believes you can handle this. But again I must ask, are you prepared to carry out this mission with every asset at your disposal, without qualms or emotional involvement?"

"If there are any doubts," Phoenix said stiffly, "perhaps it would be better if another agent is assigned."

"No. The committee has faith in you, and I'll have to do the same." She typed a quick note on her tab. "There'll be a more detailed report, your eyes only, waiting for you in your quarters, outlining your cover stories and the support you'll receive from the Agency. Not to be shared with anyone, is that clear?"

"Yes, ma'am. Very clear."

"Then you're dismissed. Be prepared to move out at 0100 hours tomorrow morning."

"Yes, Director." Phoenix rose, turned and walked out of the office. Her heart was pounding, but not with fear. She'd have a chance to show them again. She wasn't that weakling orphan anymore, and she would never stop proving it.

No matter what it took.

Chapter 2

"Move them along," Drakon told Brita, all too aware that it was only a few hours until dawn and there was always the chance that the authorities would be waiting for just the right moment to strike. There were only a few secret ways in and out of San Francisco that remained unknown to Aegis and the Enforcers, in those less regularly patrolled areas along the Enclave's southern Wall and right in the heart of the Fringe.

That, Drakon thought, was the only reason this passage hadn't been discovered. Even the Enforcers were wary of the Fringe, since more than a few had died here.

Brita hustled the last few emigrants out of the concealed hole in the Wall and had a brief word with the hired gun who was to escort them to the boat. Drakon didn't trust the man, but the coyotes knew better than to betray the Boss they knew as Sammael.

They knew he would hunt them down and kill them. They didn't know he was an Opir.

They didn't have to.

"Done," Brita said as the others sealed and hid the exit with heaps of trash and artfully scattered pieces of twisted metal and broken concrete. She slapped her hands together as if to rid them of something she hadn't wanted to touch.

"Damn it, Sammael," she said, "you know this isn't worth the risk. The crew is starting to question why they should be involved in this at all."

Scanning the other members of his crew, who were just finishing their work, Drakon smiled coldly. "We're paid well enough," he said.

"Sure, by the ones with rich relatives who don't want members of their family deported to Erebus," she said. "But what about the ones you help for free?" She jerked her head toward the hidden passage. "Some of them didn't have a single Armistice dollar to their names."

"Why should you care, Brita? It hardly affects you."

"It's dangerous. Just like every time we make a trade, the crew thinks about how much money they could get for the product you save for the Scrappers out of your own cut."

"Half of the crew were Scrappers themselves," Drakon said, referring to the poor Fringers who survived on any scraps of food or any other necessities they could find. "It's not my concern if they have no compassion for their own kind. They obey, and they get their percentage. They don't, and they face me."

"And what if they just desert?"

Drakon had given up counting the number of times he and Brita had had this same argument, and he was weary of it. "And go where?" he asked. "To The Preacher? The members of his crew seem to die with distressing regularity. Dirty Harry brings in big hauls, but loses plenty just as big because of his lack of judgment."

"That's right," Brita said, scuffing her worn boots in the dirt. "But you're assuming everyone in the crew has a brain."

She knew damned well he assumed no such thing. Brita was one of the few people he trusted with his life, but he had never made the mistake of trusting the rest of his crew.

Listening and watching carefully, Drakon walked away, Brita on his heels. He could hear the others following, relying—as he supposedly did—on their dim headlamps to find their way in the dark. Drakon could never let them suspect he didn't need the light at all.

He knew there might come a time when he slipped and one or more of the crew recognized his superior strength and his aversion to the sun, no matter how carefully he tried to hide both.

He looked human. As human as any of them, with his genetically altered reddish-brown hair and light gray eyes. *That* camouflage the scientists in Erebus had given him, but they couldn't change the essentials of his nature.

"We gonna make it in time to the handoff?" Repo asked, trotting alongside Drakon like a puppy eager to please his master. He was the smallest of Drakon's crew, and though he was as tough as any of them, he'd been treated like a runt for most of his life, the victim of every bully in the Fringe until Drakon had stepped in.

"They'll wait," Brita snapped.

Yes, Drakon thought, The Preacher would wait. He needed the product Drakon and his crew had smuggled into the city. Just as *he* needed the camouflage that being a Fringe Boss brought him. Drakon, Brita, Repo and the rest made their way through the abandoned, garbage-strewn streets, beyond the pale of the city proper. The meeting place changed every time; tonight it was in the

virtually abandoned section of San Francisco once known
as the Mission District.

As if they knew what was up—and, inevitably, they
did—the Scrappers had fled the area and remained undercover, well out of the reach of the not-unthinkable
chance that The Preacher might "recruit" one or more of
them, especially unwilling women.

The Boss in question was standing just behind a small
fire, the light casting his craggy face in dramatic shadow.
Drakon had never been impressed by The Preacher's the-
atrics, and they were usually dangerous. A fire in the
Fringe was an invitation to the Enforcers.

Aware of the ever-present danger, Drakon approached
the fire and signaled for the others, except Brita, to stay
behind him.

"Well met, Angel of Darkness," The Preacher said,
smiling through his beard. The band of very dangerous-
looking men behind him smiled almost as unpleasantly.
"Do you have the shipment?"

Drakon narrowed his eyes at the unexpected brevity of
The Preacher's overture. "In a hurry, Preacher?"

"Tonight's not good," the Boss said, his grin never wa-
vering. "Feel it in my bones. Let's do this."

Brita stepped forward with the tiny box that held the
keys to the storage facility. One of The Preacher's men,
twice her size, looked it over as if he actually doubted
what it contained.

Drakon and The Preacher had been trading for over a
year, and the other Boss knew damned well that Drakon
always stood by his word. The Preacher's man passed
Brita a box in return.

"You sure you don't want to come over to our side?"
the man asked Brita with an ugly leer.

Her lips puckered, ready to spit. "Stand down," Drakon said softly. "Tell your thugs to keep their mouths shut, Preacher."

The other Boss shrugged. "Lay off, Copperhead. We ain't here to buy women." He nodded to Drakon. "Good to do business with you, as always. Don't spend it all in one place."

His crew laughed, all guttural male voices, since female followers were considered property of the crew, not full members. Drakon kept his mouth closed, remembering again not to show his teeth. Though he wore caps to conceal his incisors, he never took unnecessary risks. Whatever Brita might believe.

In spite of his contempt for his fellow smuggler—whose specialty was reselling Drakon's items at a very marked-up price to "middle class" citizens north of the Fringe—Drakon made the traditional offer of his hand. The Preacher made no attempt to reciprocate.

Brita opened her mouth to say something inadvisable when a woman came running out of the darkness. She halted suddenly when she saw the Fringe crews, looking about wildly as if to seek escape.

The first thing Drakon noticed about her was the cloud of dark hair flying around her panicked face. The second was that she was quite beautiful. And clearly not of the Fringe.

"Shit," Brita said, pulling her illegal sidearm. "A raid?"

"I don't know," Drakon said, gesturing toward the rest of his crew, who had automatically begun to take up defensive positions. "Get everyone back to the Hold. If there are Enforcers on the way, I'll—"

Before he could finish, Copperhead went straight for the young woman and grabbed her arm before she could dash off into the darkness. Acting purely on instinct, Drakon moved in, shoved the man out of the way and took the woman from him none too gently.

She gasped as he gripped her arm, and he eased up a little. Her hair obscured her face, but he could see her parted lips, hear her gasping for breath. She'd been running hard for some time.

"Are you—" She swept her hair out of her face with a trembling hand. "Are you The Preacher?"

"That would be me," the other Boss said, stepping around the fire. "What do you need, my dear?"

Drakon stepped between him and the woman. "I don't know who you are," he said close to her ear, "why you're running, or what you want with him. But you're not from the Fringe, or you wouldn't be asking for a Boss who'll keep you on your back for the rest of your life."

She stared from him to The Preacher, who smiled enticingly.

"Whatever you need," The Preacher said, "I'll gladly provide it, pretty thing."

"Your choice," Drakon said, his tone indifferent but the rest of him far from it. Touching her was like making contact with a live wire. His whole body seemed to catch fire, and he could not only feel the blood pumping through her body but smell it, as well. As he could smell the woman's hair, the clean scent of it, though her clothes were torn and her face splotched with dirt. Her body held the faint musk of perspiration and that indescribable scent unique to women of both species. His cock stiffened, though the time for arousal couldn't be worse.

Her eyes narrowed, as if she'd felt the physical change in him. For a moment he wasn't sure if she'd bolt right into The Preacher's willing arms. Drakon was inexplicably tempted to drag her away, willing or not.

"What's your name?" she asked, astonishing him with the clarity of her voice and the sudden, fearless intensity in her eyes.

"We need to get out of here," Brita said, cutting off his answer. "If she's running from Enforcers...."

"I told you what to do," Drakon snapped. "Get them home."

With an openly hostile glance at the woman, Brita signaled to the others. As they melted into the darkness, The Preacher stamped the fire out with one heavy boot.

"I'll give you five hundred A-dollars for her," he said.

The woman reached down and gripped Drakon's hand as if for dear life, and he understood the unspoken message in her eyes. He knew he was acting against sense, against reason, against the dictates of his mission, but he couldn't let her go. He ran, pulling her with him, making his way easily in darkness that would confound his rivals.

"Who's after you?" he said, not even slightly winded.

"I..." The woman gasped, and it was clear she wasn't in any state to explain.

"You're leading Enforcers into the Fringe," he said.

She didn't answer, and he didn't stop until they were far enough into the Fringe that the only illumination came from the scant light of false dawn in the west. He was running out of time.

But he still needed a few answers before he took her into the very heart of his hard-won turf.

As he came to a stop, she bent over, hands on knees, to catch her breath. He saw that her clothing was some kind of uniform, though a very generic one, the kind of standard issue that would be given a city or Enclave employee—known in the Fringe as a govrat, a citizen with a clearance rating high enough for government work.

As she straightened, he studied her face, making a rapid assessment: features somehow delicate and strong at the same time, stubborn jaw, smudges and scratches on her face that did nothing to lessen her beauty. Her body was slender and fit, that of a woman able to handle herself in a fight.

"Who are you?" he asked.

"My name is Lark," she said, glancing over her shoulder.

"Who's after you?"

She met his gaze, half-defiant and half-afraid. "The Enforcers."

Exactly what he and Brita had suspected. "Why?" he asked.

"If we don't move soon, it won't matter."

He almost laughed at her bravado. "Why did you come with me?"

"I don't know. I was told to find The Preacher."

"Why?"

"They said he could get me out of the city."

"He wouldn't," Drakon said. "You were given very bad advice."

"Can you help me?"

"If you're running from Aegis or the Enforcers," he said, "you're not my enemy. If this is a trick, you won't get out of this alive."

"A trick?" she said with a burble of choked laughter. "What kind of trick?"

Drakon considered that he might have jumped to conclusions a little too quickly. Something about this woman almost convinced him that her fear was real.

"What can you pay for my help in getting out?" he asked.

"Information. But you won't get it until I know I'm safe and none of your Fringer friends are going to hurt me."

The sound of fast-moving vehicles thrummed from less than a quarter mile away. Whether she was leading them or running from them didn't matter now. Drakon seized her wrist again, and they ran until Lark—if that was really her name—was panting hoarsely and beginning to stumble. Drakon turned a sharp corner into an alley. She leaned against him as if she might fall without his support. He wasn't thinking at all when he put his arm around her.

He could still smell her blood. Almost feel it inside him.

He reached inside his jacket pocket with his free hand and pulled out one of the blindfolds he and the crew had used on the emigrants. "Turn around," he said.

Her gaze fell to the cloth in his hand. "You're kidding. If you think I'd ever—"

"I'm not letting you into my Hold without this. I give you my word that you'll come to no harm."

"The word of a—"

"Criminal, a fugitive from justice? Enclave justice?" Drakon turned her and tied the blindfold around her head before she could even think of struggling.

"I must be crazy," she said, her voice rasping with exhaustion.

"No," he said. "You've made the only possible choice." Taking her arm again, he led her alongside the building, constantly listening, and took a very circuitous course toward the Hold, dodging the sounds of approaching troops. They didn't seem to be gaining ground, perhaps more concerned about ambush than moving too recklessly.

He continued on by one of the many hidden pathways he and his crew had devised over the past year, frequently doubling back to make certain they weren't being followed. Dawn was beginning to break when they finally negotiated the last obstacles and entered the Hold.

The building didn't stand out from the other half-collapsed structures throughout the Fringe, but there were traps set at every possible entrance, and guards at every boarded window. The widely spaced lights were flickering and dim. The common rooms, mess and meeting room were protected by many external walls, like a castle keep. No one could reach Drakon and his crew without the use of explosives. Like so many other of the black-market items Drakon and the other Bosses dealt in, those were hard to come by.

Repo was crouched right outside the inner door. He sprang to his feet and stared at the woman in astonishment.

"You brought *her?*" he asked.

"No questions now." Drakon pulled Lark through the maze of corridors, passing the occasional crew member without pausing for explanation, and took her straight to his private quarters.

"Sit," he said, half-pushing her down on his narrow bed.

She probed the firm surface with her hands. "Where am I?"

"Where no one else will bother us."

She tensed, and he knew immediately what she was thinking. "I am not The Preacher," he said. "I have no intention of molesting you. But I can't protect you until I get more information."

"Protect me from whom?" she asked, turning her head slowly as if to take in any sounds that might help her get her bearings. "I thought *you* were the Boss here."

"Most of my crew have the option of going elsewhere if I seem too soft."

She turned her face toward him as if she would be staring if he could see her eyes, and he realized he'd just admitted something to her he wouldn't say to anyone but Brita.

"Soft because you agreed to help me?" she asked.

"I haven't agreed yet."

"But they won't be happy with what you've done. Would one of them challenge you?"

It was too late to retreat from the subject now, and he still had complete power over her in spite of her troubling insight. "You seem to know a great deal about the Fringe for a Cit," he said.

Cocking her head, she smiled. It was a particularly lovely and enticing smile. "You're unexpectedly honest and well-spoken for a condemned criminal," she said.

Drakon pulled the room's single chair close to the bed. "You work for the government," he said, a statement of fact.

Her smile faded. "I did."

"You're on the run from your own kind, and yet you've somehow convinced yourself that only the ignorant and deceitful have been deported?"

When she didn't answer, he pressed on. "*Why* are you running?"

"Do you think I could get some water?" she asked. "I haven't had anything to drink in a while."

Her sudden change of tone put Drakon even more on his guard. "I'll have to tie you up."

"I won't resist."

Far from trusting her, Drakon removed a heavy pair of shackles and short chain from a locked drawer. "Get up and turn around," he said.

She obeyed without protest, and Drakon bound her hands together behind her. "Members of my crew are scattered everywhere throughout the Hold," he said. "If you attempt to escape, they will almost certainly kill you."

Chapter 3

"Your orders?" Lark said, resuming her seat on the bed after Drakon had her shackles in place.

"No one will take the risk of letting you escape."

"I came here willingly, didn't I?"

Drakon didn't bother to answer. He went out into the corridor—where, as expected, Repo was keeping watch—and sent the man for water. When Repo returned, he was obviously near bursting with questions.

"Be patient," Drakon said. "Find out what the others are saying, and report back to me."

"Yes, Boss." Repo hurried off, and Drakon went back into his room. He undid the shackles and handed Lark the slightly cracked glass, which she drained quickly.

"More?" he asked.

"Not now, thanks." She ran the back of her hand across her lips...those full, enticing lips. Drakon swallowed. He wondered just how much she'd be willing to trade for her safety.

And felt no better than the other Bosses, whom he despised.

"Then let's get back to the essentials," he said. "Who are you?"

"I told you," she said. "My name is Lark."

"Lark what?"

"What difference does it make?"

"You do realize that you are completely in my power?"

"Ooh, scary," she said, her mouth twisting into an ironic smile. "Have you ever read the pre-war literature known as 'comic books?'"

Drakon froze, caught one of the thousands of memories he had managed to bury deep in his mind since his deportation. A little boy, laughing in delight because his father had managed to buy him a very rare bound edition of *The Iron Corps* for Christmas. It hadn't been black market, but Drakon—the man he had been then—had saved up a portion of many months' salary to buy it, even though Mark had still been a little too young to understand all the words.

"I know of them," he said coldly.

"Then I don't have to explain." She shifted her weight, and even that slight movement brought his attention back to her body and the aching hardness that refused to be banished even by a firm act of will.

It's the blood, he told himself. Like fine wine, human blood came in many vintages.

And he'd never smelled anything so rich and sweet. He wanted it, badly. But he knew his reaction now was fueled as much by hunger as inconvenient lust.

He would have to access his stores very soon. They had been going down more quickly than he'd expected and would need to be replenished, not a task he could entrust to any member of his crew. "Lark," he said, pushing his hunger aside. "You still haven't answered my question."

She pulled a few strands of her dark hair out of the blindfold. "I've been branded a traitor by the government."

"Why?" he asked.

She plucked at the blouse of her torn uniform. "I was an Admin. Very low clearance. I came across confidential information I wasn't supposed to be able to access. Someone found out, and—"

"What kind of information?" he interrupted.

"Let's just say that it would be more than a little embarrassing for the higher-ups, and possibly make trouble for certain parties involved in the election."

Suddenly, Drakon was interested in Lark for more than her blood, her beauty and her spirit. "And what?" he prompted.

"They regard any breach very seriously. Rather than take a chance I might use it, they trumped up charges against me and were going to have me executed. I was able to—"

"Executed?" he interrupted. "Not deported?"

"They don't deport traitors," Lark said, a grim set to her mouth.

"And *are* you one?"

She suggested he do something anatomically impossible. Drakon let it pass. Whatever she'd discovered, it couldn't just be *"embarrassing for the higher-ups."* Drakon knew well enough that the Enclave government could be as ruthless as the Citadel's Council, and would sooner kill than take the slightest chance of a security risk.

"So you think you'll be safer out of the city," he said.

Her blindfold shifted, suggesting eyes widening in astonishment. "Wouldn't you, if you didn't have such a good thing going here?"

He leaned over the bed. "What do you know of my business?"

Her body quivered as if it recognized the threat of a predator. "Only what I saw, back there. What you told me. And what everyone knows about the Fringe."

"That there are ways of getting out in this part of the city? Why do you think such exits exist?"

"You are kidding, right?"

"I'm deadly serious."

"Everyone remotely connected to the government knows that such passages exist. Most of them have been shut down by the Enforcers, but someone always manages to find another one. It's common knowledge that convicts can be smuggled out of the city for the right price."

"The price." Drakon straightened and circled the room, his heart beating fast. "Why do you believe we have use for information on the foibles of a government official?"

"That's not all I have," she said. "Some of it might be very useful to your...operations."

He came to a stop before her. "If you have something valuable to us, why do you believe you can withhold anything we choose to take from you?"

"You mean by torturing me? Or do whatever you thought this Preacher guy would do?" She shook her head. "That would be a mistake. You see, even the lowest-level govrats—to use your Fringe lingo—are given anti-torture conditioning. It's not much, but usually it works by triggering a fatal chemical reaction in our bodies after a significant amount of pain is applied."

"This is the first time I've heard of such conditioning," Drakon said.

"It's new. They want to keep it secret, of course. But I'm telling you now because I have nothing to lose, and you'd be better off taking what I'm willing to give you instead of losing all of it. I promise you that what you'll get from me will be worth what I'm asking."

Drakon took the chair again.

"Assuming you have such information," he asked, "how are we to substantiate it without risk to ourselves?"

"I never said it was without risk," she said, "just as I knew it could be a fatal risk coming out here."

Perhaps even worse than merely fatal, if he acted as loyalty dictated. He had no reason to trust her. If he found a chance to pass her on to Erebusian agents who could get her to the Citadel, she could be extremely valuable as a source of intelligence.

But he couldn't envision taking such a drastic step, and he certainly wouldn't return her to her Enclave hunters. His mission had been clearly defined, and once completed would have virtually the same effect as if he were to tear the government down with his own two hands.

One highly popular mayor, in the midst of a highly contentious election, dead. The mayor who claimed to want to end the deportation of criminals to Erebus, cut off the tribute of blood serfs who were so essential to maintaining Opiri society in the Citadel of Night. Essential to maintaining the Armistice and preventing another devastating war.

Aaron Shepherd. One of the two men in all the world Drakon wanted dead more than he wanted to live.

Phoenix couldn't see the man's face, but she didn't have to. She'd memorized it the first time she'd glimpsed him, when he'd snatched her away from the leering henchman of The Preacher, the Boss she'd been sent to find.

Either someone at Aegis had given her very bad information, as this man had told her, or her instincts had been dangerously off. But she didn't think hearing a man offer to buy her for *"five hundred A-dollars"* would inspire much confidence in even the most desperate fugitive.

She could honestly say she'd been incredibly lucky. This Boss's treatment of her had been no worse than she might have expected from any one of his kind, likely better than most. He was handsome, most definitely, with his defined features, gray eyes and auburn hair. Strong and fast, his movements swift and graceful. He had struck her right away as being someone extraordinary.

Even so, she hadn't been sure until she'd seen the faint red reflection behind his otherwise very normal-looking eyes. His incisors were covered in some way she couldn't quite define. She'd been luckier—or unluckier—than she or Aegis could possibly have imagined.

The man who had "saved" her from The Preacher wasn't human. After the first shock had passed, Phoenix had quickly realized that neither his fellow Boss nor either of their crews knew what he was. His coloring told her he must be a Daysider—one of those very human-looking "mutant" Opiri who could walk in daylight without suffering fatal burns—and Daysiders looked very human to most non-Opiri. The headlamp he wore wasn't just protective camouflage, since his breed couldn't see nearly as well in the dark as dhampires or other Nightsiders. But he seemed to have forgotten that no ordinary man or woman could keep up with him, and that he was supposedly leading a human female to safety.

What he *believed* to be a human female.

He didn't seem even remotely concerned about what he might have revealed, but if he believed her story, he wouldn't expect a govrat to be looking for Opiri in the city.

And *this* Opir had done very well for himself by becoming a turf Boss. He couldn't be the assassin Drakon, since no one less than a Freeblood—the lowest rank among full-blooded Opiri—could be trusted with such a task, and only a true Nightsider could operate in the dark with complete freedom.

But any Opir in the Enclave had to know who and where

the assassin was hiding. This was too big an operation for one agent to handle alone. Others would be helping him make preparations. All resources would be thrown behind the killer, regardless of the danger to the other spies in San Francisco.

"I knew it could be a fatal risk coming out here," she'd told him. She had been warned that the Fringe could be dangerous, but now that she'd seen it—seen how people were forced to live, families scraping by on whatever discarded material they could find, raiding garbage bins in the Mids, forced into theft and worse by the very need to survive and protect those under their care—she understood why the Fringers might attack an outsider.

It had made her feel sick, this suffering…a feeling she'd had to force aside as a distraction she couldn't afford. And any trouble from the people here was by far outweighed by the incredibly delicate and deadly task of prying information out of her "captor" without getting herself summarily killed or, almost as likely, smuggled out of the city and shipped right off to Erebus for interrogation.

Phoenix wondered if he'd accepted her implausible story about the new anti-torture conditioning. What she did have was an implant in one of her molars, the old reliable standby of covert agents since well before the War.

But she wasn't nearly ready to die. She'd completed Phase One of the operation: making a connection with someone influential in the Fringe, one who could help her locate an Opir operative. The Preacher, or another like him, was to have provided the necessary access, but she'd bypassed that step entirely. Phase Two, finding an Opir spy, was also complete.

That was all she was supposed to do. Phase Three, pinning down the location of the assassin Drakon's hiding place, was to be the work of a more experienced agent.

She should have been making plans to escape and return to Aegis.

But not yet. Not quite yet. She was in too good a position to give it up now. Even though Aegis wouldn't know how far she'd already come, they'd follow through with their part of the plan by continuing the search for the "fugitive." And when she finally did return, she'd have plenty to give them.

Now the Daysider's silence was heavy, as if his mind was focused on weighty matters…as well it should be. But she knew he was thinking of other, more personal subjects, as well, not the least of which was her body.

She'd been well aware of his arousal; it had been impossible not to be, given the impressive size of his package. She could still smell his desire for her like a heady perfume, even though she could no longer see the way his pale gray eyes followed every slight move of her body.

She'd planned to keep him from realizing that she knew what he was as long as possible, and prevent *him* from finding out what *she* was, until she had no other choice but to consciously make use of her true nature. But if part of his nearly instantaneous and obviously powerful attraction to her was due to the scent of her part-dhampir blood, she had no idea how long her secret could last.

"Lark," he said.

She almost—*almost*—forgot to respond to her alias.

"Was the information you plan to sell to me the reason your government believed you'd betray them?" he asked, resuming their conversation as if there had never been a break. "Or was it something else?"

Phoenix thought through her cover story. There was still something about her claims he wasn't buying.

"Okay," she said with a shrug. "I found some…stuff that I thought might bring in a little extra income. They don't pay us govrats that much, you know. Not at my clearance level."

"What *stuff?*" he asked, his husky baritone sending unwelcome shivers down her spine.

"Just a little persuasion," she said. "A politician who'd rather not have anyone know he keeps a little something on the side."

He snorted. "And they caught you?"

"They only found out at the last minute who did it."

"And you were stupid enough to risk so much without taking sufficient precautions."

"Maybe I needed the money fast."

"Why?"

"Do I have to tell you my life story to get you to help me?"

"You'll have to provide a lot more than that if you want our help."

"Isn't that what this conversation is all about?"

The chair he was sitting on creaked, and she turned her head to follow the sound of his progress around the small room.

"It isn't only the Enforcers who are chasing you," he said. "Not if you've been declared a traitor. Traitors are the ones who might reveal things to the bloodsuckers that could bring the Enclave down."

"And you think I—" She gulped in a breath. "I don't have *that* kind of information. And everyone knows the Nightsiders are evil monsters. Why would any Cit pass Enclave secrets on to those who would only enslave her?"

"Aegis must think you *have* those kinds of secrets," he said. "They could be sweeping the Fringe in an hour."

"I didn't access Aegis files! I can't even get near them!"

His weight—his heat, his warmth, his maleness—settled beside her on the bed. "Are you telling me the truth?" he asked, very softly.

"I—" For a moment she forgot what she was about to say, enveloped in the blatant desire emanating from him.

"It would be safer for me to turn you in," he said. "Anonymously, of course."

"You wouldn't do that."

His breath sighed very close to her lips. "You don't know what I'm capable of," he said.

"You warned me about The Preacher, even before he—"

"Maybe my motives weren't very different from his."

"Didn't you say you wouldn't molest me?"

"I wouldn't take any woman against her will."

But the rough purr in his voice told her exactly what he meant by *will*. She'd been prepared for this. She'd been ready to offer her body in payment for what she had to have, regarding it as no more than part of her mission.

The problem was that her body was responding to his nearness, his potent masculinity, as powerfully as he was reacting to her. And her mind was refusing to think of using that body as just a tool in a war for the Enclave's survival. Her nerves hummed in response to the aura of sheer sexual need that surrounded him, and she realized that she had somehow developed a very personal, visceral interest in her "savior."

Her enemy.

"Before we go any further," she said, "would you mind telling me your name?"

Her question broke the spell. "Sammael," he said, slight annoyance in his voice.

"That sounds familiar," she said.

"An archangel," he said. "Some call him the 'Angel of Death.'"

"Now you're trying to scare me again."

"Perhaps my bark is worse than my bite."

She nearly burst into highly inappropriate laughter. "Is that what the other Bosses say?"

"Ask the ones who tried to invade my turf."

"Very reassuring. Okay, about that information. It could make it a lot easier for you crimin... Your smugglers to establish better contacts and get access to valuable goods outside the Fringe. And I do have a way for you to check on it before you commit yourself."

"What is it?"

"I want your word that you won't kill me as soon as I tell you."

He laughed, a sound that would have been pleasant under other circumstances. "That shouldn't be a problem," he said, running his warm, calloused hand down her arm, his skin caressing where it brushed over the hole in her uniform blouse.

Oh, God, she thought, feeling all the heat in her body rushing to a very precise location between her thighs. "Until you...until you have a good reason to believe me," she stammered, "you'll continue to wonder if what I'm offering is worth your help. Just give me a chance to... prove myself."

"And what will you do once you're free of the Enclave?"

Phoenix found it increasingly difficult to concentrate on the conversation. "What do the other emigrants do?" she asked, her heart beginning to race. "Make a life somewhere in the Zone?"

"Where they may starve or be picked up by bloodsuckers," he said.

"Obviously, that's a chance they're willing to take." She steadied her voice. "If my choices are blood-slavery, execution or a very unlikely chance at life and freedom, I'll take the last, thank you very much."

"No matter how slim the odds?"

"Yes. Will you give me a chance?"

It didn't seem possible that he could move any closer, but he did. "There is no question of your leaving the Hold until your background story is thoroughly checked, your initial information proves genuine and all risks have been carefully weighed."

She bit her lip. She might as well bring the subject out into the open.

"You mean you think I'm leading the Enforcers into the Fringe," she said.

He met her gaze sharply. "Are you?"

"You're thinking that I was out to find Bosses and expose them, aren't you?"

"A good guess," he said grimly. "It's been tried before."

"I was looking for The Preacher, but there was no guarantee I'd find him. And the only reason I'd do anything like that is if I were some kind of spy." She laughed. "I can't believe you'd think that for a moment. Not about someone like me, a humble govrat."

"I don't know you."

"You're right." She frowned. "So what are you going to do to check out my story?"

"That doesn't concern you. I'll make the decision about whether or not you stay. My crew will abide by my decision once the situation has been explained to them."

"What if they don't?"

His voice dropped to a low growl. "If you're afraid any of them might hurt you, you can stop worrying. You're under my protection."

Another silence fell, seething with sexual awareness. *Use it,* she told herself. *Distract him. Bind him to you. Give him a reason to take this situation personally. Very personally.*

She knew she wasn't at any risk that he might take her blood and learn what she really was. He'd be giving *himself* away. And she couldn't think of any sane reason he'd do so, just as he knew he couldn't be taking blood from his crew.

But where he obtained his blood was a disturbing question she had to set aside for now. Deliberately striking a pose she knew would emphasize the curve of her breasts under her shirt, she turned her head toward him, sensing without sight how close his lips were to hers.

"Perhaps you'd like a more immediate gesture of goodwill," she said. "I'm prepared to give you something I know you want."

"And what is that, Lark?" he said, though Phoenix knew very well that this was only a kind of formality between them. A maneuver with only one possible ending.

She licked her lips. "Me," she said. "Right here, right now."

Chapter 4

Sammael's weight shifted as he drew back. "You *would* sell yourself, then," he said roughly.

"Isn't that what you were hinting at all along?" she asked. "Isn't it possible I want you, too?" She reached out blindly and touched his jaw. The muscles bunched under her fingertips. "Even if I can't see your face right now, I seem to remember you're not hard on the eyes." Her fingers skated down his chest and ridged stomach and came to rest on his cock, straining against the confinement of his pants. "But you're certainly hard in other ways."

Sammael didn't so much as twitch. "You expect to manipulate me with sex. You must have a very low opinion of my intelligence."

With an effort, Phoenix kept herself from flinching. His body certainly wasn't faking its interest, and yet he seemed almost offended by her offer. *After* putting the moves on her with his caresses and insinuating voice.

Was this a game to him? Did he think he was manip-ulating *her*?

She outlined his cock with the palm of her hand. "You seem to have a very *'high'* opinion of my physical as-sets," she said.

"I can find women who have a better reason to share my bed."

"You said my life is yours. My life includes my body."

He slipped out of her grasp. "I don't take advantage of powerless women."

"So you said." She laughed. "Which is the true Boss, I wonder? The one who makes clear he wants a woman in his bed, or the gallant protector who treats a fugitive like a virgin princess?" She stretched, feeling her nipples aching under her thin bra. "I want you. There's no reason not to mix business with pleasure."

"Do you make a habit of sleeping with men you don't know, especially criminals?"

"I'm a criminal now, too. As you pointed out." She pressed against him again, wrapping her arms around his neck, straddling him so her thighs were clasped around his waist.

Suddenly, he was kissing her, pushing his tongue inside her mouth and cupping her bottom as he ground into her.

And she enjoyed it. This wasn't some sacrifice she had to brace herself to endure. Heaven help her, these feelings of attraction—desire—hadn't been imaginary. He was an Opir, and she was ready…eager…to have sex with him.

She hated herself for it. She was too close to stepping over the line, forgetting that this was all part of the job—and the minute she did, all objectivity would be gone. It had happened before, and it had started the same way. With passionate, heedless sex.

This wouldn't be heedless. All she had to do was unzip

his pants and her own, drag him back to the bed, pull him on top of her, inside her...

It almost worked. She had his zipper down and his cock in her hand. He slipped his palms under her shirt to cup her breasts and kissed her again, spreading her thighs with his knees.

An instant later his heat was gone, and she was alone again.

"Your method needs refining," he said. "You know you're desirable, and you pretend to be willing. But no man or woman attains power in the Fringe without the ability to separate truth from lies."

"Was my body lying?" she asked, pulling her legs together as she sat up on the bed.

"It was *your* test," he said. "You wanted to see if I'd lied about taking advantage of you. I'm not playing along. You won't buy my trust that way."

He was angry. Very angry. And there was contempt in his voice, as if he didn't believe a woman had as much a right as any man to freely express her desires.

That's not why you're here, she reminded herself. *This is a job. Nothing more.*

"You have nothing to gain by this," he said. "Either your information is useful, or it isn't. You'll be left alone until I've made my decision."

Phoenix breathed deeply, concentrating on slowing her heartbeat. "Where are you going to keep me? Do you have a cell for prisoners in this Hold of yours?"

He paused, as if he hadn't expected the question. "You'll stay here."

"In your room?"

"For the time being. You'll have only minimal contact with the others. You'll wear the blindfold when you do leave this room, and then only in my company. When you're here alone, you can take it off. I'll be locking you in."

"Thanks," Phoenix said wryly. She pulled the fabric off and tossed it on the bed. His expression was rigidly controlled, jaw clenched, eyes hard. He was mastering his desire, but with a great deal of effort.

He'd said he had women willing to share his bed, and Phoenix had absolutely no doubt that he was telling the truth. It wasn't only because of his position of power in the Fringe or his good looks, but because he exuded need as well as strength, an odd kind of gentleness as well as indisputable masculinity and a sense of leashed danger tempered only by a peculiar kind of thieves' honor.

Gentleness? she thought. *All Opiri are killers by nature, Daysider or not.*

No reluctant kindness or self-control could change that.

"What are the sleeping arrangements?" she asked, waiting for her eyes to adjust to the dim light from a tiny lamp on the bedside table.

"I'll sleep on the floor."

"I can sleep anywhere. I'll take the floor."

"I wouldn't dream of subjecting a guest to such treatment."

"So now I'm a guest? How flattering."

"Don't push it," he said, turning toward the door. "I have business to attend to. Remember, your life and freedom depend on your good behavior and what you tell me."

"You've made that very clear."

He met her gaze again, his eyes searching her face. How ironic that he was the one Boss she couldn't hope to fight, either through the use of her superior senses or by physical means.

A trade-off, she thought, as he walked out the door and locked it behind him. Sammael would know about the assassin as no human would. But she was going to be fighting in other ways—fighting his nature and her own—if she hoped to get the information she wanted.

Because if she didn't figure out how to carry out this mission without losing her head, it was already over.

"So who is she?" Brita asked as Drakon sat down at the battered meeting room table.

Remembering Brita's warning, Drakon scanned the faces of his crew. Very few of them would be considered desirable companions by ordinary Enclave citizens. Some, both men and women, had suffered ugly lives of poverty and abuse. The majority of them had been condemned to deportation for relatively minor crimes, and had chosen to brave the dangers of the Fringe rather than submit. A few were simply dissidents with revolutionary ideas who had found their lives made "uncomfortable" by the Enclave authorities.

The ones he considered likely troublemakers were slumped in their mismatched chairs, clearly disgruntled by Drakon's decision to bring an outsider into the Hold without consulting anyone else. Others seemed openly curious, but the majority were waiting for an explanation, their expressions neutral.

Brita was in the last group, and as Sammael's lieutenant she had the right to speak first. Drakon nodded to her.

"Who is she?" Brita repeated impatiently.

"A fugitive," he said. "An administrative assistant who gained access to certain restricted information that may be of use to us."

"A fugitive," Shank said, sitting up a little straighter in his chair. "Just what we need, more Enforcers on our backs."

"They never even got near us," Drakon said, staring

into Shank's eyes. "She wanted help, and I determined that the benefits outweighed the risks."

"You mean you wanted her for yourself instead of selling her to The Preacher. She's quite the looker." Shank licked his lips. "I wouldn't refuse, either, if I was you."

"If you know my mind so well, Shank, what am I thinking now?"

The human quickly dropped his gaze, but his posture remained defiant. In spite of Brita's repeated warnings, Drakon wasn't concerned. If necessary, he'd make an example of the man, or any others who challenged him. He had to maintain his cover. And his connections.

"What did she do?" Ferret, lean and tall, asked quietly. "Try to sell this information? Blackmail?"

"I haven't had time to learn the details yet. I'll know soon enough."

"You went too easy on her," Brita muttered.

"She's been here less than an hour," Drakon said. "She wants out of the city, and is willing to pay."

"And you think she's telling the truth?" Repo asked.

"Have you ever had cause to doubt my instincts?" Drakon said, sweeping the crew with his gaze a second time.

No one had the nerve to answer him. Brita alone shook her head. "Don't waste your time, Sammael," she said. "I can get this *'information'* out of her without the bargaining."

"She's to remain alone and untouched, in my room."

"So Shank was right," Beachboy said, tossing his shaggy blond hair away from his forehead.

Drakon rose abruptly. Beachboy shrank in his seat.

"My only interest in this female is what she can give us in return for her escape," he said. "And I'll make sure it's worth our help."

"And if it isn't?" Brita asked.

Drakon's silence gave them their answer. Glances were

exchanged, and Brita shook her head, clearly disgusted. Drakon ignored her.

"So what's next, Boss?" asked Grimm, folding his thick arms over his protruding belly. "We gonna make some real money this time?"

"We have a shipment of fresh produce coming in from the South Bay agricultural compound tomorrow night," Drakon said. "My contacts have arranged for one of the ships to be rerouted to the Hunters Point shipyard for repairs. From there, we'll have to get the cargo into the city."

"And you'll give half the stuff away to the Scrappers, like always," Shank complained.

"You know how I do business. The Scrappers know things even we don't, because no one pays attention to them. We feed them, and they help us."

"Fear is enough to keep 'em in line," Shank said.

"Would you like to test that theory?" Drakon said, planting his fists on the table and leaning toward the human.

Again, Shank backed down. A charged silence fell over the room.

"I'm going to send most of the crew to watch the passage and make the run to the shipyard," Drakon said. "I'll need a few of you with me to take care of other business. Brita, you'll remain at the Hold and keep an eye on Lark. Make sure she gets food and fresh clothes."

"Sammael—"

"I need you here. No interrogation. Just provide her with necessities until I return."

"And if she makes trouble?"

"There are shackles and a blindfold there if you need them. But she's not to leave my room."

"Fair enough," Brita said, though she was clearly peeved at being left behind.

"The rest of you will receive your instructions at 1300

hours," Drakon said. He walked away from the table, indicating that the meeting was over. The whispers and mutterings he heard as he left the room were no more than he expected under the circumstances.

Listening carefully to make sure no one followed, he strode to the roofless room where he kept his blood stores. The refrigeration unit ran on solar power, but the door was flush with the intact room adjoining it. Drakon had no need to step into the dangerous morning sunlight. He opened the two manual locks, noting again that his supplies seemed more thin than he remembered, and withdrew a vial of blood. He took a careful, measured amount—just enough to keep him strong and alert, but never quite sufficient to ease his hunger completely.

It seemed all he had become was hunger. Hunger for blood, for peace, for revenge. And now for a woman he'd only met a few hours ago.

He locked the blood away again, boarded up the room and returned to the labyrinthine corridors of the Hold. Lark's unique scent seemed to permeate the entire building, and his new and constant state of arousal was worse than a week without blood.

"Be careful," Brita said, coming up behind him.

Drakon turned to face her. "More rumblings from the crew?" he asked.

"I've known you too long," she said. "Don't forget I've *seen* the stray kitten you brought in."

"Your point?"

"You usually don't have any problem with women, but that female's got you riled, and you aren't thinking clearly."

"You don't know me as well as you think you do," he said softly.

She shrugged. "Whatever you plan to do with her when you have the information you want, be careful. Shank could be right—she might be a spy for the Enforcers, just waiting for the perfect time to signal them."

"I had considered that," he said drily. "I'll take your advice under consideration."

"Just don't put it off too long." With a shake of her head, she walked away.

Damn her, Drakon thought. He should never have let it become so obvious. But Brita was right. In a matter of hours he seemed to have developed some kind of unprecedented obsession with his captive, and it wasn't normal. Not normal at all.

He didn't like puzzles. He never had. In his old life, everything had seemed clear-cut, the rules easy to follow. All that had ended with his conversion.

Now he had begun to realize that not everything had changed. Once he'd been capable of real emotion. Humans believed that even new-made Opiri lost their ability to "feel," and Drakon had believed they were right.

But they were wrong. And Drakon was beginning to realize just *how* wrong. What troubled him most wasn't just the way Lark aroused physical need, but that she also touched parts of him he'd believed long dead. The ability to admire courage, to recognize the admirable traits among those he'd once served.

And to make dangerous mistakes.

He returned to his room, collected himself outside the door and went in. Lark was sitting on the bed with her knees drawn up and her eyes closed. Her lovely face was almost haggard, with shadows under her eyes and tension above her brows that couldn't be feigned.

"How was your meeting?" she asked, opening her eyes. "Has your crew decided to throw me to The Preacher's tender mercies?"

"No," he said, standing very still as her scent washed

over him and produced what had become his body's inevitable response.

"What next, then?"

Drakon sat on the chair. "Tonight we have a job, and you'll be left here under guard. When we're done, we'll test the validity of your information."

"I'm not going to run, you know."

"We'll know how much you can be trusted soon enough."

Leaning forward, Lark wrapped her arms around her knees. "Who are you, Sammael? What brought an obviously educated and cultured man such as yourself to become a Fringe Boss dealing in stolen goods?"

Drakon laughed to himself. Yes, in his old life he had received a fairly decent, rudimentary schooling, the one afforded all Enclave citizens. But Lark spoke of *education* in a difference sense, and her use of the word *culture* was meant to convey some kind of status far above the one he'd been born with.

He'd never been one of the Enclave's elite. What he'd learned of *"culture"* had come from his Opir Sire, who had seen something in him worth cultivating and had boosted Drakon up the Opir ladder from serf to vassal to Freeblood in a remarkably short period of time. He had stopped aging at twenty-nine, five years ago. It seemed an eternity.

"I was one of those *dissidents* the government is so fond of denouncing," he said, skirting very close to the truth. "I spoke out against certain unjust laws and restrictions, the forced separation of families under the Deportation Act."

"Then you agree with the mayor," she said with what seemed to be real interest. "You'd like to see an end to deportation."

"I would like to see some other means of dealing with

the problem of satisfying the Opiri," he said. "But I spoke out on these matters before Shepherd came to office, and I was warned in advance that I was to be taken in for questioning. So I escaped."

"Shepherd held the same views then, and he was a senator...."

"I had no reason to trust any political authority, whatever his or her promises."

A spark of anger flashed in Lark's eyes, but she covered it quickly. "You're right," she said. "They can't be trusted."

And you didn't like hearing me criticize the government, he thought.

"Patterson and Shepherd are very much the same, in spite of their supposedly opposing views on peace and deportation," he said. "And whatever their earlier ideas might have been, power has a strange effect on people. It changes their commitments and alters their promises."

"How has power affected *you?*" she asked sharply. "Everyone knows it's dog-eat-dog in the Fringe. How many people have you killed, just to keep your power?"

"I do whatever is necessary to protect those under my care."

"Your *care?* Stealing food from people who need it, dealing in contraband, trading on citizens' fear of deportation by demanding everything of value they have just so they can—"

"And yet you came here knowing all this," he interrupted. "You worked for those who abused the people from whom I steal *'everything of value.'* What benefits did you receive from *your* employment, Lark?"

Flushing, Lark looked away. "I'm sorry," she said, as if she meant it. "We've all become harder since the War."

"No," Drakon said. "People haven't changed. Only the circumstances."

"The entire human race never had to fight for its very survival before."

"And now the Opir race does the same."

"You're *defending them?*"

Drakon knew he'd almost revealed too much. There was something about this woman that threw him so far off balance that he thought he could actually confide in her. Let her see something of himself that he'd shown no one else since he'd been with Lord Julius. Explain why he had to…

"I'll have a tray brought to you," he said, turning to leave.

"Wait," she said, swinging her legs over the side of the bed.

He turned halfway, his hand on the doorknob.

"Don't you want the test information?"

"Tell me," he said.

She did, in brisk detail, as if he were a military commander and she a soldier making a formal report. Drakon could find nothing suspicious in what she said, but that meant nothing at all.

"You'll remain here for the day," he said. "You may not see me again for some time, but my lieutenant, Brita, will see to your needs."

"And will you keep me chained while you're away?"

"Should I?"

Her direct gaze met his. "I promise to be good," she said with a wry half smile.

Instinct—blind, animal instinct—almost drove Drakon to join Lark on the bed and take her up on her earlier offer. But once again he controlled himself, remembering that they had nothing in common except that she was human, and he had once been.

"Keep your promise, Lark," he said, striding to the door. "Be very, very good."

Chapter 5

"He's crazy."

The woman with the short black hair and nose ring took the chair, folded her arms and stared at Phoenix balefully. Phoenix had seen Sammael's lieutenant when she'd run into his meeting with The Preacher, but hadn't really met Brita until she had brought a breakfast tray bearing an odd combination of nutrient bars and surprisingly fresh vegetables, along with a change of clothing. She came again at lunchtime, when she'd escorted Phoenix to one of the shared bathrooms to clean up.

Phoenix had seen and heard enough to know that Sammael and Brita didn't always see eye to eye. But Phoenix had no idea where Sammael had gone, and Brita hadn't enlightened her. In fact, the woman had barely spoken, and on the third visit, when she'd brought a sparse dinner, she'd left Phoenix alone for well over eight hours.

By Phoenix's estimation, it was probably about four

in the morning…an odd time for Sammael's second-in-command to come calling.

"Why?" Phoenix asked. "Because he believes me? Or has he done something else you don't approve of?"

Brita scowled. "I got a message from one of the crew," she said. "I guess your information must have panned out."

That didn't sound right to Phoenix. Sammael hadn't said he planned to check on it when he'd left. And even if he had, it wouldn't have been possible for him to act on what he'd learned either last night or this morning.

Studying the woman's grim face, Phoenix pretended to be relieved…which wasn't so far from the truth.

"Then I guess he's not so crazy after all," she said. "Maybe it's time you started to trust me, as he does."

"Not likely. I'm just following orders."

"It sounds as if you don't trust Sammael's judgment."

"I was against keeping you here," Brita said, the words sounding almost bitter. "If I were him, I'd have killed you on sight."

Phoenix sat very lightly on the edge of the bed, her feet planted firmly on the floor. "Really?" she said. "It seems to me that your obvious dislike of me isn't just concern over who I am and what I may be doing here. You're personally worried about Sammael, aren't you?" She smiled. "Afraid that I might have some…undue influence over him?"

"*You?*" Brita snorted. "I know you've been offering him every asset you have, but he hasn't taken you up on your offer, has he?"

Phoenix clenched her jaw, wondering exactly how much Sammael had told Brita. "All I want to do is get out of San Francisco," she said.

"And you think he sees you as anything but a tool? He's had better than you a hundred times."

That was just the kind of reaction that told Phoenix she had to keep pushing. She knew next to nothing about this woman, who clearly had almost as much authority over the crew as Sammael did.

She had to uncover Brita's motives, decipher her relationship with Sammael, and learn just how much of an obstruction she might be to Phoenix's mission.

There was no sign that Brita had any idea what Sammael really was. But what if she did? If she was as close to him as she seemed...

Surely not. No free human would aid an Opir spy, even assuming she also knew nothing of what Erebus intended for the mayor.

Still, this was the Fringe, where anything was possible and hostility against the government was rampant. Phoenix had to be certain. She had to risk asking questions of a woman who obviously despised her.

Even if she wasn't sure she wanted to know the answers.

"Are you his lover?" she asked bluntly.

Brita's muscles tensed as if she were about to fling herself on Phoenix. Phoenix braced herself for attack.

"His *lover?*" Brita spat, visibly struggling to get her anger under control. "Neither one of us has time for that."

Phoenix released her breath slowly. At least she wasn't dealing with jealousy, which was a very dangerous and irrational emotion.

What troubled Phoenix was that her relief wasn't in the least objective. It was uncomfortably *personal,* as if she couldn't bear the thought that—

"By the way," Brita said, abruptly derailing Phoenix's uneasy train of thought. "Sammael said to move you to a new room of your own."

Phoenix stared at the Fringer woman in surprise, noting that her body had relaxed as if there had never been any tension between her and the prisoner.

And that made Phoenix very, very suspicious.

"I don't understand," Phoenix said. "I thought Sammael wanted me to stay here."

Brita stretched out her long legs and crossed her ankles. "He doesn't want you to leave the premises, but you may be staying here for a while, and you can't spend all your time locked up in this room."

"Sammael's orders?" Phoenix asked.

Brita didn't answer. She rose and jerked her head toward the door. "Come on. I'll show you to your new digs."

She strode through the door without once looking back. Phoenix followed slowly, half-expecting an ambush.

The corridor outside was damp and cold. The only light came from Brita's headlamp, which she turned on as soon as they left Sammael's room, and a few flickering lights spaced several yards apart. Phoenix assumed they conserved energy whenever possible, since the Fringe's access to the city's power grid was strictly limited.

Brita escorted Phoenix along several corridors and stopped before a warped door. "About as good as any room you'll find here," she said, "and it has a decent bed."

She led Phoenix inside. "If you need anything," she said, "bang on the door. This place gave up being soundproof a long time ago, if it ever was. But you wouldn't be very smart to try and leave this room without an escort. Every exit from this building is guarded by a whole network of booby traps and alarms, and they have to be disarmed very carefully."

"How many prisoners do you have here, anyway?" Phoenix asked.

"Just do as I tell you." Brita closed the door, locking it from the outside. Phoenix listened for a while after Brita's footsteps had receded into the distance.

This was obviously some kind of test…or a trap. And Phoenix was by no means sure that it was Sammael's idea. She would certainly learn the truth when Sammael and his crew returned. Since they worked at night, they'd be finishing up their current *"business"* by dawn or soon after…only a couple of hours away.

Brita had told her not to leave the room, and Phoenix knew it would be dangerous to try. On the other hand, she might never have a better shot at looking for evidence that Sammael was in direct communication with Drakon, and how he might lead her to the assassin. The odds that anything obvious would turn up were probably thousands to one, but the odds weren't her concern. The looking *was*.

Still, she didn't attempt to leave until she heard voices that seemed to be coming from outside the building, too indistinct for her to decipher the words but clear enough for her to identify one of the speakers as Brita.

After a few moments' careful consideration, Phoenix decided to take the risk. She tested the door and quickly discovered that the lock was broken—more proof that this might very well be a trap. She paused outside, listening again.

Brita definitely wasn't in the building, and Phoenix was finally able to pinpoint the direction of the voices. Before she did anything else, she had to know what Sammael's lieutenant was up to.

Still, she hesitated, sensing something out of kilter besides the obviously ineffective lock. It took her a few minutes to find the webwork of nearly invisible wires stretched between floor and ceiling on each side of the door, clearly meant to trigger an alarm on contact. Or perhaps do something much worse.

But Brita clearly didn't know that this govrat's training had included such esoteric skills as disarming bombs and alarm systems.

In five minutes, Phoenix had found the trigger and disabled it. She used every one of her half-dhampir skills to make her way through the maze of corridors while avoiding the surveillance cameras she spotted at each end of every hall or corridor. She found a rear exit and searched the area for the *"booby traps"* Brita had mentioned.

As she'd suspected, there didn't seem to be any safeguards to prevent escape, only to keep potential enemies out. If Sammael's crew did take prisoners or hostages, they certainly weren't confined in rooms with half-broken locks.

Once she was certain she wasn't going to trip any alarms, Phoenix carefully moved through the outer door. It was hidden from the view of outside observers by the strategic placement of old crates and pieces of discarded metal and wood, but the voices grew more distinct, and soon she could make out the words.

"I told you I'm happy where I am," Brita said. "I don't care what you offer me. I'm not switching crews now."

"Even though everyone in the Fringe knows that Sammael's crew is getting restless because he gives half your booty away?" the man's voice asked.

"He gives a shit about the people who live here. And you're wrong about his crew. I grew up in the Fringe. I know what it's like, and I know how to survive here. Sammael's no weakling, and you're never getting to him through me."

"We can always find someone else."

"You don't think Sammael's watching? You think he's so soft that he'd let some traitor go over to your Boss?"

There was a long silence, and Phoenix could almost hear the man's shrug.

"Your funeral," he said. "But The Preacher's gonna come for Sammael's turf sooner or later, and it's gonna be a nasty war. Whoever loses is gonna take his crew down with him, so you better make sure you're on the right side."

"And you better make sure you don't come here again, or I'll kill you myself."

The man laughed. "You can try."

The sound of his footsteps receded, and then there was only the darkness and silence.

Phoenix retreated just inside the door and waited until Brita returned, disarmed the alarms and stepped into the Hold. Her pupils were huge in the darkness, and when she saw Phoenix she stopped in apparent shock.

"You were talking to someone from The Preacher's crew," Phoenix said, leaning against the wall.

Brita's eyes narrowed. "You got past the web."

"You were laying a trap for me," Phoenix said, dodging the question. "Why?"

"Because you're not who you say you are."

As you are not, Phoenix thought. "You've obviously believed that from the beginning," she said aloud, taking a step toward Sammael's lieutenant. "Who do you think I am, Brita?"

"You're not human."

Phoenix wasn't shocked. If she recognized Brita, then it was bound to work the other way. But she had to be sure. "Why would you think that?" she asked calmly.

"Maybe Sammael is blind, but I'm not."

"And what do you see so clearly that he doesn't?"

"Things like how easily you move in the dark. And other—" She cut the air with her hand. "I don't have to explain myself to you. I just know."

"Do I look inhuman?"

"Looks can deceive."

Indeed they can, Phoenix thought. "If what you believe is true," she said, preparing herself for a fight she didn't want, "why didn't you tell Sammael at the beginning?"

Brita turned on Phoenix again, ignoring her question. "If you're not human, you have to be with Aegis," she said. "You're here to find and expose Sammael, and whatever Bosses you can take down with him."

"You're Sammael's lieutenant," Phoenix said. "If you're so sure about this, you have an obligation to tell him, don't you?"

"Why are you so eager for him to find out?" Brita asked.

"Why are you so willing to keep it from him?"

"Because..." Brita nearly trembled with anger. "You *know* why."

"Could it be that you think I might let him know about enemy Bosses sending envoys to his lieutenant? He might wonder how often you've done this before."

"You have nothing on me," Brita snarled.

"Does he know you're not quite human, either?"

Brita froze. "What the hell are you talking about?"

"You were out there with no light, and it's dark as pitch in here. You aren't wearing a headlamp, but you saw me as soon as you walked through the door."

Lips pressed tightly together, Brita rearmed the alarm system. "You're wrong."

"I doubt it. It's true that you don't look like a dhampir, and you aren't a Daysider if you can see so well in the dark, but—"

"A Daysider?" Brita raised a clenched fist. "You're calling me one of *them*? Is that what you're saying?"

Brita did an excellent job of feigning rage, Phoenix thought. A reaction like that couldn't easily be faked.

But why would someone neither human nor dhampir nor Daysider, evidently unknown to Aegis, be in the Fringe working for a Boss who happened to be an Opir agent?

It couldn't be a coincidence. She and Sammael had

worked too closely together to hide from each other. No... Brita knew what Sammael was, and she was working *with* him...working to help the assassin prepare for his strike.

Phoenix knew *he* had to be a Daysider, and that Brita was just as potentially dangerous as Sammael. He was still almost certainly the one in charge, but that was little comfort under the circumstances.

But what *was* she? She had human coloring and seemed to lack the sharp incisors, but she could easily be hiding her teeth under caps. She could be a blood-drinker.

Or was she, like Phoenix, more human than Opir? She obviously wasn't a serf. Why would the Opiri, who despised humans, use someone like her to forward their designs? "I'm not calling you one of 'them,'" Phoenix said.

"But I'm calling you an Aegis operative," Brita said.

"Now you're the crazy one," Phoenix said. "Sure, I'm not completely human. But some of us don't *want* to work for Aegis, and the only way to avoid that is to get out of the city." She met Brita's gaze. "I'd guess it's the same with you, isn't it?"

"I saw you run right toward the fire, right into danger, when you were supposedly trying to escape the Enforcers," Brita said, jerking up her chin. "I know you're in the Fringe to locate Bosses and turn them over to the government."

"You *know?*" Phoenix asked mockingly. "Sammael has harbored the same suspicions, hasn't he? Why hasn't he taken action?"

"Because...because you..."

"Have him under my spell?" She snorted. "If I were after the Bosses, I'd have had two of them right where the Enforcers could find them. You'll notice I didn't alert them."

"Because maybe you wanted to catch more than two fish."

"But I haven't tried to escape, and by now—if you were right about me—I'd have realized that my odds of exposing any of the other Bosses would be just about impossible. Maybe we should just agree that you aren't ready to defect to another crew and I'm not here to betray Sammael, and go on about our business as if nothing has changed."

"No deal."

"Even if I tell him what you were doing out there with one of The Preacher's crew?" Phoenix sighed. "Look, I'm not asking you to trust me. Just let me get out of the city."

"Not good enough."

"What *do* you want, Brita? I was right before, wasn't I? It's not just a matter of your own survival and freedom. You may not be Sammael's lover, but you're more than merely his lieutenant."

Brita seemed ready to object, but suddenly her shoulders sagged and she looked away.

"I owe him a lot," she said. Most Bosses use people who aren't members of their crews like disposable objects. The Scrappers, everyone who tries to survive here in the Fringe, don't matter except when they can be useful. And since Bosses only recruit the strongest and meanest people in the Fringe, it's always the weakest who end up being victims."

"And you used to be one of the victims, even though you're more than human? You must have grown up having to hide what you are." Phoenix rubbed her lower lip. "What is that, anyway? Not Opir, not dhampir, not Daysider....what are you?"

They stared at each other. Brita finally broke the impasse.

"Sammael took chances on a lot of us," she said. "But we learned fast, and pretty soon we were as good as the other crews. Maybe better, because we didn't take anything for granted." She ran her hands through her spiked hair. "If it matters to you at all, Sammael gets food and other necessities to the Scrappers, keeps the worst-off from starving. He holds back some of our booty just for that, even if it comes out of his share."

"You make him sound like a paragon of virtue."

"He can be as ruthless as any of the others if he's riled enough. I've seen him take down two Bosses, which is why not even The Preacher messes with him, big as he talks. But he's one of the good guys, if someone like you can see anything past what you're taught by your government masters."

"Not *my* masters."

"So you keep saying. But now your excuse is that you just want to get out of working for Aegis. It's all lies."

"It doesn't matter what I've done or who I am. I'm not here to expose anyone. Sammael will sell me what I need because he can use what I'll pay him. And once I'm outside the city, you won't have to worry about my motives, will you?"

"If you even plan to leave the city."

"We're talking in circles now, Brita," Phoenix said. "But tell me...does Sammael know what *you* are?"

She waited for a tense, extended moment for Brita to inadvertently betray her true relationship with the Daysider. But Brita's answer was firm and simple.

"No," she said. "And I *will* kill you if you tell him."

"Then we do understand each other."

Brita stared at Phoenix for a long time. "I'm going to show you something," she said. "I want you to see this before you go back and betray him to the Enforcers."

"I told you I'm not—"

"I'll have to take you outside the Hold."

"I don't think Sammael will like that, do you?"

"This won't be a trap, if that's what you're worried

about. I know you want to know more about him, and I'm going to give you that chance."

The other woman's sudden change of attitude both worried and intrigued Phoenix. She couldn't very well turn down any chance to see more of the Hold or anything else Brita was willing to show her, even though Brita was almost certainly lying about her own motives. "So will you try to slit my throat as soon as we're outside?" Phoenix asked.

"I'll give you fair warning when I'm ready," Brita said.

"That's very kind of you."

Brita shrugged. "You stay here." She strode off, leaving Phoenix right in front of the armed entrance. She returned a few minutes later with the blindfold in her hand.

"What's the point in taking me to see something if I can't see it?" Phoenix asked. "Or are you going to put me up in front of a firing squad?"

"It's only until we get there," Brita said, moving behind Phoenix to tie the cloth around her head. "Then you'll see everything, I promise."

Possibly even my own death, Phoenix thought. But she was still ready to fight, and she wasn't going down without one.

Chapter 6

Brita took Phoenix's arm, and then they were outside in the damp coolness of early morning, the smell of the bay carried on a chill predawn breeze from the east. Phoenix took particular care to note and memorize the various small changes in scent along their path, the many turns and double-backs, everything that might help her find this way again.

After a very short while, Phoenix realized they were heading south, toward the Wall. Her heart jumped in her chest. Was Brita going to let Phoenix out of the city without Sammael's knowledge?

Soon enough, Phoenix realized her guess was wrong. Brita removed her blindfold and Phoenix saw that they were near the corner of one of the countless decrepit buildings that provided such unreliable shelter for the *"citizens"* of the Fringe. Brita gestured for Phoenix to stay where she was.

From her position, Phoenix could see the Wall rising

up above the shorter buildings, separated from them by an empty lot. The barrier was studded with thick shards of glass and every other conceivable sharp surface, capable of stopping a would-be human escapee or slowing a Nightsider invader. The top of the Wall was crowned by coil after coil of razor and barbed wire, extending the barrier's height by another good twenty feet.

But there were clearly weaker spots in the Wall—small cracks deepened by time and changes in weather, crumbling concrete here and there, evidence of efforts to file down the sharp points that made even touching the Wall so deadly. And along the base, stretching to either side as far as Phoenix could see, were mountains of boxes and metal scraps and every kind of abandoned appliance and machine, arranged in such a way as to appear like garbage thrown against the Wall. It was exactly the deceptive kind of barrier used to block the entrances to Sammael's Hold.

A concentrated effort by Aegis or the Enforcers could clear it away in a matter of days, exposing the hidden passages the Bosses kept finding...or creating. But there were never enough Enforcers to waste on patrolling the south Wall and preventing a handful of lawbreakers from escaping every few weeks.

Phoenix was about to ask what she should be looking for when the faint beam of a headlamp pierced the darkness and a small group of people—men, women and children—crept out of the shadows. Two of Sammael's crew seemed to be leading them, while several others, armed with stolen Enforcer rifles, followed behind, walking backward to watch for any pursuers.

Sammael came last. His headlamp was barely bright enough to extend a few inches beyond his face, but he moved easily, as if this place was very familiar to him. He spoke to his crew in a voice too low for Phoenix to hear, and then joined the emigrants.

There were about a dozen of them, huddled together with their meager belongings. Meager, in some cases, because their owners could only carry so much out of the city. It was evident that one family was from the Mids, another couple almost certainly from the Nobs. But the mingled fear and hope was the same on every face.

These were people condemned for deportation for minor crimes such as shoplifting or running a red light— foolish little infractions that showed how desperate the government was becoming in its search for convicts to send to Erebus as blood serfs. Some were accompanied by family members who would give up everything to remain with their loved ones, even brave the dangers of the southern Zone and risk their own very possible deaths.

Phoenix leaned against the wall of the building, taking deep breaths to ease her distress. She had never been so close to one of these unfortunate people. Aegis had kept her protected from such sights, from such thoughts.

Now there was no escape from reality. She had always disliked the practice of deportation, but the situation was complicated and very volatile. That was why the two main political factions, Patterson's and Shepherd's, were so hostile to each other. No one *wanted* deportation, but those who supported Patterson believed an end to it would lead to another devastating war, while Shepherd's supporters claimed that there had to be another way to negotiate a new, permanent kind of peace.

She turned her troubled attention back to the waiting emigrants. A wealthy-looking couple was clinging to each other, the fiftyish woman with a tearstained face and the man staring about him in apparent confusion, as if he couldn't guess how he'd come to be in such a place. Their money obviously hadn't been enough to buy their way out of punishment.

The Mids family, consisting of two young children

and a single man, sat together in a small circle of misery. The girl, perhaps ten, simply looked blank. The boy, a few years younger, was crying. The father's face was wretched with misery.

Was he leaving a wife behind, a wife already condemned? Did he hate this city, one of the last refuges for humanity on the West Coast of the former United States?

"There will be additional supplies waiting for you outside the walls," Sammael was saying, cutting into her thoughts. "You'll be in the Zone for the most of the next hundred miles south of the city. Avoid the agricultural Enclaves. There are said to be several unauthorized human settlements between here and the Los Angeles Enclave. I can't vouch for their safety, but you'll be better off with other people around you."

The man with the two children pushed his hand inside his pants pocket and pulled out a crumpled wad of A-bills. "I'm sorry I don't have more," he whispered, his voice thick with unshed tears. "If I did…"

"Keep it," Sammael said, stepping back. "You may eventually find them useful, and I don't need your money."

"But I understood…"

"I don't need your money," Sammael repeated. He knelt to face the little boy, stroking the child's dirty hair away from his forehead. "Don't be afraid," he said. He smiled at the girl. "You'll take care of your little brother, won't you?"

The girl's face lost its blank look, and she focused on Sammael's face. "Yes," she said. "I'll take care of him."

Sammael took her hand and squeezed it very gently. "That's a brave girl," he said. He got up, nodded to the father and turned his attention to the wealthy-looking couple.

"Two hundred A's are all I need from you," he said.

The woman's moist eyes widened. "That's all?"

"You'll have a hard enough time adapting as it is," Sammael said. He hesitated, lowering his voice. "You do understand you may die out there, or be taken by rogue Freebloods."

"We understand," the man said. "At least we have a chance." He held out his hand. "Thank you."

Sammael ignored the hand, and the man let it fall. "There will be no turning back," he said.

A series of nods, a sob, a sharp breath followed his announcement, but no one seemed interested in backing out. A few moments later, Sammael joined his crew in chivying the frightened people into what seemed to be a solid stack of concrete blocks.

Phoenix continued to stare long after they had disappeared from view. Her bones seemed to have melted, and only a sheer act of will kept her on her feet.

Sammael had let those people out for nothing, or almost nothing. He'd risked his life and those of his crew out of sheer altruism, just as Brita had described.

No, not just altruism. Compassion. A Daysider showing compassion to his enemies, people he was supposedly willing to help destroy by aiding in the mayor's assassination.

It was a paradox. He had no stake in these peoples' lives, no reason to want to help them.

"Only three Bosses smuggle people out," Brita whispered, "and the price the others charge is very high. With The Preacher, it's a miracle if you get out at all. Sammael does it because he wants to help."

Does he? Phoenix thought. Or was all this some kind of trick to upset what Brita believed to be Phoenix's plan? Was it possible that Sammael was pushing these people right into the arms of bloodsuckers waiting to ambush them outside the walls? Wasn't that just as likely...*more* likely coming from an Opir?

No, she thought. Not from a man who had touched the little boy with such gentleness, spoken to the little girl in just the right way to give her a purpose, a reason to go on.

None of it made any sense.

"Come on," Brita whispered, grabbing Phoenix's arm again. "We need to get back before they do."

Phoenix resisted her tug. "You showed me this because you think it would change my mind about exposing Sammael and your crew...*if* that were my intention, and if I could get out of here alive?"

Brita didn't answer. She blindfolded Phoenix again and hurried her back to the Hold by the usual circuitous route. But every moment, Phoenix was aware that she was being given a chance to escape, that Brita must have had more than one reason for taking the *"guest"* out to observe Sammael's act of apparently selfless philanthropy.

Was Brita hoping that she could force "Lark" to act recklessly to expose Sammael and the secret passage? Did she want an excuse for a fight and a chance to kill? Phoenix didn't give her what she wanted. Once they were back at the Hold, Brita escorted Phoenix to her room, followed her in and closed the door.

"You didn't run," she said.

"But you expected me to try," Phoenix said, standing near the bed.

"I don't know what to make of you, and I don't like—"

"Not knowing," Phoenix finished. "Believe me, I understand."

Brita snorted. "I'll give you the benefit of the doubt, for now," she said. "That doesn't mean I won't be watching."

"And I'll keep your secrets as long as you keep mine."

"And what you just saw this morning?"

"I'm not planning on telling anyone. It might backfire on me, too." She offered her hand, which Brita pretended not to see.

"The others will be back anytime now," the lieutenant said. "I suggest you get some rest."

She left, played with the lock outside—presumably with the intent of hiding the fact that it had never been functional in the first place—and walked away, her footsteps barely audible in the corridor.

Twisting her hair into the usual ponytail and tying it with a scrap of twine, Phoenix considered what she'd learned. There was so much she had yet to understand. Once again she weighed instinct against her orders. If she were to follow her instructions precisely, this would be the time to return to Aegis with the intelligence she had collected…presuming she could escape now that she'd let several opportunities pass. She'd made direct contact with an Opir spy, after all. And more.

But that wasn't good enough. Even if she could manage to get away, she still didn't know exactly what role Sammael was playing in the assassination. If she could pin that down, she could return to Aegis having done everything she could.

That meant she had to keep pretending to want to escape the city and still find a way to stay with Sammael until she understood his connection to Drakon. And she couldn't forget her purpose, though part of her wished she *could* get away from the Enclave…from duty, from doubt and all the other emotions she shouldn't be feeling. From wondering if Sammael's actions with the emigrants had been done out of genuine compassion Opiri weren't supposed to possess. That no agent of murderers *could* possess.

She sat on the bed and massaged her temples. Wasn't the fact that she wanted to believe proof that she hadn't been the right choice for the job after all? They should have sent someone harder, more focused, more dedicated. Like her father. Someone who wouldn't be thinking that maybe she wanted to stay with her enemy...not out of necessity, but because she was beginning to—

Care. About an Opir who took in the weak of the Fringe, shared his *"take"* of profits with the poor, helped human convicts escape and refused to take advantage of a prisoner he badly wanted.

She laughed. She kept assuming all that was true. God help her.

But it wasn't too late. There was still time to pull herself back from the brink and harden her heart, remembering that Sammael's supposed *goodness* to the fugitives and the people of the Fringe meant nothing in the end. His breed had killed Dad, would keep killing until they'd won their war and enslaved all mankind.

Turning off her troubling thoughts, she slept fitfully for the next two hours, trained, as were all agents, to rest whenever the opportunity arose but with senses tuned for any change in the immediate environment. By dawn— which she couldn't see but sensed as clearly as if she were looking out a window—she woke to the sound of the crew returning to the Hold.

But she didn't hear Sammael's voice. She rolled off the bed and half-ran to the door, every muscle tense and heart beating fast. Other voices rose in argument, and she knew something had gone wrong.

Sammael hadn't returned. Phoenix was struck by the sudden fear that the Enforcers *scouring* the Fringe, supposedly looking for *the treacherous govrat,* had taken Sammael against orders, anyway. Could his helping the emigrants have exposed him somehow?

There was another, just as chilling, possibility. Phoenix had heard the very unsubtle threats leveled at Brita by The Preacher's representative. What if one of his followers, or a whole crew of them, had caught Sammael somewhere alone?

She banged on the door for a good minute before it swung open with a loud creak. Standing in the doorway was a small, wiry man she hadn't met.

"Brita said to check up on you," the man said, gazing at her with pointed curiosity.

"Where is she?"

"Busy. You need the bathroom or something?"

"I want to talk to Brita," she said, trying to balance the tone of her voice between worried concern and stubborn insistence.

"She ain't available. I'll tell her you asked after her when she's free." He began to close the door, but Phoenix wedged her boot in the crack.

"What's your name?" she asked.

"Repo."

"Where's Sammael?" she asked. "Did something happen to him?"

"Why do you think that?"

"I've heard a lot of arguing, but not his voice."

Repo shrugged.

"He didn't return with your crew, did he?"

"That ain't none of your business. It ain't smart to pry into stuff that ain't your business, not in the Fringe."

"It's my business when he's the one who's supposed to get me out of the city."

"He's Boss. He can do what he wants, and he don't report to nobody. If your info checks out, he'll keep his word."

The door groaned as Repo closed it behind him. Phoenix hardly noticed.

If your info checks out, the man had said. So Brita *had* been lying about Sammael already knowing that Phoenix had been telling the *"truth"* about her information.

But why? Just to throw Phoenix off her guard even more?

Someone's voice—a man's—rose above the others Phoenix could hear in another part of the building.

Sammael's. He was back. Safe.

Finding her way to the bed, Phoenix sat down heavily. She felt as if she had won a sudden and unexpected reprieve from some terrible punishment, and yet she was ashamed. Ashamed that she'd cared about Sammael's welfare, not just about losing her chance to learn the nature of his connection to Drakon.

Ashamed that she could imagine his fingers pushing her hair back as tenderly as he had the boy's, speaking to her just as gently.

Could she make him care for her? Not simply desire her, but care in a way that he wouldn't want her to leave his side until his work was done?

No. She had to concentrate on what she knew was real...the sexual desire he refused to act on for reasons of his own. If it was weakness he feared, she had to make him believe he was in no danger of falling into a trap by making love to her. If it was her dhampir blood that drew him to her, so much the better. He wouldn't give himself away by trying to take it, but there still might be a way to use his craving against him.

If Brita hadn't already told him that Phoenix was part Opir.

It had been a very close call.

The crew was nervous, exchanging uneasy whispers, fidgeting, glancing right and left as if they expected Enforcers to burst in on the Hold at any moment.

That, Drakon thought, wasn't going to happen. The men and women who'd finished up with the shipment had narrowly escaped the Enforcers, it was true, but they weren't anywhere near the Hold, and the crew would settle down once they knew they were safe.

But every moment of the debriefing, as Drakon covered each small error and moment of nearly fatal inattention, he thought of Lark. He had been thinking of her when they had been in the midst of unloading the shipment of produce and hiding it as close to the city Wall as possible, in preparation for bringing it through after the next nightfall made it safer to move the material.

He'd been thinking of her when they'd run into the Enforcer patrol soon after releasing the fugitive humans. He'd thought of her when he had come so very close to capture—to losing his life, since he was required and intended to die first—after he'd deliberately caught the Enforcers' attention and led them on what once had been commonly known as a *"wild-goose chase."*

And he'd imagined her body, her warm lips, her welcoming arms as he made it to the Hold just before dawn, half regretting that he had survived. Knowing that she had, at best, offered herself to him only because it was a way of buying her escape from the Enclave.

Knowing, too, that she might even have been behind the Enforcers' attack.

Now, as he discussed the operation with his crew, he could think only of going to her. Brita had moved Lark to new quarters—ignoring Drakon's express orders to keep her firmly locked up in his room—and had reported that their *guest* had been very cooperative ever since.

Perhaps *too* cooperative.

Recalling himself to the task at hand, Drakon finished the debriefing. "Go eat and rest," he said, rising as he dismissed the crew. Brita and most of the others left, but a few lingered.

"What you gonna do now?" Shank said with a leering glance. "Go check on the client, maybe give her a little personal attention?" He glanced around the table at the others who had remained. "It's *her* fault there're so many

Enforcers around, whether they're really chasing her or she brought them with her."

Drakon walked around the table and backhanded the human, sending him flying halfway across the room. It was always a risk to display his more-than-human strength, but he had to keep Shank in line before he encouraged others to defy his Boss.

When Shank lifted himself off the floor, groaning and swearing, Drakon was standing over him.

"You can leave now," he said, "or stay and keep your mouth shut. But if you run and pass on information that can damage this Hold or any of the crew, I will personally hunt you down. Understand?"

Shank wiped his bloody lip with the back of his hand. "I get it," he said sullenly.

For a moment all Drakon could do was stare at the blood on Shank's mouth. Fresh blood. So long since he'd had it. So easy to take.

So deadly to his purpose.

"Sleep," he told the others, quickly backing away. "I'm sending most of you out tonight to finish the job. Those who don't want to risk it and forfeit their share of the profit are free to do so."

With many glances at the unfortunate Shank, the last of the crew filed out of the meeting room. Drakon spent a good half-hour walking aimlessly through the corridors, trying to convince himself not to go to Lark's new quarters. He didn't succeed.

He found the lock broken, but if the prisoner had made any attempt to escape, Brita hadn't reported it. Lark was standing in the center of the small, damp room as if she had been expecting him.

"Did you do it?" he demanded, striding to stand directly in front of her, toe to toe, face-to-face.

She searched his eyes, her own slightly moist, as if she'd been weeping. "Do what?" she asked.

"Bring the Enforcers in to hunt us down?"

"What are you talking about?"

He grabbed Lark by the shoulders, not gently. "You know. And now I have reason to think we were almost ambushed because of you."

"Ambushed?" Her chin jerked up. "You seem to have forgotten that Brita was with me all night."

Of course Lark was right. Brita had been very clear on the matter, though she obviously trusted Lark no more than she had before. "That means nothing," he said, "if your plan was to make everyone in the Fringe believe the Enforcers were only interested in you, and that everyone else was reasonably safe."

Shaking him off, she gave him a look of utter contempt. "Safe?" she said. "I'm not telepathic, able to figure out where you and your crew were going to be doing *'business'* last night."

Her logical response hardly set Drakon at ease. In the year he'd been leading his crew, not once had they walked into a trap. When it had finally happened, the one who might be responsible had a clear-cut alibi.

And Lark's sincerity—now that he was with her, smelling her, feeling her heat—only increased his uncertainty. *Someone* among the crew would have had to inform the Enforcers, but it hadn't been this woman.

That would mean he had a traitor among his crew. And that he couldn't accept.

Why? he asked himself, *when* you *are the ultimate traitor?*

"How many Enforcers attacked you?" she asked, her brow creased in a very good approximation of worry.

"Nine," he said, his anger draining away.

"Nine." She laughed shortly. "Even if Brita hadn't been

here and I'd been in touch with the Enforcers, do you really think I'd have thought that nine of them would be enough to take on you *and* your crew?"

Once again, Drakon had to admit that she was either the best liar in the Enclave or he was the greatest fool here *or* in Erebus.

But one fact couldn't be denied. The Enforcers were in the Fringe because of Lark, one way or another. Ultimately, she would have been the cause if any of the crew had been caught or killed.

And she was *his* responsibility.

He turned away from her and paced across the room. "What am I to do with you?" he asked.

"You haven't checked out my information, have you?"

"When would I have done that?" he demanded, turning to face her again.

Lark shrugged, a slight shift in her expression suggesting that she had been about to speak and had thought better of it. His suspicion flared again.

"Look," she said, "put me in a concrete-walled cell with a bucket and a pile of straw, if that'll make you feel better. But I can't tell you anything I don't know, or confess to something I didn't do." She returned to the bed and lay down, closing her eyes as if she knew she had nothing to fear. "Maybe you should look among your own people for a leak. And tell me if you find anything interesting."

Chapter 7

Lark's dismissive manner aroused Drakon's anger all over again. "You seem very comfortable here all of a sudden," he said, moving closer to the bed.

She opened her eyes and sighed. "You may have noticed by now that I'm not the type to beg and whimper. Believe it or not, I don't want anyone to get killed on my behalf. The sooner you can get me out—"

"We know they're watching the Wall much more carefully than they ever have before," he said. "We have one last job to finish, but after what happened this morning, I'm not taking my crew out again until I can find a way to solve our current problem."

She sat up, her back against the wall, plucking at the tumbled sheets. "Okay. I've accepted that I may be here for a while. What else do you want me to say?"

Drakon wondered what he *did* want her to say. He turned to leave.

"Brita and I had a talk while you were gone," Lark said.

Very much on his guard, Drakon turned again and stalked toward her. "What kind of a talk?" he asked.

"Well, first she moved me out of your room. She didn't say it right out, but I think she was worried that you'd fall prey to my feminine wiles." Lark grinned, an expression which, under the circumstances, seemed more than a little crazy. "But we know that didn't work, don't we? You're not interested." She sobered again with the same startling suddenness. "Brita did seem to want me to understand you better, or at least what you do here. I don't know why."

Neither did Drakon. "What did she say?" he asked, taking up his pacing again.

"She told me what you do for the people of the Fringe, and how well you treat the convicts you smuggle out of the city."

Drakon almost laughed. In his former life, he hadn't been able to ignore the suffering here, though for the first few years he'd tried to block out everything he hadn't wanted to see. In so many ways, he'd been far worse than merely blind.

Now he saw far too much. And what he did now could never make up for what was coming.

"Is this why you feel so safe?" he asked harshly. "Because Brita told you these stories about my many kindnesses? You shouldn't believe her."

He felt her gaze tracking his agitated strides across the room and back again. "I was wrong about you," she said. "You know, since I came here, I've seen things I never let myself think about before. I've had a real look at people who don't have anything except a tiny government stipend to live on, no decent housing, never enough food. People who have to scrounge for whatever they can find to make life bearable."

"And how do you feel now that you know these things?" Drakon asked without slowing his pace.

"Helpless," she said. "Even if I stayed in San Francisco, I wouldn't know how to make a difference."

She couldn't make a difference, Drakon thought. No one could, not with the Enclave run as it was now.

Again and again he had tried to justify his purpose here. What he was going to do… Could it result in anything worse than what already existed in this city?

Yes, the death of one important man might achieve what the Citadel intended. The entire Enclave might collapse from within. He couldn't pretend otherwise.

But the Opiri seemed to forget, again and again, how resilient and stubborn human beings could be. The mayor's assassination and the resulting chaos might finally force the government, with all its corruption, to acknowledge the weakness in the system they had built since the end of the War. The Senate would realize that simply stopping the tribute wouldn't lead to peace, only a conflict as bad as or worse than the one before. But the Enforcers and their reign of terror would have to come to an end, as well.

A new way would have to be found. The Enclave could even become stronger, able to fully hold its own against Erebus far into the foreseeable future. And if it did, Erebus would also have to change.

So he told himself, when he was at his weakest. When he doubted. When he thought of the Scrappers and those desperate to avoid deportation, the ones his guilt and former convictions bound him to help.

When he forgot to hate.

"There's nothing you can do," he said, coming to a stop.

"But something has to be done, doesn't it?"

Once again she threw him off balance, leaving him

with an anger that could only turn on itself. "What do you suggest?" he asked, wondering what she'd say if she knew what he was.

"All it takes is more people doing what *you* are. And if…" She swallowed and looked up. "If you need to turn me in to the Enforcers so you can keep doing it—"

"You'd surrender so easily, after all the trouble you've gone to in order to escape?"

"So you *do* believe that's what I want?"

He released an explosive breath. "If you were like this with your former employers, I wonder why they didn't strangle you long before you had the opportunity to access that restricted information."

"They were tempted more than once, I imagine," she said, bitter self-deprecation in her voice.

Drakon moved closer to her. "You weren't happy there," he said. "Maybe the blackmail wasn't just because you needed money."

"Do you want my employment history now? My résumé, perhaps? Do you have a position in mind?"

Now, Drakon thought, was not the time to tell her the position he imagined her in.

"Who are you, Lark?" he asked, suddenly needing to know. To know *everything*: about her past, her likes and dislikes, her family, all the little secrets she kept from him.

"I could ask you the same," she said. "You're a mass of contradictions. The difference between us is that you're already trying to change things, even if it's only a little at a time."

"I'm no hero," he said.

"Most heroes don't think they *are*," she said.

"Don't worry, Lark," he said, leaning over her. "There's no need for all this noble posturing. I *will* get you out of this city."

Her gaze dropped to her lap, and Drakon could feel himself beginning to slide down a dangerous slope, one that called on an emotion even more deadly than sympathy. His body was causing him enough trouble, reminding him that becoming an Opir far from reduced physical desire. In many ways the transformation only increased it, especially if there was blood involved.

For the hundredth time he tried, unsuccessfully, not to imagine that slender neck bent back, those breasts bared to his mouth, those strong, round thighs open beneath him....

Her touch snapped him out of imagination and into a reality more jarring than anything he could create in his mind. Suddenly, her face was very close to his, her scent swirling about his head like the most potent aphrodisiac.

"Posturing," she said, the word hardly more than a breath. "Is that what you think I'm doing? Ready to make the ultimate sacrifice like some heroine stepping in front of a train to save a crowd of orphans?"

The image almost made him laugh, though it really wasn't funny at all. Sacrifices weren't always noble.

"It's not just for them, you know," she said softly, her fingertip brushing his chin.

He caught her hand to still it. "What are you talking about?"

"Brita told me you almost died out there."

His body shut down cold. "Brita? But you said she spoke to you before I—"

"She came here again as your meeting was breaking up," Lark said. "She had a lot of the same questions you did about how the Enforcers might have found you. She said you were solely responsible for leading the Enforcers away, and that you'd never have let yourself be taken alive."

He stepped back, his movement as jerky as a newborn foal's. "She wasn't with us. I was never in any danger."

"She said Repo told her otherwise."

Furious with both Brita and Repo, Drakon started for the door again. Moving more quickly and silently than he would have thought possible, Lark stepped right into his path.

"I'm sorry," she said quietly. "I'm truly sorry I brought this down on you."

Drakon tried to brush her aside without hurting her. "There's no need for this," he said.

"It's not because I'm attracted to you, though I am," she said, holding her ground. "Maybe it's something I just…" She looked away, flushing. "I feel for you."

"Feel?" he repeated mockingly. "In a little more than twenty-four hours you've developed…*feelings* for someone you don't know, a Fringe criminal, because of a few fairy tales?"

"You wanted to know about me," she said. "I've been alone most of my life. Both my parents died when I was quite young. I developed certain instincts. I learned something about reading people. I learned well enough that I was able to pass the gov exams and get a decent position without any help or any connections."

"And yet these *'instincts'* initially told you that I stole from the desperate and that I could be sexually manipulated," he said. "And I seem to remember that you got yourself into trouble by blackmailing someone you should have left alone."

"Those were both mistakes," she said quietly. "But I don't think I'm making a mistake now."

"And you tell me this…why?" he snapped, alarmed at the emotion her words seemed to be awakening in *him*. "What more do you have to gain?"

"Your life."

"I've given strict orders that if anything happens to me, Brita will still get you out."

"You almost speak as if you wish you were dead."

Her insight hit him hard. How often had he wished just that, unable to shake off either the memories of the old life or the obligations of the new?

"I think you lost something very important to you," she said. "Some*one*. I did, too. Maybe that's why—"

"You know nothing," he snarled, pushing her aside. But she caught at him with unexpected strength and swung him around. She rose on the balls of her feet and kissed him, recklessly, hungrily, as if he were her only connection to life—not merely survival, but life itself.

And he lost the battle. Every human and Opir instinct deserted him, the knowledge that this was dangerous… wrong, according to his old code, the code he'd been forced to set aside when he'd been converted. It had been so long since he had wanted a woman this much. So long since he'd done more than simply satisfy his carnal urges.

It wasn't like that with Lark, and he didn't know why. He couldn't make sense of it. Admiration for her courage and level head wasn't enough. Her concern for him—her *feelings*—weren't enough.

But suddenly his tongue was thrusting between her lips and her hands were digging into his back as he cupped her bottom. She pressed her hips against him, rubbing his swollen cock through his clothing and hers.

A few moments later they were on her slightly sagging bed, and Drakon wasn't thinking at all. There were endless seconds of urgent fumbling as he worked at the buttons of her borrowed shirt and she his fly.

There was no undressing. He suckled on her nipple through her thin T-shirt as she kicked off her pants. He didn't even bother to remove the slip of damp, silky cloth beneath; he simply pulled it aside and thrust into her wetness, some part of him remembering to move slowly until her thighs tightened around his waist to draw him deeper. After that it was all fast, hard rhythm and Lark's little gasps and moans, her back arching and her eyes closed, murmuring the occasional hoarse demand that he move still harder and faster.

Somehow, they both made it last. When he felt himself, or her, come too close to completion, he slowed and buried his head in the curve of her neck, smelling the blood, feeling it beat in time with his, wanting it so badly that he thought he might lose control, utterly.

She bent her head farther back as if she knew what he wanted, as if *she* wanted it, too. But she didn't know what he was. Could this be the kind of instinct sometimes found in serfs…that the giving of blood could sometimes result in the kind of ecstatic sexual pleasure few humans ever knew?

His teeth ached, and he knew he could no longer restrain his need for release. He pounded into her, and she cried out as her body tightened and throbbed around him. He followed an instant later, shuddering, his muscles tensing and relaxing until he pulled out and rolled over, bathed in sweat.

Lark lay quietly, making no attempt to move closer to him or even touch him. She stared up at the ceiling as if she had no idea what she'd done. As if the whole encounter had been as much beyond her volition as it had been beyond his.

"Lark," he said.

She moved her head slightly toward him without meeting his gaze. "I didn't…" She swallowed. "It wasn't what I expected."

Suddenly, he was angry again—irrationally, furiously angry. "Not the tender lover you expected?"

"That isn't it." She finally rolled over to face him, her

expression grave rather than relaxed and sated. "I already told you…" Tears filled her eyes. "I don't expect you to understand."

She turned away from him, folding in on herself. Drakon felt something in his heart give way, dammed emotion that wasn't only anger, after all. He touched her shoulder gently.

"You're imagining these feelings, Lark," he said.

Hiding behind the shield of her tangled hair, she shook her head. "You're making fun of me."

As if that were the worst thing he could do to her, he thought. "I'm not making fun of you," he said, pulling a strand of hair out of her face. "You're naive. I'm not."

"No. You're just stubborn. And blind."

Drakon sat up and swung his legs over the side of the bed, yanking on the zipper of his fly. "There can't be anything more than this."

She rolled over again and smiled a sad smile, her hair fanned across the pillow. "Maybe not," she said. "But I still want you to have the information I was going to trade for my escape, no matter what else happens."

"I want nothing more from you."

"But you'll take it, because you can do more good for the people here if you do. And I'll show you. Personally."

"No."

"Because you still think I'd betray you."

Stifling a laugh, he tucked his shirt into his pants. "Strangely enough, I don't."

She got up, tugged on her pants and came to stand behind him. "Then let me help."

Drakon knew he was insane for even listening to her. She'd been good. Very good. She'd given him more than any woman ever had. And he'd felt something when he'd been inside her. Something other than mere physical pleasure.

He turned to face her, longing to push the perspiration-damp hair out of her face again, kiss her, fall into bed with her, *into* her....

All he had to do was make one mistake, and it was over.

"I'll consider it," he said.

"That's all I ask. But..."

"But what?" he said through clenched teeth.

"At least you could stick around a little longer. Talk to me."

"About what?" he asked. "After you're gone—"

"I told you something about myself," she said. "Quid pro quo."

"I'm not interested in talking about myself."

"At least you could tell me a little more about how you came to be Boss of this outfit and chose to help people the way you do."

Drakon glanced at the door. There was no earthly reason to stay. The idea of repeating his cover story—so closely built on his own life—one more time seemed like an abomination.

"You already implied that I must have killed to get where I am," he said.

"If you ever killed anyone, it was in self-defense or to protect someone else."

In spite of himself—his frank recognition of the dangers of getting to know anything more about her, or vice versa—Drakon found himself responding. "Just how much violence have you seen in *your* life?" he asked.

Chapter 8

A flicker of some unreadable emotion passed behind Lark's beautiful hazel eyes. Drakon was momentarily distracted by the way they changed, seeming to shift from brown to gray to green all within a few seconds.

"I didn't grow up with the kind of hardship the people here do," she said, retreating to sit on the bed again. "Before my parents died, we were…well, not exactly rich, but not poor, either. In a regular kind of neighborhood, in the usual middling kind of apartment."

Like one of the many high-rise apartment buildings that covered the majority of San Francisco, Drakon thought, built after the devastation of the War to replace the many varied neighborhoods of single and two-story family homes. Too many people to cram into one city, every square mile of space needed to house survivors who had lived in countless towns and smaller cities throughout what had once been known as the Bay Area.

"How did you..." He swallowed, almost unable to speak the words. "How did you lose your family?"

"My father was doing a dangerous job for the government, and when he died, my mother...she couldn't bear to go on without him."

Drakon looked away. "I'm sorry," he said.

"I moved into a group home until I was old enough to apply for a job," she said, her face expressionless. "There were many of us living in close quarters, and I didn't have a lot of friends. After my gov application was accepted, I moved to a dorm and lived pretty comfortably with other men and women in my position. I never wanted for anything, really. But I already told you that." She met his gaze. "Now it's your turn."

With a sigh, Drakon dragged the chair halfway across the room and straddled it backward, his arms crossed and leaning on its wobbly back. "You want to know how I became Boss?" He smiled in a way meant to chill rather than encourage. "What if you're wrong? What if I *have* killed? Maybe more than once?"

"I don't believe it," she said.

"Naive," he said, though he spoke as much of himself as of her. "I did kill someone. The previous Boss." He hesitated, wondering why he should have to justify himself to Lark at all. "It was necessary."

"You did it to save someone else."

"I'm sure Brita will be happy to tell you all about it."

"Was it her life you saved?" Lark asked with what seemed to be more than mere curiosity.

He couldn't manage to make himself lie to her. "As I said, ask Brita," he said. "But keep in mind that she tends to embellish."

"Somehow, I doubt that," Lark said softly. "You pretend not to have ideals, but you do. Ideals and a philosophy that gives you some reason to treat people with decency."

Drakon realized it really had gone too far. "I have dealings with evil men," he said. "I trade with them, haggle with them, work with them. What does that make me?"

"Human."

Drakon came very close to simply walking out of the room again. But somehow, with her voice, with her utter lack of judgment, he felt the urge, the need, to talk of a past long dead.

"I grew up in the Mids, as you did," he said. "I had a regular job, as you did. But my..." He paused, hardly able to believe he could admit so much to a stranger. "I had a family. I was married. I had a child."

"Oh," Lark whispered, drawing her knees up to her chest.

"And you want to know what happened?" he said, hearing his own voice turn harsh again, beating at her as well as himself. "They were in the wrong place at the wrong time."

"I'm sorry," she said. "Truly sorry."

"I made a mistake," he said. "Someone I trusted turned against me."

Lark was quiet for a long time, her chin resting on her knees, her eyes downcast. "You trust Brita," she said slowly.

He stared at her intently. "Is there some reason you think I shouldn't?"

"No. It only proves that whatever happened in your past, you're still able to trust *some*one."

Drakon wondered if she was speaking more of herself than him. "You never finished *your* story," he said. "What did you do after you got your job? Obviously, you didn't leave anyone important behind when you ran."

"No."

"No lovers?" he asked, meaning to be cruel.

She glanced away. "A few," she said. "No one who ever meant much to me."

A strange, disturbing mingling of satisfaction and anger coiled in Drakon's chest. He couldn't bear to think of those other men touching her, caressing her, moving inside her.

"I find that hard to believe," he said.

"Why?"

"You're beautiful, desirable, good in—"

"Bed?"

"I should have said brave, stubborn, determined, too intelligent to hold a low-level government position."

"Maybe that's all I wanted. A simple life."

"I don't think so. Maybe it was ambition that led you to access information above your security rating, not a mistake."

"I can't make you believe what you don't want to believe," she said, "but I've never been ambitious."

"Then what are you, Lark?"

"Like you. Human."

It was the second time she'd said it, and Drakon no longer trusted his ability to maintain his mask. "Is there anything else you want to know?" he asked, climbing off the chair.

"Everything. But it can wait." She rose. "Are you going to let me show you what I have for you, Sammael?"

It was his name on her lips that made him decide, though he knew it was sheer madness. He had to know.

Because if his gut was wrong, if she did betray him after all, he would have to escape. He'd find another hiding place, and Lark's treachery would give him the final incentive. All his doubts would be gone forever.

But there was a sickness in him as he thought of it, a feeling that part of him would already be dead. If he had ever been a superstitious man, one prone to believing in the supernatural, he might have believed this woman had bewitched him.

But he had never been superstitious. "We'll do it," he said. "Tonight, while my crew is handling other business. But only on the condition that you swear not to let yourself be taken by the Enforcers if we meet them."

"The most important thing is for you to get away if we find ourselves in that position."

He crossed the space between them and grasped her arms. "You'll do what I tell you. That's the condition."

"Only if you listen to my advice when it comes to taking risks. When are we leaving?"

"I'll come for you at sunset," he told her, and finally walked out of the room, his body moving against the pull of his desire. He needed to speak to Brita, find out why it had been necessary for her to convince Lark that he was a merciful man.

He was anything but. And when he was finished, he never could be again.

Phoenix sat on the bed for a good half-hour before she felt capable of moving again.

It had all been part of the job, she told herself over and over again, their fierce lovemaking. The most potent sex she'd ever had in her life.

But she hadn't been thinking of the mission when she'd responded so ardently to Sammael's aggressive passion. She'd wanted it. Wanted *him*. Had felt nothing but need and indescribable pleasure as he'd moved inside her. Nothing but sheer, thoughtless lust.

She hadn't needed to tell him about *feelings* to get him into bed. *"It's not because I'm attracted to you, though I am,"* she'd said. *"Maybe it's something I just feel for you."*

And he'd mocked her, quite justifiably. Mockery she'd

deserved. Twenty-four hours. It wasn't possible, and she didn't know why she'd said something more apt to drive him away than attract him.

But she'd doubled down after they'd finished in bed. He'd called her naive. She'd called him stubborn, and blind. *"There can't be anything more than this,"* he'd replied.

Phoenix dropped her head into her hands. She knew that. Whatever part he was playing in the Citadel's scheme, she knew she couldn't appeal to any compassion he might feel for humanity, even if—as seemed to be the case—Brita, for her own obscure reasons, hadn't told him of Phoenix's true heritage. Of course he might be pretending not to know, but she didn't believe he could fake what had just happened between them.

The problem was, she was now utterly convinced that Sammael was the very opposite of the stereotypical, evil, tyrannical vampire. He'd lost a wife and child. *"At the wrong place at the wrong time."*

That could mean anything. But he'd lost loved ones, as she had. And it had hurt him, deeply. She had felt it as vividly as she felt her own pain when *she* remembered.

Except that what he'd said...wasn't possible.

She looked up, frozen with realization. Could Daysiders have wives and children? Opiri didn't live like humans. They didn't marry. Their *"children"* were the vassals they created with their own blood. And even if Daysiders were outside the mainstream of Opir life, they still didn't have *normal* relationships.

So he had to be lying. And because he looked and acted so *human,* because she wanted to believe him, she'd fallen into the trap. She'd told him more about herself than she'd ever intended.

Rising, she walked unsteadily around the room. *"No*

lovers?" he'd asked, as if it really mattered to him. As if *he* could be jealous.

He had been manipulating her all along, not the other way around. And Brita had almost certainly helped his cause by showing her his *work at the Wall.*

Because they still believed she was here to set them up. She'd wanted to be her father's daughter. Instead, she'd failed. Failed completely.

Nearly walking into the wall, she stared at the peeling paint and forced herself to think. There still might be a way of salvaging the situation. What if she could use her bewilderment, her tangled feelings, her desire, in ways that could benefit her mission? Take advantage of Sammael's assumption of her weakness, his knowledge of her background and her apparent willingness to turn herself in to her pursuers to save the lives of those endangered by the Enforcers?

It still troubled her that the Enforcers had pursued Sammael and his crew. Could Sammael and Brita also have been lying when they spoke of his being pursued and nearly taken? Could it be yet another test on Brita's part?

There were still too many variables, too many unknowns. Phoenix had to be ready for attack while pretending to be completely out of her depth in every possible way.

Which she very nearly was.

Casting off her self-pity, Phoenix walked slowly around the room again, frowning at the pockmarked floor. Her main concern now was to determine how going with Sammael to check out her *story* could work to her advantage, how she could continue to seem ready to *"sacrifice"* herself without actually doing it. He'd made her swear not to let herself be taken by the Enforcers, but he'd be ready to stop her if he believed for a second that she might reveal herself to the patrolmen, and him along with her.

With a sigh, Phoenix prepared to wait out the day, listening for voices that might reveal anything of interest. Repo brought her breakfast, and another woman served lunch and dinner. She ate only to maintain her strength, and because her body needed more protein than full-blooded humans. Soon after sunset, Sammael came for her. He deliberately kept his distance from her, seldom meeting her eyes, and explained in a clipped voice what she was to do.

There wasn't quite enough moonlight for an average human to see by, which mean that Sammael had to wear his headlamp, out of necessity as well as for camouflage. Phoenix knew she had to be very careful not to reveal her own very good night vision at any point during their dangerous excursion. She pretended to rely on her own headlamp, moving cautiously even though she could clearly see what lay ahead of them and on every side: the same half-collapsed buildings, the squalor of the poorest citizens trying to survive, the leftovers of society.

It made her as sick to see it now as it had before, but she couldn't let on that she saw it at all. Or that she was aware of the presence of Enforcers in the area at the same time Sammael sensed it. She followed Sammael's lead in dodging them, pretending to defer to his greater knowledge of his stomping grounds.

However, once she and Sammael approached the universally accepted *border* of the Fringe, at the edge of the least prosperous area of the Mids, she could safely act with confidence in leading Sammael to their destination. Before she'd left on her mission, it had been arranged that she should give a certain signal to indicate that she'd come with the man or woman whom she'd convinced to help her *"escape."* From there, everything should go smoothly, according to plan.

And it did. Phoenix led Sammael through backstreets,

conveniently devoid of cops or Enforcers, to a particular bayside warehouse where goods from the Agricultural Enclaves were stored under heavy guard. She'd already explained how the patrol schedules had recently been changed—no less rigid, but altered from the original pattern because of some obscure administrative decision.

Nevertheless, Sammael was extremely cautious as she led him closer to the warehouse. He cast her frequent and suspicious glances, narrow-eyed and undeniably dangerous.

Together they crouched in the nearest safe cover and watched the heavily armed guards pace out their rounds, until, at 3:00 a.m., the relief appeared.

In that brief span of time, there was a moment when a small section of the warehouse was left unguarded. Phoenix moved boldly in spite of Sammael's whispered protest, turning off her headlamp and pretending to rely on the spotlights from the warehouse as she moved closer, paused to find fresh cover and ran closer still.

Sammael caught up with her, his breathing sharp not with exertion but with anger. His gaze snapped in every direction.

"*This* is what you brought me out here to see?" he asked as the new guards gradually took their assigned posts. "There's almost no gap at all. And what about surveillance cameras?"

"I never said it would be easy," she whispered. "But I also have access to codes that can disable the cameras. I'm sure that some of your clients won't come anywhere near a Boss's turf in the Fringe. I thought it would be worth your while."

Sammael's lips set in a grim line. "I could lose half my crew in an operation like this."

"But at least you have a chance. The new routine hasn't been established. The new guards don't know the old ones yet, and vice versa. You'll have to watch carefully, but there will be screwups. There always are."

"You're surprisingly knowledgeable for a humble Admin," Sammael said.

"I'm not stupid. These guards are trained to shoot at anything that moves, but they aren't Aegis agents. They aren't even Enforcers. You just have to get your crew close enough to stun a couple of the guards, replace them with your own people and get inside the warehouse."

"Just," he said with a quiet laugh.

"Look at it this way. If the Enforcers are concentrated in the area of the Wall, they'll be less likely to patrol *this* area."

Sammael grunted, watching the guards intently. She followed his gaze.

"I told you I didn't want anyone killed because of me," she said. "All I have to do is walk out there and turn myself in. You should be able to get away without any trouble, since they'll be busy with me. And I swear to you that I'll never tell them where to find you or your Hold."

His silence made her throat tighten—not with fear, though she knew he could destroy her mission in a heartbeat—but because she didn't want to leave him. It seemed no amount of determination could protect her from either emotional or physical attraction. She was still painfully aware of the warmth of his body—so unlike the ancient legends of vampire-kind—his graceful strength, his striking and handsome face.

And the kindness she was forced to doubt but couldn't forget.

"I can't take your word for that," he said coldly. "But this is good enough for now. I'll want the rest of the information as soon as it's safe to get you out."

Chapter 9

Phoenix released her breath slowly. Sammael would probably never trust her completely—that would be madness on his part— but she thought he was sincere in his satisfaction with what she'd shown him. He didn't suspect that everything had been prearranged.

"We're done here," Sammael said tersely. "Let's go."

They headed back for the Fringe by a different but equally circuitous route, pausing often to watch and listen. Phoenix was reasonably confident that the Enforcers would obey their orders and continue to stay out of her way, even though there would be at least one watching every possible route to and from the Fringe.

She didn't realize she'd been too optimistic until Sammael suddenly disappeared, she heard the faint sound of a scuffle and he returned dragging a helmetless and clearly unconscious young Enforcer by the collar of his dark uniform.

"I caught one of your hunters," Sammael said, his voice

icy as the wind off the Bay in winter. "I'm surprised they let such a green recruit work without a partner."

"How can you tell he's green?" she asked with a calm she was far from feeling.

"Look at him," Sammael said, nudging the man's leg with the toe of his boot. "Young and stupid, hardly out of his teens. They must be getting desperate."

Struggling to keep her fear from showing, Phoenix looked more closely into the young man's face. "I think he's a little older than he seems," she said. "You're not going to hurt him, are you?"

He gave her a long, penetrating look. "What do *you* think I should do?"

"Leave him somewhere no one will find him for a while. He can't do any harm now."

"But he would have, if he'd managed to send for his comrades before I got to him. He might even have killed you. Or me."

Phoenix allowed herself a very small measure of hope. Sammael didn't know who his prisoner was…or was pretending not to. She knelt beside the young man, feeling for his pulse. Steady and strong. He wasn't in any danger. Yet.

"The patrolmen are doing their jobs," she said, rising again, "and it's not their fault if their superiors believe I'm a traitor."

"As you *are*."

"Yes. But this one is no threat to you or your crew. Just leave him somewhere out of the way, and let's go on."

He stared at her for a long time. "No," he said. "I think I'll bring him along. We might find out what they intend to do if they can't find you…if they plan to bring an even larger force into the Fringe, maybe even Aegis operatives."

By questioning him, Phoenix thought with a sinking

heart. *You want to be absolutely certain the Enforcers are doing what I claimed.*

"If he disappears," she said, trying to conceal the desperation in her voice, "they'll send more Enforcers, anyway."

"I don't think so. They expect some of their own to fall performing their duties."

"You obviously don't know much about cops, or soldiers," she said. She touched his shoulder hesitantly, aware that she was taking another big chance with him. "I have another idea. Even if you can't risk getting me out of the city now, maybe you could set it up to seem as if I'm gone. That would get the agents looking in the southern Zone outside the Wall and out of the Fringe, wouldn't it?"

"And how am I to get that information to your pursuers?" he asked.

"We can think of something. You can still keep me around until you're absolutely sure I'm not working for your enemies."

He looked into her eyes with an intensity that made her shiver. "Where is your former urgency?" he asked. "It almost seems as if you *want* to stay at the Hold. Is it because of these *'feelings'* you believe you have for me? Because you believe I could return them?"

"I wouldn't be stupid enough to expect that," she said, lifting her chin.

Drakon stared at her a moment longer, heaved the Enforcer over his shoulder and waited for Phoenix to precede him. For a moment, she seriously considered using her superior night vision to create some kind of diversion and signal the other watching Enforcers to rescue their comrade while she pulled Sammael to *safety.*

But she knew if she made any rash moves, the young Enforcer might be the one to pay. And that would be far more of a disaster than she dared tell Sammael.

All she could hope for was that she could convince Sammael not to harm him. And that he wouldn't break under questioning and give her—or himself—away.

Constantly aware of Sammael on her heels, Phoenix let him herd her into the Fringe by paths only the inhabitants could negotiate without difficulty. Once they were within a quarter mile of the Hold, he dropped the young Enforcer and spent a good while simply watching and listening. At least, Phoenix thought, the other Enforcers were keeping their distance.

But she and Sammael weren't to be left alone after all. She heard the rustling of footsteps around them a few seconds after Sammael jerked up his head and tensed his muscles, ready for a fight. Out of the darkness, moving almost as silently as a dhampir, came a ragged man, and then a woman and a child followed by a small crowd of Scrappers. They spread out to form a loose circle around Phoenix, Sammael and his prisoner. Sammael relaxed, and Phoenix guessed that they knew him…and he, them.

The young boy—no more than ten years old—moved closer, staring down at the Enforcer. His face was smudged with dirt and gaunt with hunger, his eyes hollow. He wore an expression weary and wise—and angry—far beyond his years.

"Look, Mama," he said to the haggard woman behind him. "A Squeezer." He looked up at Sammael, and Phoenix saw fierce admiration in his eyes. "Where'd you get him, Boss?"

Sammael cast a brief, warning glance at Phoenix. "He was dogging us," he said to the boy in a deliberately casual voice. "You know how many Squeezers have been hanging around here lately."

"Yeah," the boy said, looking at the other silent observers. "They're doing sweeps now. Like the one when they took Dad."

There was a low, hostile murmuring that Phoenix pretended not to notice.

"The way they took my Lisa," a tall man said, his voice breaking. "She never did anything. We never did anything but be useless to the government. So we came here, and even in the Fringe it wasn't safe from them." He pointed an accusing finger at the unconscious Enforcer.

There were more murmurs—of family members arrested and shipped off to the bloodsucker city, of unreasonable laws that condemned even the most minor lawbreakers, of constant hiding from Enforcer sweeps to maintain their fragile freedom, the right to live this hard and brutal life.

Almost as if he'd heard them, the young Enforcer groaned, and his eyelids fluttered. Sammael heaved him to his feet, bunched his fist and hit the boy square in the jaw. The Enforcer slumped again, and Phoenix suppressed the urge to hit Sammael just as hard.

"Where you taking him, Boss?" one of the male Scrappers said, his voice nearly trembling with hatred.

"Back to the Hold for questioning," Sammael said, reaching down to grab the Enforcer's collar. "Find out what they're planning."

"But we know why they're here," the young boy's mother said. "Everyone knows they're after someone who came to the Fringe to get away." Her gazed fixed on Phoenix. "Who's she? Never seen her before."

"A new recruit from another Boss's turf," Sammael said. His voice held an unmistakable note of authority that strongly discouraged further questions. But the Scrappers were tough, and even Sammael couldn't deter them.

"Rumor says the one the Squeezers are after is a govrat looking for a way out of the city," said an older man, his body hunched with years of hard labor.

"Like many others, Elder," Sammael said, holding the man's stare.

Glances were exchanged in heavy silence. Phoenix felt no fear of what they might do to her, only a deep pity and shame that was becoming all too familiar.

"This govrat they're looking for," a man with a gravelly voice said, "we heard she found you during a parlay with The Preacher."

"She did," Sammael said. "She ran before I could speak to her."

"No one knows where she is now," the first woman said. "As long as the Squeezers are here, none of us get any peace."

"You know if *we* find her," the boy said, displaying a gap-toothed grin, "we'll give her to the Squeezers."

"We don't want you in no trouble," the gravel-voiced man said. "You help us, we help you. The way it's always been." He kicked at the Enforcer's boot. "Give him to us. They'll never find out what happened to him, but maybe they'll remember it ain't safe to come to our neighborhood unless they have a whole army with them."

Phoenix was painfully aware of a taut sense of eagerness in the crowd, the primal anticipation of the persecuted waiting for a chance to punish one who had taken part in their persecution. This was no sudden whim, but a deep, long-standing resentment. She had no doubt that they would kill the young man…eventually.

The truly frightening thing was that Sammael was obviously considering their offer. His eyes were harder than she'd ever seen them.

Maybe he agreed with the Scrappers. Maybe he didn't think whatever he'd learn by questioning the boy was worth the effort and the potential danger to him and his crew.

He began to lift the young man by the collar again,

pushing him toward the Scrappers, but Phoenix moved to stand between him and the mob.

"Wait!" she said.

Everyone stared at her. The young Enforcer began to stir again.

Moving faster than she ever had, Phoenix tore off her headlamp, snatched the young man's collar from Sammael's loose grip and ran, half-dragging, half-carrying the Enforcer away from the Scrappers. There were shouts behind her, quickly muffled. Sunrise wasn't far away, and once it was light she doubted either Sammael or the Scrappers would try to catch the Enforcer in a place where his fellow cops might see them.

She'd been placed in an impossible position. If she took the young man to the nearest Enforcer, she'd lose any chance to continue her mission. She'd have to return to Aegis in defeat.

But Sammael might very well kill the patrolman anyway, even if he'd never intended to give him over to the Scrappers. She couldn't let that happen.

Casting her senses wide, she began searching for one of the hidden Enforcer teams. She heard and smelled a man and a woman a little to the north and set out at a run, the patrolman slung over her shoulder. She'd gone about half the distance when Brita ran right into her path.

"What are you doing out here?" the lieutenant asked, panting a little.

"I could ask you the same question," Phoenix said, changing course toward the nearest abandoned building as if she'd been headed that way all along. She eased the young man to the ground just inside the open doorway and straightened to face Brita.

"Where's Sammael?" the other woman said, catching up to her.

"We went out so I could show him the value of the information I promised."

"Why in hell didn't he tell anyone?" Brita asked. "How could he go out there with you alone?"

"Why did you tell me my information had already checked out?" Phoenix countered.

Brita's expression made clear she wasn't about to answer. She stared down at the man. "Where did *he* come from?"

"Sammael caught him following us," Phoenix said, whispering a swift prayer of thanks that Brita didn't seem to recognize the patrolman, either. "He's...been drawing this guy's friends away so we could—"

"What is he thinking? What can he gain by doing this?"

"He said he wanted to question him about the Enforcers' intentions," Phoenix said.

"We *know* what their intentions are, if you've been telling the truth," Brita said, taking a menacing step toward Phoenix.

"Maybe Sammael has some other idea he didn't share with me."

"And now you're alone out here without protection, and so is Sammael. After I told you what nearly happened to him before."

Brita was so very good at pretending to believe that Sammael was merely a vulnerable human, Phoenix thought, without an Opir's means of defending himself. "It wasn't my choice," she said.

Sammael's lieutenant glanced from Phoenix to the young Enforcer at her feet. "Something about this stinks to high heaven, and—"

Phoenix lifted her hand, suddenly aware of unfamiliar scents and the scuffling of feet not far away. "Someone's coming," she said.

Brita's nostrils flared. "Damn. I know who it is. They all smell the same."

"Who?"

"The Preacher's men. And they're headed this way."

"Maybe they followed you," Phoenix said.

"Not possible," Brita said, though her attention remained focused on the street. "I don't know why they're here, but I'd say there are about ten of them, and they know where we are."

"So we'll have to fight," Phoenix said.

"You can bet some of them will go straight for this Enforcer, but they probably won't bother holding him hostage."

Like the angry Scrappers, Phoenix thought. "You'd let him be killed?"

"I'd throw him to a pack of starving wolves to keep them off my tail," Brita said. But she glanced again at the young Enforcer, a deep frown between her eyes.

"You're right," she said. "I wouldn't let them have my worst enemy. I'll get him to the Hold."

Phoenix's mind raced. She had no reason to believe Brita would treat this man better than The Preacher's crew, or the Scrappers. But the alternative was to see the patrolman die here and now.

"Sammael said he wasn't to be harmed," she said, holding Brita's gaze. "Will you leave him alone?"

"I'm sure that's exactly what *you* want," Brita said. "But Sammael's still my Boss. I'll wait."

"Then you take him. I'll hold these guys off as long as I can."

"You never did tell me what you are," Brita said as she bent to grab the Enforcer.

"As I recall, you avoided the same question."

Brita barked a laugh, lifted the Enforcer in a fireman's carry and hurried away, vanishing into the mist that had settled over the Fringe. Phoenix crouched just inside the doorway of the building, watching as The Preacher's men emerged out of the low-lying fog and advanced, some breaking off from the larger group and circling to either side of the building.

Ten. Using both her Aegis training and half-dhampir strength and speed, she could probably take five of them down in quick succession. But the others would be coming at her at the same time.

If Sammael were with her, they could do it together. But she wanted him well away from this. After what she'd done, he might simply choose to let The Preacher have her.

Never, she thought. But now that she knew she might die at his enemies' hands, her thoughts drifted to the impossible what-ifs: What if she and Sammael had been born on the same side of the war? What if they could have been true lovers? Not just for sex, but—

Her foolish dreams ended when the first three Fringers ran straight for her, wielding highly illegal burners, knives and rebar welded into clubs. The burners were the most dangerous, and Phoenix let the advance guard think they had her before she feinted to one side, darted in and grabbed one of the weapons, smashing the trigger and tossing it aside.

Immediately the other man with the burner fired at her, and Phoenix barely got out of the way, rolling and springing to her feet just in time to avoid another blast. She charged the man, struck him hard in the face and wrenched the burner out of his hand. She turned it on the third man, who was almost on top of her. He stopped, staring at the deadly weapon in her grip.

By then, another five of The Preacher's men were coming at her, fortunately armed only with hand weapons more easily countered. Phoenix torched the ground in front of them, and they fell back, their faces contorted with rage and the uninhibited desire to do any number of terrible, ugly things to her before they killed her.

"If you're after the Enforcer," she called, "he's gone."

"Because you let him go!" one of her opponents shouted back at her. "We know why you're here! If you give yourself up, we may decide just to sell you back to the Squeezers instead of…" He grinned, showing a mouthful of black and missing teeth.

He said they knew why she was here, Phoenix thought as she weighed her next move. But did they mean they knew she wanted out of the city, which must be common knowledge by now, or that she was working for the Enforcers, or Aegis?

They couldn't know that she was part dhampir, or they would have been more cautious in attacking her. Checking the burner again, Phoenix realized that the magazine was nearly empty. It wouldn't be good much longer. And she could hear the men who had split off from the group moving behind her. Two of them were coming through the building, one around the side. She might avoid them, but she had six still-viable fighters facing her.

She decided again on the direct approach and ran straight at the closest man, grabbing his arm and twisting it until he was forced to drop his club. She swung the club at the next nearest opponent, hitting him square in the jaw. Bone snapped, and he fell back with a scream. Two other men came at her, and she felled one with a roundhouse kick but narrowly missed another, who was nimble enough to dodge out of her way.

But the other three were still behind her, and she had to divert her attention long enough to take one of them out. A sudden light caught her eyes, and for a moment she was blind. Something struck her hard on the shoulder, leaving her numb on one side and utterly unable to defend herself.

She blinked as the two men who had been behind her were lifted off the ground, feet dangling, collars twisted into their necks by hands stronger than any human's. Sammael knocked the men together and tossed them to the side like torn sacks of Fringe garbage.

The few men still standing took one look at Sammael and stumbled away. The sun broke through the mist, glinting over the tops of the low buildings to the east. The Preacher's crew ran without looking back. Phoenix let them go, and Sammael made no move to follow.

Instead, he backed away, head bent, until he was inside the building's doorway. Phoenix followed quickly. She knew at once that he was hurt in some way, though his clothing seemed intact and unbloodied. His headlamp was gone.

The moment she was inside he leaned against the nearest wall, gripping his arm. He looked up and met her gaze.

His face was red and blistered, but it was his expression that stopped her cold.

"What are you?" he asked, his voice hoarse and rough. "I saw you fight. You shouldn't have been able to see well enough in the dark to get here, or stay ahead of me." He blinked, his eyes watering through the puffiness of his eyelids. "Dhampir?" He breathed in sharply and winced. "No. The eyes are wrong."

Phoenix knew she had to be honest with him now, as honest as she could. Some part of the truth would be so much more convincing than lies she couldn't back up.

But it was very hard to think when she was looking straight into his badly burned face.

Chapter 10

"You're right," Phoenix said, calmly holding Sammael's stare. "I'm not completely human. But I'm not a dhampir, either. They haven't got a word yet for what I am. My father was a dhampir, sent on a suicide mission by Aegis. My mother was human, and she died soon after my father failed to return."

Sammael laughed, the sound as raw as if he had swallowed fire. "I should have seen it. There were signs, if only I'd—"

Phoenix swept down before he could finish and grabbed him as he fell. She eased him to the floor.

"What happened to you?" she demanded, looking him over more carefully. "Your face, and your hands…"

"Burners…will do that," he said, no longer looking at her.

"If one caught you in the face, you're lucky to have your eyes or any of your features," she said, thinking desperately of some way to treat his wounds. She knew the pain must be excruciating.

"Looks worse than it is," he whispered hoarsely. "Just leave it alone."

Phoenix didn't even bother to respond. She had no ready source of water, no cold packs or bandages, nothing to help him.

But he was a Daysider. He would heal, certainly more quickly than a human. She didn't know if he would scar, but she was simply grateful he was alive and in one piece.

"You weren't burned when you saved my life," she said.

His eyes, frigid with hostility, met hers again. "I wasn't burned by those men. I got these while I was on my way to you."

"More of The Preacher's men?"

He grunted in answer.

She decided not to press for details. "How do you know so much about dhampires?" she asked.

"Who doesn't?" he said with a curl of his lip. "I asked you before if you worked for Aegis. You denied it. But if you're even part dhampir, you have to be with them. They don't let non-humans run around the Enclave unsupervised."

"No, they don't," Phoenix said, sitting beside him. "But I'm not good enough to serve as an agent. I did work in the lower levels of Aegis, and I did get unsupervised access to classified information. I intended to use it against the Agency somehow, but I never got the chance before they realized what had happened."

"You *intended* to use it against them?"

"For what they did to my father and mother. Losing him killed her. The Agency raised me like some kind of estranged aunt who didn't want the burden of a niece she'd never met. I didn't belong anywhere. I have no reason to be loyal to them, and every reason to make them realize that dhampir agents aren't just objects to be thrown away to keep humans safe."

She stopped herself before she was tempted to embellish the story, which he was going to doubt, anyway. But there was something in his face that suggested he found her tale more plausible than the one she'd told him before. As if the idea of revenge made perfect sense to him.

"So you still want to escape the city?" he asked. "Then why did you turn on me?"

"I'm sorry, but I couldn't let you throw that Enforcer to the Scrappers, even if they have every right to want to tear him to pieces."

"You believed that was what I intended?"

"I couldn't take the chance."

"Where is he now?"

"I ran into Brita, literally. She took him back to the Hold."

"Why would you think she wouldn't just kill him?"

Sammael, of course, still had no idea that she knew what Brita was, but he also knew what any Opir was capable of.

"She'd probably give him a quicker death," Phoenix said, "and I wasn't going to run into the arms of the nearest Enforcers just to save him."

He stared at her, jaw set. "You've won *him* a reprieve," he said, "but unless you leave immediately, I will be keeping you at the Hold indefinitely."

She shrugged. "Thanks for the generous offer, but given the condition you seem to be in, you can't very well keep me. I could get away anytime. But I don't plan to leave until I have a sure way out."

"I may decide never to help you escape."

"I'll take my chances."

He shifted, the muscles under his seared skin contracting. "Why haven't they sent Aegis after you?" he asked.

"I don't know. It may simply be because they figure the Enforcers can handle me."

"Have they seen you fight?"

"I never got the chance to show them."

He clearly knew she was still holding something back, as she had so many times before. "So you're an outcast after revenge," he said, "but you still don't want to hurt the ones hunting you."

"Maybe revenge means killing to you. It doesn't to me."

He closed his eyes. "I know you can find your way back to the Hold. Go and take care of your Enforcer. I need..." He averted his damaged face. "I need to rest."

"I can carry you back."

"I don't think so." He took in another ragged breath. "Just leave me alone."

He began to rise, gasped and thumped against the wall. Phoenix grabbed his arm and forced him to sit again, aware as she did so how violently he flinched at her touch.

She backed away and sat on the floor a safe distance away. "You're not completely human, either, are you?" she asked, deciding she had nothing to lose by revealing her knowledge when he couldn't hurt her.

And because she didn't believe he would. Not even to protect himself and his mission. His face had swollen with the burns, but she couldn't mistake the change in his expression. He was genuinely startled, as if he'd expected her to say something else entirely.

"How long have you known?" he asked.

"For a while," she said. "I realized you couldn't be full Opir, or your teeth would show it." She touched her own normal incisors. "I assume you don't drink blood."

"Then what do you think I am?"

"Why don't you tell me?"

"I'd like a few answers first," he said, his body visibly relaxing. "How is it that *you* had a dhampir father, when nearly all of them were children at the end of the War?"

"Nearly all," she said. "But some were fathered before the War began, before the Awakening, from humans the Opiri Elders took as serfs when they were the only Nightsiders roaming the earth. My father escaped to the Enclave in the middle of the War, and found sanctuary here. Back then, half-Opir children were treated no better than serfs by the full-blooded. But they were valuable, the same way they are now."

"For their blood," Sammael said. "An aphrodisiac with potentially addictive qualities." He laughed. "When you tried to seduce me, were you hoping to use your blood against me?"

"Aegis doesn't believe that a half-dhampir's blood would have the same effect," she said.

"Yet even true dhampir children were abandoned in droves once the War was near its end," Sammael said.

"Most of the Opiri who abused and abandoned our women were masterless Freebloods. They weren't interested in hanging around to care for any children they fathered." She paused. "But you know all that." She sighed. "Now it's your turn."

"My mother was a dhampir," he said slowly. "She also escaped, toward the end of the War."

"Is she still alive?"

"They're both dead, like your parents."

Phoenix's heart ached that it was so easy for him to spin such a lie, a past that so deliberately echoed her own. "What happened?" she asked.

"My mother was killed by humans because of her Opir blood," he said, utterly without expression. "My father attempted to take revenge and was killed by Enforcers.

That is why I became a dissenter and an enemy of the government."

"My God," she said. He was so convincing. She could almost believe he was exactly what he claimed to be.

"I understand why you hate Enforcers," she said, "and why you'd want to kill your captive. But I'd have to try to stop you if you tried."

"I don't understand why you care about him at all."

"Maybe I just admire his courage. As I know you do. But I do wonder why you help humans when they killed your father and mother."

"I don't blame everyone for the work of a few."

But he'd help kill them, anyway, Phoenix thought with anguish. "I guess being a Fringe Boss is a way of spitting in the face of the people you *do* hate."

"You're very perceptive," he said.

But not enough, Phoenix thought. Not enough to understand how he could be the man he was and still be part of the potential destruction of the Enclave.

"You need to get back to the Hold," she said, "so those burns can be properly looked after."

"Rest is what I need now," he said. "And since—as you so accurately pointed out—I can't very well hold you prisoner, *you* go back. I'll follow when I can."

His stubbornness left her at a loss. Yes, he needed rest, but they weren't so far from the Hold, and he now knew that she could carry him.

Maybe it was simply that he wanted her to think he was much weaker than he was, so he wouldn't reveal what she knew to be true…that he was really a Daysider.

"All right," she said, getting to her feet. "But I'm going to find some water first. You're going to need it."

She searched the building for any sign of plumbing that still functioned, but found nothing. That was only to be expected, since it would be inhabited if the Scrappers had the necessary resources available.

She had more luck in one of the adjacent buildings, where there were, in fact, several families of Scrappers getting by with whatever was available. Unlike the ones she'd met with Sammael and the young Enforcer, these people were more suspicious than hostile and were willing to share a bit of water when she told them that a friend had been burned by The Preacher's men. She thanked them profusely and returned to Sammael.

He was fast asleep, though she was amazed he'd permit himself to take the risk. She set the bowl of water down, along with clean scraps of fabric, and bathed his face with extreme care. Once he was partly awake, she made him drink and half-carried, half-pulled him into deeper cover under a stairwell, making him as comfortable as possible. He was too exhausted to fight her.

There was no question of leaving him alone now. But by late morning Brita had returned, and she ran off immediately to fetch a pair of Sammael's larger male crew members. They carried him back to the Hold, Brita in the lead and Phoenix following, alert for the slightest hint of danger. Brita looked at Phoenix narrowly, but seemed satisfied that Sammael's *"guest"* hadn't learned more than she should know about the Boss. She believed Sammael's secret was still safe. For now.

Once they reached the Hold and the men set Sammael down, he shook them off and stepped back. He seemed better than he had, Phoenix noted—his face less swollen, less pain in his eyes, more grace in his movements.

"I'll see the prisoner now," he said.

Brita and Phoenix began to protest, but he gave each of them a look that silenced them both. Though he appeared to be stronger, Phoenix didn't doubt for a moment that he needed more rest and whatever treatment she could offer to augment his natural healing abilities.

Claiming to have important business to attend to, Brita left. Phoenix followed as Sammael strode down the corridor with the big men at his heels. Before he entered the room, he beckoned to Phoenix. "I want you to come in when I rap on the door," he said.

"Why?" Phoenix asked cautiously.

"Maybe you can shed a little more light on why he behaved the way he did."

"I'll do my best," she said.

"I think you will," he said, and closed the door between them.

"Who are you?" the young Enforcer asked, his voice strained with the effort to conceal his fear.

Drakon paced slowly back and forth in front of the prisoner's chair, concealing his pain and exhaustion as he passed in and out of the circle of light focused on the Enforcer's face. He truly *was* little more than a boy, probably no more than twenty, with a slightly square jaw that still had a bit of softness to it. If he were anything like his father, he'd have nothing left of that softness soon enough.

But Drakon was amazed that the young man had been permitted to become an Enforcer, let alone work without an experienced partner at his side. If Drakon had had any choice at all, he'd never have taken the boy. But he hadn't been left with a choice.

Then. But now…

"Who do you think I am?" Drakon said.

"You were with the traitor," the Enforcer said, turning his blindfolded head this way and that as he tried to gauge the size and dimensions of his surroundings. "You're going to be in big trouble for taking me, but maybe if you give her up…"

"I don't think I'm the one in trouble," Drakon said. He glanced at the door. Several of the crew were outside, awaiting his decision.

Having the young man eliminated would still be the simplest course, as long as Drakon was very careful to make it look like an accident or the work of one of the other Bosses. More specifically, The Preacher's.

And Drakon was tempted. One of the two men he most hated would suffer greatly because of his death. But Lark had threatened to stop him—or try to—if he attempted to carry out the most extreme option. And Drakon didn't want to hurt her unless he had absolutely no alternative.

"The patrolmen are doing their jobs," she'd said, *"and it's not their fault if their superiors believe I'm a traitor."*

Doing their jobs, Drakon thought bitterly. Just as he had done in his human life, before he had seen his error, before he had been deported to become a serf in the Opir Citadel.

As his fellow Enforcers had done their duties by betraying him as a *traitor,* worthy of the worst penalty the Enclave could impose. Was it their fault that a brother Enforcer's wife and child had died because of a superior's vindictive command?

He began pacing again, aware of the young man's well-trained silence. The longer he was missing, the more risk that every Enforcer, cop and Aegis operative in the city would descend on the Fringe. And likely round up or kill anyone in their way.

"I asked you who you think I am," he said to the Enforcer in a calm, level voice devoid of threat.

"This is a Hold," Patterson said. "There are lots of people here, but they're scattered all over. So you belong to a crew, and you have to have influence or you wouldn't be the one questioning me and giving orders. Maybe you're the Boss." He shifted, stretching his shoulder against the pull of the ropes. "I don't know why you were with the fugitive, but she was obviously leading you somewhere, so you're helping her somehow. Or she's helping you."

"If I'm a Boss, why would I need the help of a fugitive with half the Enforcers in the city on her tail?" he asked.

The Enforcer must have realized he'd already said too much. He fell silent. Drakon squatted before him. "Let me fill you in," he said. "She was an Admin for the government, and she's got classified information. She could sell it for help getting out of the city. That's what she wants, isn't it?"

That presumption, Drakon thought, would undoubtedly be held by this young man's peers, the common patrolmen. But the officers of the various Enforcer units had to know what they were really chasing. That she wasn't entirely human.

"What surprised me," Drakon said, "is why you were working alone and decided it was a good idea to tackle the traitor and a male companion without backup. Are you Enforcers spread so thin?"

The young man's lips tightened. "I was following orders."

"Or perhaps bending them so that you could take credit for capturing the fugitive yourself."

"I said I was following orders," the Enforcer said through gritted teeth. "Look, I never got a good look at your face. I can offer an assurance on behalf of the Bureau that you won't be harassed if you return the prisoner to us."

"Can you?" Drakon asked. "A few moments ago you threatened me, said I would be in *'big trouble'* for taking you and presumably helping the fugitive."

The young man sat very still, obviously composing himself. "It was a stupid thing to say," he admitted slowly.

"But I mean what I'm telling you now. They don't want you, or any of the Bosses. They only want *her.*"

"And you have the authority to offer such a bargain? I don't see any indication of it on your uniform. Or are you really an officer posing as a regular patrolman? Perhaps you even wanted to be captured, hoping you could obtain useful information."

"I'd have to be crazy to do that," the Enforcer said. "I know you could have killed me anytime since then if you thought I was a threat. So why am I here? Do you really think I'm going to tell you something useful?"

"You just indicated you had nothing useful to tell me."

"Then maybe you'll consider the idea that we'll not only leave you alone, but pay you more than the traitor ever could if you turn her over to us."

"I'd consider that you're afraid that what she can tell me is very valuable, indeed," Drakon said, rising.

"She…" the Enforcer swallowed with obvious nervousness. "She could hurt the entire Enclave with what she knows, including the Fringe."

"Interesting," Drakon said. "But again, I ask how you hold the authority to make such bargains on your organization's behalf?"

"I—"

"I'll tell you what *I* believe," Drakon said. "Whatever rank you hold, you personally are of some value to the government. You took a stupid risk, and now you've placed yourself in a position where someone might pay a great deal to get you back, even without your so-called '*traitor.*'"

"You're wrong," the Enforcer said. "I'm just a regular—"

"We're not quite as isolated here as you in the Nobs

seem to believe," Drakon said. "Your name is Lieutenant Matthew Patterson, your father is Senator Patterson, and he'd do anything in the world to get you back alive."

Chapter 11

Patterson clamped his lips together in a way that told Drakon he wasn't likely to offer any confirmation of his true identity.

But there were other things Drakon wanted from the Enforcer at the moment. He needed to know if the average patrolman knew that their quarry wasn't human, and that they were on the hunt for her under orders from Aegis. He needed to confirm Lark's story about her past, her parents' deaths, her *adoption* by Aegis. He needed to find out if her employers believed she was seeking revenge by using what she'd supposedly stolen. And what exactly they thought that revenge would be.

But this Enforcer seemed to have courage, conviction and devotion to the cause he fought for. He wasn't likely to give Drakon the answers he sought.

Was that the real reason Lark had saved him? Not just because she hadn't wanted to see an *innocent* young man killed, but because she'd recognized him as the son of the influential senator, just as he had?

He laughed, making young Patterson jump. He still wanted to accept Lark's explanations, even as his doubts grew stronger. So soon after she'd seemed to prove herself worthy of his trust by revealing the usefulness of her stolen intelligence, he'd been forced to realize how stupid he'd been in not recognizing that she was more than human.

Now he could understand why he was so sexually aroused in her presence. It wasn't just her enthusiasm and beauty and desire for him. Even if he couldn't become addicted by it, he had unconsciously recognized her dhampir blood. And now he wanted very, very badly to taste it.

"I'm not good enough to serve as an agent," she had said. If she seemed an outsider, a misfit, she could be a far more effective operative under certain circumstances. If his worst suspicions proved true, why hadn't she taken Matthew to safety when she'd had the chance? Wouldn't returning him to his influential father have been more important than whatever her mission might be? Or had Brita actually stopped her?

Drakon clenched his aching hands. He knew she wasn't afraid of him, and he'd no more be able to force answers from her than he could from Matthew Patterson.

But he'd looked into her eyes when she'd inspected his injuries, recognized emotions he'd seen in Cynthia's eyes so many times before her death. She'd claimed such feelings before, and he had begun to believe they were genuine, even if they ran contrary to her purpose in the Fringe. Maybe he could make use of those feelings now.

What if he were to offer to get her out of the city this coming night? Her reaction might prove—

Young Patterson sucked in a breath, and Drakon snapped back to the task at hand. He retreated to the far corner of the room and let the Enforcer stew in silence a good half-hour before he rapped on the inside of the door. Lark entered as he'd instructed, her expression wary. Now he'd get a better chance to see how she and the Enforcer would interact under very different circumstances.

"You've been questioning him?" Lark asked, though the answer was obvious.

"He's told me very little," Drakon said.

She moved closer to the young man, and Drakon saw a muscle twitch under her eye. "It's all right," she said to Patterson. "No one's going to hurt you."

"Who are you?" the young man asked.

"Lark," she said. "Lark Bennet."

Patterson's face crumpled in dismay and disgust. He looked as if he'd liked to have spit in her face.

"What have you told him?" he demanded.

"Please," Lark whispered. "You don't—"

"You're worse than any scum in the Fringe," Patterson said. "Why haven't you bought your way out of the city yet?"

"Be silent," Drakon barked. "She had no choice. This woman is my prisoner."

"Your *prisoner?*" He laughed under his breath. "What happened, Bennet? Your information not good enough? Couldn't make him do what you wanted? Or are you enjoying being his whore too much?"

"I told you to be quiet," Drakon said in a very soft voice. "She may be a traitor in your eyes, but she's no one's whore."

The Enforcer turned toward Lark again. "They hired you even though your evaluations said you were unbalanced. They gave you a rating way above what you ever should have—"

"How do you know all this?" Drakon cut in. "Did Senator Patterson tell you?"

Lark cast Drakon a look of astonishment. *Almost convincing,* he thought.

"Don't pretend you didn't know who he was from the moment we took him," Drakon said to her.

She had the sense not to deny it. Instead, she leaned closer to Matthew as if to confide some secret to him. "The government decided to execute me without a trial, without giving me a chance to defend myself," she said. "Why shouldn't I run? Why shouldn't I use whatever information I have to get out of the city?"

The prisoner turned his head aside. "Do you want me to intercede with the senator and beg for your life? He won't listen to me, even if I'd give you another chance."

"But you said you could guarantee that the Enforcers would leave the Fringe if I gave this woman up to you and let you go," Drakon said.

"He told you that?" Lark asked. "I—"

Drakon took Lark's arm, pulled her to her feet and led her out of the room.

"He doesn't realize what you really are, does he?" he asked.

"No!" She pulled her arm out of his grasp. "I...did recognize him as soon as you caught him. But he wouldn't—"

"That was a very pretty performance," he said, "but hardly convincing. Young Patterson needs acting lessons."

"What?"

"It was too well-rehearsed," he said. "He offered too much information about you, whether he knows you're part dhampir or not. He also just happened to fall into our path like an overripe apple. I admit I wasn't completely sure before, but your pleading with him convinced me otherwise." He backed her up against the wall. "He let himself be taken, didn't he? He was part of your plan."

"Let himself be taken?" she asked, appearing genuinely shocked. "When he knew you might kill him? He had nothing to do with this!"

"Why don't you tell me why the Enforcers put on this act of wanting to capture you, when that's the last thing they intend to do?"

She met his gaze with a long, direct stare. "You're right," she said. "It's all an act."

He trapped her with his body, his hands planted to either side of her head. "Variations on a theme," he said. "One lie built upon another, each a little more convincing than the last."

"If you'll only listen…"

He stared at her parted lips, wishing he could kiss her senseless, feel her naked thighs wrap around him, enter her right here in the corridor until she gasped and cried out and lost herself completely. He wanted to sink his teeth—the teeth he dared not show—into her neck and take her blood until he was drunk with it.

"I'm listening," he said, closing his eyes as he breathed in her complex and intoxicating scent.

"I had a chance to be completely honest with you after we fought The Preacher's men," she whispered, arching against him—whether purposefully or instinctively, he didn't know. "But I was still afraid."

Drakon felt a tightness in his chest that almost made him forget how much he had lied to *her*. Was lying with every breath even as he condemned her for the same betrayal.

"Go on," he said coldly.

"It was all a setup, making it seem as if I were running from Aegis and the government so I could have a legitimate reason to go looking for a way out of the city." She met his gaze, sorrow in her eyes. "You were right in your suspicions. I was sent to identify and expose the Holds of as many Bosses as possible, so the Enforcers could take down at least some of the worst criminals in the Fringe and close up the hidden passages."

Drakon released his breath. It was still possible that this story was true. He prayed it was.

"Why send a non-human operative on such a job?" he asked.

"The humans weren't having any success."

"But you've located only one Hold so far," he said. "Leaving the Enclave would never have served your purpose. Is that why the Enforcers stepped up their patrols around the Wall? To give you a plausible reason for remaining?"

"I knew nothing about that," she said, "though I admit it did serve my purpose."

"As did my attraction to you."

She laughed a little hoarsely. "In some ways, it was easier than I expected. But it backfired on me. You were one of the men I was hunting. But the sex was good for both of us. No matter what else has happened, that part was true."

Nothing in this world was true, Drakon thought. Nothing real. Nothing that survived. He had learned that long ago.

"Neither one of us was thinking then, were we?" he said. "What of the information you were prepared to trade? The warehouse you showed me?"

"Also a setup, so you'd believe whatever else I had to give you was real."

"And now you've succeeded in destroying your mission after all. That doesn't sound like Aegis to me."

"I told you I was never considered qualified for the important jobs," she said, edging out of his reach. "I obviously wasn't qualified for this one, either."

The bitterness in her voice was very convincing, Drakon thought. Very convincing, indeed.

"Are you only half-dhampir, as you claimed?"

"Do I look like a full dhampir to you?"

Drakon stalked away. "If I took you into that room and subjected you to the kind of interrogation you thought I intended for Matthew Patterson," he said, "would that finally persuade you to stop lying to me?"

"If you mean you'd torture me," Lark said. "I know you wouldn't."

"Do you truly think you know me after three days?"

"I've already admitted I've made a mess of things. But I can't do you any harm now, can I?"

He laughed, hating that she thought him so weak.

"Why is Aegis suddenly so interested in the Fringe and the Bosses?" he asked. "The city couldn't operate without smuggling. Corruption runs through every facet of human civilization, and the Enclave's no different. There are always enough officials who will work to prevent any long-term efforts to destroy us."

"But this time," she said, "the faction supporting Shepherd wants an end to deportation. You even said you agreed with his policy."

"I said I'd look for some other means of solving the problem," he said. "So who is behind this, then? Patterson and his cronies?"

"The mayor was…pressured into allowing Aegis to send a few agents to explore the possibility of closing up the illicit exits and round up a few Fringers to—"

"Keep the Enclave from descending into a state of virtual war between the opposing factions before the election begins," Drakon finished for her. "And you agreed with this plan?"

"It was never my decision to make."

"Doing your duty," he said heavily. "You told me you'd seen things here you'd never let yourself think about before. People living in misery without decent housing or food, scrounging for what they need to survive. But you would have brought even greater misery to people who already lack hope."

She looked away, a suspicious moisture in her eyes. "The Bosses and their crews cause plenty of suffering without help from anyone else. Maybe even you, Sammael. What have *you* been getting out of your selfless philanthropy?"

A desperate grasp at redemption, he thought. Redemption that would never come.

"You said yourself that you deal with evil men," she said into his silence. "No matter which side we're on, we make compromises. The only difference is in our motives."

"And yours is to serve Aegis without question."

Her lips pressed together, holding back words she was obviously afraid she'd regret. He desperately wanted to kiss those lips. Even now.

"We were both born more than human," he said. "We chose different paths. I would have done anything to keep out of the government's hands. The only way to do that was to hide. And I wasn't going to live like a cockroach scuttling out of the light."

"But that's exactly what you do, isn't it?"

"Make up your mind," he said. "Either I'm like The Preacher, exploiting innocent people for my own gain, or I'm a generous benefactor who helps them stay alive. Either I'm a traitor, or I'm a survivor. Which is it?"

"I wish I knew," she said, folding her arms across her chest. "But I can guarantee that Matthew Patterson won't know any more than I've told you. You realized that he was acting. The Enforcers knew I wasn't supposed to be caught. They weren't to make any attempt to take other prisoners."

"Strange that they seemed so intent on capturing *me* yesterday, out by the Wall."

"I thought you were lying about that," she said, "you and Brita both, though I didn't know why. In any case, I didn't tell them to do it. Even if they'd thought you might be a Boss, it wasn't in their orders."

"With the elections so close, and nothing to show for what Mayor Shepherd *'authorized'*?"

Her eyes held his without fear. "You'll never believe anything I say now. But as far as Matthew Patterson is concerned, common sense will tell you that holding him will bring the whole city down on your head. He's not only the senator's son—he's considered a hero for acts of valor facing down several murderers who escaped detention. He's also one of the generation who seems willing to consider new solutions with the Opiri."

"Like you?" He laughed under his breath. "Will the good Senator Patterson bargain to get him back?"

"I don't know," she said slowly. "But I'm beginning to realize that…there's something wrong about all this. Even if you sent me back now, I'd leave without really understanding why things are as they are, here in the Fringe, in the rest of the city."

"You *know* why. The people here are a burden on the Mids and Nobs. The higher-ups would deport them if they could get away with it."

"You can mock me," she said, meeting his gaze. "I did say that I didn't question my duty, not at first. But any person has the right to change her mind. Even against her duty."

Drakon didn't believe her sudden change of heart. It had come too quickly, like everything else.

"Are you prepared to accept the consequences if you choose to betray your own people?" he asked bluntly.

"You said it yourself. There must be another way of

solving the problems we face as a society, and with the Nightsiders."

"And what do *you* see as the solution, Lark?"

"I don't know!" She took one step toward him and then another, until their faces were literally inches apart. "I don't know the answer. To anything."

She put her arms around him and kissed him, hungrily, madly, and as Drakon returned the kiss he felt that urge to strip her clothes from her body, take her against the wall, indifferent to those who might pass by.

Lark gasped and let go as if she'd been reading his thoughts. Her skin was flushed and hot, her breath and heartbeat racing. She reached down and grasped his hand.

"Not here," she said, her voice little more than a pant. "My room. Or yours. I don't care. I just want to feel you—"

Drakon turned his hand and tightened his fingers around hers. "Don't even try," he said, fighting his lust down to a more manageable desire. "Come with me."

He pulled her into the room where young Patterson was waiting. She stopped near the door.

"I won't tell you!" Patterson snarled. "If that bitch is still here…"

"Give it up, boy," Drakon said. "I know it's all been a trick from the beginning, and what your *'fugitive'* was sent to do."

"You *told* him?" the young man said, turning his head in Lark's direction.

"To save your life," Drakon said. "Just as she did before, when the Scrappers would have taken you. The people of the Fringe are just looking for a way to get back at the Enforcers. I'd just as soon have fed you to them."

"You should have let me die," Patterson said, turning his head toward Lark. "You've made it easier for the Bosses to defend themselves against us, haven't you?

You've told them our plans, everything we've worked for!"

He spat to the side of the chair. Drakon stepped behind the young Enforcer and yanked the blindfold off his head. Patterson blinked several times, struggling to bring his vision into focus. Drakon moved again to face the young man, gently pushing Lark aside. "Look at me."

The Enforcer blinked again. "I still don't know you," he said.

Drakon slowly released his breath. "No," he said. "You don't know me. But your father was the most brutal captain and commissioner the Force has ever known. And even if the mayor authorized this sweep, Patterson was behind it."

Matthew's eyes widened. "What are you talking about? My father…he has nothing to do with this!"

"Your father has been behind every major sweep by the Enforcers over the past six years," Drakon said, barely controlling his rage.

"Yes!" Matthew said, trying to rise. "He helped keep this city alive!"

Drakon caught the young man's jaw in his hand. "Hunting men and women like dogs, violently separating families, sending the most petty criminals to Erebus…"

"Necessary!" Matthew said, his voice muffled by Drakon's merciless grip. "To save us…just like now!"

"Stop!" Lark grabbed Drakon's hand and pulled it away. "You have nothing to gain by—"

"It doesn't matter," Drakon said, releasing Patterson and leaning down to stare into the young man's eyes. "I never believed your operative's claims about possessing secret information and wanting to escape the city. I would never have let her leave this Hold alive. And you'll only get out if your father pays the price."

Lark stared at him, almost as pale as the Enforcer. "Sammael," she said. "Please. Let me talk to you outside."

"You've said enough!" Matthew shouted. "You're obviously on his side now. What turned you into a traitor? His skill at—"

Moving more quickly than the young man could possibly detect, Drakon yanked up the untied blindfold and pulled it between the Enforcer's teeth as if it were a bit on an unruly horse.

"*You've* said enough, I think," he said, tightening the knot at the base of Patterson's skull. "This game is over." He turned to Lark. "You have more to say to me?"

"Yes." She swallowed. "I want to know why your hatred for John Patterson is so personal."

Chapter 12

Phoenix left the interrogation room before Sammael could drag her out, wondering if she'd made a mistake. Instinct had demanded that she throw Sammael off balance again, but it was more than that. She truly wanted to know why he hated Patterson.

Sammael had called Matthew's father a cruel leader. But it didn't make sense that such hatred was related to the death of Sammael's father, since his story couldn't be true. He was a Daysider, and though no one knew exactly how Daysiders were created, his forebears would never have been in the Enclave. It was highly unlikely that Sammael would have encountered Patterson in the Zone, since Enforcers seldom ventured outside the city Wall.

The large men who had carried Sammael to the Hold were waiting in the corridor as if they'd been summoned to arrive at a specific time. "Keep him under guard," Sammael told them as he walked out. "No one is to speak to him. Understood?"

One of the men saluted, and the other nodded.

"My room," Sammael said to Phoenix, not waiting for her to follow.

She caught up with him quickly, but didn't attempt to speak until they had reached his quarters and he'd closed the door with more than necessary force. She sat in the chair, forcing herself to relax as he took up his usual pacing.

"You once asked me about my background," he said suddenly, never breaking stride. "I told you I came from the Mids, as you did. I told you I was married. Had a son. I told you they were in the wrong place at the wrong time." His burned fists closed, and his face tightened with a show of agony as much emotional as physical. "My father wasn't the only one in my family to suffer at the hands of Enforcers. My wife and son were two of many innocents caught between a team of Enforcers and a small crowd of protesters. The protesters were no danger to anyone, and my family was only passing through the area when the Enforcers opened fire."

He was so utterly sincere that Phoenix began to feel tears in her eyes again. The unwilling sympathy made it that much easier to pretend she believed him.

"I'm...so sorry," she whispered.

His rigid expression didn't change. "One man led the assault, though his deliberate malice, his intent to kill and not just control, was covered up later as a small error in judgment."

"John Patterson," Phoenix whispered. "And you want the son to pay for the father's sins. Matthew may defend his father, but he might not fully understand the extremes Senator Patterson went to during his military career."

"And I still don't plan to kill him," Sammael said. "As long as his father will pay to get him back."

Phoenix released her breath slowly. "How?"

"'Common sense will tell you that holding young Patterson will bring the whole city down on your head,'" he quoted her mockingly. "The boy's a hero, according to you. Even if the mayor was pressured into this sweep for political reasons, he can't oppose saving his rival's son." He met her gaze. "The only other way is to dump Matthew's body in another Boss's turf. And even then, if anyone else knew where he was or what he was doing when he disappeared…"

"What *is* your plan?" she asked.

"Much of it will depend on you, Lark. On your courage and cleverness."

Phoenix managed to maintain her composure. "What do you want me to do?"

"I want you to return to Aegis—to one of your superiors, one you believe you can trust—and tell her that one of the Bosses you've been investigating has Matthew Patterson. You will tell this superior that, in exchange for Matthew's life, you must deliver all files connected to John Patterson's career with the Bureau, particularly records about the incident in which he killed my family. Do whatever you must to convince them to let you take those files. And then you will tell Patterson that his son will be killed unless he and certain politicians meet at the border of the Fringe at a specific time one week from today."

"But why? They'll never agree to—"

"I'm betting they will. They can bring all the security they like. I intend to bring those files with me when I return Matthew and read them to the assembled politicians. It may do nothing to harm Patterson, but at least the information will be on public record."

"You think I'll just…go along with this, and not betray you?" Phoenix asked, unable to believe that Sammael genuinely thought his plan would work.

Unless he had a plan within a plan. Since he hadn't

lost a family that had never existed, maybe he thought he
could use the situation to aid the assassin in—

"Yes," he said, mercifully interrupting her thoughts.
"And you won't lead them back here, because you'll know
the whole time that young Patterson's life is at stake. I
give you the choice, Lark. Choose to let me have my revenge, or let Patterson's son die."

With a sick feeling in the pit of her stomach, Phoenix
realized that what she did now could determine the fate
of everyone in the Fringe. In the city itself. She hadn't
yet found a way to question Sammael about rumors of
an assassin, let alone search the Hold for proof of his af-
filiation with other Opiri spies in the city.

Understanding hit her so hard and fast that she almost
doubled over. Sammael wasn't only asking her to gain
access to files that might not even exist, but expecting
her to hold the Enforcers off for a full week. Maybe that
had always been his intention. If he was actively helping the assassin, the killer would probably act during
that very week.

But she still might have a chance of surprising Sammael, disable him somehow and turn him over to Aegis
for questioning. She would have to fulfill Sammael's de-
mands very quickly if she was to have any hope of helping prevent the assassination attempt.

And Matthew could easily die during such an operation. What would the death of a senator's son, popular in
his own right, do to the city?

"Don't do this, Sammael," she said, making no attempt
to conceal her anguish. "No revenge is worth the kind
of risk you're talking about. Send Matthew back. Leave
him in some neutral area far from the Hold and let them
come get him."

"And allow him to report all the questions I asked, the
things I told him?"

"They'll kill you the second they have Matthew."

"Do you think I'm that stupid, Lark? I'll take plenty of precautions, and you'll stay out of the way."

Phoenix recognized the futility and danger of arguing with Sammael again. "All right," she said. "Assuming I can get these files and can get back to you, the Enforcers back off and these politicians agree, what will you do when Matthew is safe? No matter what happens to Patterson, do you think they won't send every Enforcer and Aegis agent back to look for you as soon as the week is up?"

He strode to the chair and stood over her, his breath coming in short puffs as if he'd just run a marathon. "I'll have arranged to move the Hold by then, warn the Bosses I consider worth saving and prepare for the next full sweep. You'll tell your superiors that I and my crew will run continuous patrols to make sure the Enforcers haven't broken the deal you make with them. We spot one Enforcer or operative, and Matthew dies."

"And the people you've helped?" she asked. "The Scrappers and desperate Cits who've come here because they have nowhere else to go? You'll risk letting them be swept up, too, when the Enforcers come back in to hunt for you?"

"I'll personally see to it that everyone who wants to leave has a chance to get out of the city first."

"In one week? That's insane."

"The southern Wall will be left unguarded."

"What about those too afraid to evacuate?" she asked.

"I'm not likely to change their minds."

Phoenix rose, turning away before he could see her wildly conflicting emotions. But Sammael came up behind her and took her by the shoulders.

"If the Bureau or Aegis had the means to take everyone in the Fringe," he said, "they'd have done so long ago. I told you there were reasons they wouldn't. But I'll do whatever I can for those who want help." He released her. "You and I have preparations to make before you go."

"When do you want me to leave?"

"Tomorrow night." Suddenly he seized her, kissing her hard. She began to return the kiss, broke free and backed away.

"You're more my enemy now than you ever were," she whispered.

"Yes," he said, his voice growing hoarse. "And when this is ov—"

He collapsed before he could finish.

Drakon woke to the feeling of cool moisture on his hands, face and chest, a soothing relief from the pain that had tormented him since he'd found Lark at the building during the attack.

Lark had made it almost easy for him to pretend he wasn't badly injured. She'd been so caught up in the drama of Matthew Patterson's interrogation, the stories they had told each other and his plans for his prisoner that he'd managed to keep his face and body from betraying his agony.

But now he found Lark looking down at him, her hazel eyes filled with mixed emotions he couldn't read. His shirt was off, and so were the rest of his clothes. A sheet was lightly draped over him, but he knew she had seen the burns. It was fortunate for him that the sunlight had barely penetrated his clothing on his shoulders, upper arms, hands and face.

"You've been asleep for a long time," Lark said quietly. "How are you feeling?"

Her simple question calmed him when he should have been most ready to act, to…

Silence her? Kill her?

But she did nothing, said nothing. She held him down gently when he tried to sit up, pressing on his stomach to avoid his injured skin.

"There's no point in struggling," she said. "There wasn't much I could do for your burns, so you might as well let your body heal itself." She sighed. "All that time with Matthew, and afterward with me, you were trying to hide this. Trying to stay on your feet, fooling everyone. But you only made it worse."

"Has anyone else seen me?" he asked.

His tone must have betrayed his concern, for Lark leaned back, her expression less worried now than wary.

"Brita dropped in briefly," she said, watching his face. "She was concerned, but oddly enough, she seemed to trust me to look after you."

Feeling an utter fool, Drakon wondered for the first time if Brita had done anything to make Lark suspect that she, too, wasn't human. But if she'd left him in Lark's care, she'd believed that Lark hadn't put two and two together and wouldn't recognize the nature of Drakon's burns.

Drakon hadn't had the chance to tell Brita that Lark had already guessed he wasn't human. Did she suspect that Lark, too, was part Opir? If Lark had done anything to make her believe that, she was in more danger than ever before.

He had to learn what Brita knew. And what she might do with that knowledge.

"Anyone else come in?" he asked Lark.

"No one except Repo, who brought the medkit."

And Repo, like the rest of the crew, didn't know his true nature. Lark was an agent of Aegis, and Brita had been wrong to think she wouldn't figure out the truth.

"I thought you were a Daysider from almost the moment I met you," she said, answering his unspoken thoughts.

He laughed. The joke was entirely on him. "But that isn't what you think now," he said.

Lark leaned over to give him a sip of water from a cracked glass. "You're a Nightsider. A full Opir."

"A bloodsucker," he said, wincing as he shifted his weight on the mattress.

"The man who saved my life from The Preacher's crew, even if I might have taken most of them down with me." She wet a fresh cloth in a bowl and dabbed at his right shoulder. "Of course I don't know why, but the fact is that you went out in the sunlight to help me, and I'm grateful."

He lifted one hand, wincing at the pull of burned skin. "Grateful," he said. "You can afford to be. I can hardly hurt you now."

"By killing me, or just taking my blood?"

He licked his lips, realizing he hadn't accessed his blood stores for three days. Lark's nearness had aroused an agony worse than the pain of his burns.

"If I'd ever taken blood from anyone here," he said, "they'd know what I am. There are enough of them to kill me, if they all turned on me at once."

"But you must have your own supply. Where do you get it?"

"It's brought to me periodically. I don't know the source."

Phoenix felt slightly ill, though she couldn't believe that he'd deliberately take blood acquired by violent means. "Stored somewhere on the premises, I presume?" she asked.

"Somewhere," he said, closing his eyes.

"I can understand why you don't want to tell me," she said. "But that's the least of your worries now, isn't it? I know the only reason you'd be hiding in the Fringe is if you're a spy for Erebus."

"Have you been hunting for Opir agents all along?" he asked wearily.

"Would you believe me if I said no?"

Drakon tensed and released the muscles of his left arm, testing the flexibility of his skin. It still hurt mightily, but he was mending.

Just not quickly enough.

"Yes," Lark said at last, sitting back in the chair as if she was relieved that at least some of the playacting was over. "I was hunting for Opir spies. Did you consider that possibility before?"

"It crossed my mind, after I learned what you were."

"Was the story you told me about your family true?"

"It was," he said, looking away.

"Everything? The Enforcers, your wife…your son?"

No, he thought. *Not everything.* "I lost them exactly as I told you," he said.

"I'm sorry," she said, with that emotion that always seemed so genuine. "I couldn't believe you before because I assumed you were a Daysider, and Daysiders don't have human wives and children. But now I know you were once—"

"Human?" he said, showing his teeth. She stared at his mouth, at the caps that made his incisors seem flush with his others.

"Yes," she said. "And the government deported you. For being a dissenter, like your parents."

He looked away, knowing he could never tell her the full truth. He could take his revenge on John Patterson if he was lucky, but his mission had to come first. During that week of respite from the Enforcers, he would do what he could to take the mayor down. If Patterson gained leadership of the Enclave after the revelation of his past misdeeds, he would inherit only chaos. Eventually, he would pay in full.

Like all the innocents who would suffer before the Enclave rebuilt itself...*if* it did before the Opiri Council came to an agreement and decided to attack.

He could still help some Fringers escape into the dubious *"freedom"* of the southern Zone. But not all would leave, and if the city fell those who remained would face lifelong serfdom.

You can stop, he told himself. *You can still back out.*

"Tell me something," Lark said, breaking into his thoughts. "Why do you look like a Daysider, or a normal human? The caps are obvious, but what about the rest of you? Are you some kind of mutation?"

In spite of himself, Drakon stiffened. He had felt a freak so long, from the moment Julius had converted him. But now, having lived among humans again for over a year...

"If I told you," he said grimly, "I'd have to kill you."

Chapter 13

It was a very bad joke. Drakon knew that both he and Lark were considering the likelihood of this situation ending in the death of one or both of them.

But then again, they always had.

"You have a very strange sense of humor," she said, "considering how many times the subject has come up under equally difficult circumstances."

Drakon swallowed the apology hovering on his tongue. "Why don't you tell *me* if *your* story of losing your parents was true?"

Her eyes glistened. "It was. But my father wasn't sent on a suicide mission. He was simply a good operative who was killed in the field. And the Agency did raise me."

"Like an estranged aunt?"

"I was different. But I found my place."

Drakon wondered if she truly had. "Why were you looking for The Preacher when you came to the Fringe with your story of being hunted?" he asked. "Were you told he had some connection to Opir agents in the city?"

"No," she said. "Not specifically. But I had to start somewhere, and we knew he was one of the most powerful Bosses in the city."

"But not that he was also the worst?"

"I knew I could defend myself, and I could escape if I had to."

He laughed, setting off another wave of pain. "If you were sent to expose Opir spies, why didn't you return to Aegis when you believed I was a Daysider? Did you think you could handle me alone?"

"I knew the odds of that were very much against me," she said. "But I thought the risk was worth it."

"You might still be able to get out of here," he said harshly. "Warn the Enforcers."

She met his gaze. "And sacrifice Matthew after all?"

"You can expose me to my crew," he said, attempting to sit up.

"And Matthew would still die, at their hands."

"So you'll present the bargain?"

"My mission is already compromised beyond recovery."

"Given what I know of you, Lark, I wouldn't bet on it." He eased himself back with a grimace. "Is Lark really your name?"

"It's Phoenix," she said.

"Lark. Phoenix. One common bird, one mythically powerful."

"I guess I couldn't get away from avians," she said. "Is your name really Sammael?"

"An Opir can have many names in his lifetime," he said. "It's as good as any."

She would know he was evading her question. But he suspected that his true Opir name was already known by

Aegis, though only through rumor. Rumor he'd always recognized might extend to suspicion that a killer from Erebus hid within the city.

Was it possible that suspicion had become certainty? Had Lark—Phoenix—been sent to find a very specific Opir agent? A Dragon to her mythical bird?

"You need more water," she said suddenly, retrieving the glass and kneeling beside him again. "And I know you'll need blood to complete your healing. You'd better tell me where your cache is."

He shook his head.

"Could it be you regret what you're doing?" she asked, leaning toward him. "Do you want to die?"

He flinched at the sound of her voice expressing the thoughts he still didn't want to face.

"You remember what it's like to be human," she said. "Did you return as a spy only because you expected you'd get a chance to take revenge on John Patterson?"

Now, Drakon thought, she was trying to trap him. He could see her struggling to make the right decision, wondering what questions she dared ask.

"Come here, Phoenix," he said.

She stared at him as if he'd gone mad. "So you can strangle me? Break my neck?"

"I believe I once told you that I would never touch you against your will," he said, meaning it with all his heart. "Are you willing now?"

She got up and sat on the edge of the bed, careful not to jar him. Heedless of the discomfort, Drakon clamped his arms around her waist, pulled her hard against his chest and kissed her. The pain was nothing to the ecstasy of holding her. She melted against him, speared her fingers in his hair and straddled his hips. She was no more gentle with him than he was with her. His cock swelled to its full size almost instantly.

Phoenix obviously felt the change. She rubbed herself against him, teasing him through the thin barrier of the sheets as he deepened the kiss. He ignored the pain in his arms and shoulders, pulling at her shirt with thick, clumsy fingers, running his palms up the skin of her belly and ribs, finding her breasts bare underneath. She tilted back her head, offering. Offering him everything.

He moaned with lust, for her body and her blood, and suddenly Phoenix stiffened. She wrenched herself free, and he swallowed a grunt of pain.

"God," she said, panic in her eyes. "I've hurt you!"

Drakon burst into a laugh of frustration and disbelief. "Yes," he said, catching his breath.

"Don't!" she ordered. "I could have—"

He grabbed for the only part of her he could reach, clamping his fingers around her wrist. "That was nothing," he said. "And I wasn't groaning in pain."

She stared at the one part of him that refused to concede defeat. The sheet might as well not have been there at all. She pulled free of his grip.

"I can't believe you were trying to seduce me in *your* condition," she said, breathless with emotion she was fighting to control.

"Seduce you?" he said, nearly as breathless. "You were the one on top of *me*."

"I wasn't… I didn't—" Phoenix broke off and clamped her lips together. Those lips Drakon had just kissed, and wanted to keep kissing until…

"I will give you one more chance," he said quietly. "You can get out of the Hold before anyone in the crew knows what you've done. You might even be able to get Matthew out as well. If you don't, I will do exactly what I vowed to do. I'll make sure the Citadel's mission is carried out."

And, in that moment, he *wanted* her to stop him. To

relieve him of his pain, his rage, his all-consuming guilt. Wanted her to end it, so he wouldn't complete his mission, wouldn't become what he had once hated so much.

He would stop hating. Stop caring. Stop remembering.

"If you don't do it," he said, "you'll always wonder if you could have stopped the Enclave from crashing down around you."

That was the moment Phoenix knew.

"Many names," Sammael had said. He wasn't merely a link in a chain, passing on information, protecting his fellow spies. This Opir knew what Erebus had planned for the mayor.

He knew because he *was* the assassin.

She sat down hard on the chair. "What was your real name?" she asked. "When you were human?"

"Charles. Charles Cruise."

"And now?"

He smiled, as if he found something secretly amusing in the midst of so much horror. "In ancient Chinese mythology," he said, "the Phoenix was the feminine symbol used to represent beauty and good luck. She was yin to the yang of the dragon, the symbol of power and good fortune."

"Good fortune?" she said, gasping out a laugh. "But you're not here to bring good fortune to the Enclave, are you...Drakon?"

"Ironic, isn't it? The two together symbolized a fruitful marriage."

He wasn't even trying to pretend. He must always have suspected that Aegis knew the name of the potential assassin, though obviously he'd been right in believing they knew little more than that. He also knew that she'd lost control of her very real attraction to him—a *Nightsider*, no matter what his appearance.

And *she* was certain that, deep in his converted heart, he didn't want to go through with his mission.

Maybe it was only wishful thinking of the worst kind. But whatever she might feel for him—or he for her, if any Opir could really feel anything of affection or love— wouldn't matter at all if she lost this chance he'd given her. If she ignored the sacrifice he was willing to make.

"Fruitful?" she said, unable to conceal the agonizing turmoil of her emotions. "There's no hope of that now." She moved just out of his reach, breathing fast. "I'm sure you've guessed by now that I was sent to track down the assassin we knew was stalking the city."

"And you, only half-dhampir, were supposed to catch him?"

"No. I was supposed to return once I had a solid idea of how we might find him or her. Once I realized you were Opir, I knew you had to be connected somehow. I chose to remain, hoping to learn more."

"To prove yourself?" he asked. "To show you're as good as any of the true dhampires?"

He knew her. How well he knew her.

"What about you?" she said. "What are *you,* Drakon? You've never behaved like a Nightsider who only cares about humans as slaves and sources of food. You—"

"I *am* one of them," he said flatly.

"Against your will. Like all the other deportees, you started as a serf in the Citadel—"

"And was Claimed by an Opir who treated his human slaves with decency. Who believed they were more than animals. I wasn't well educated before I went to Erebus. By the time I became his vassal, I knew more about both human and Opir history than most humans learn in their entire lives."

"But you're not a vassal now," she said.

"I'm a Freeblood," he said, "able to make my own choices."

She was quiet a moment, thinking things through. "I understand your desire to get revenge on Patterson," she said. "But what about Shepherd? Drakon, I want to understand."

"What does it matter?"

"It matters to *me*."

He sighed. "I told you the Bloodlord who Claimed me in Erebus became my mentor," he said. "But he was more like a father to me. Julius believed, as I did, that there must be a way to communicate with the Enclave—not via diplomats or small acts of aggression, but through the agents who actually patrol the Zone. Agents of Aegis and the Council, meeting in peace."

"He sounds like a…good man," Phoenix said softly.

Drakon seemed not to hear her. "Many Opiri in the Citadel had begun to question the Expansionists who wanted a new war, but some of these dissenters recognized the possible benefits of tearing down the old and rebuilding, even if it might lead to a smaller war."

A smaller war, Phoenix thought with a shudder. "Political expediency," she said, "meant to stop something even worse."

"As in the Enclave." He clenched his teeth. "My Sire sent me out to warn Enclave agents. But Julius learned that the Expansionists on the Council had acted alone and had sent their own operatives to kill any Opiri in the Zone who were not explicitly authorized to be there. He risked his own life to warn me. But Aegis captured him, tortured him and left him for dead. I found him and held him while he died of his wounds and exposure to the sun. There was hardly anything left of him but charred skin and bone."

"My God," Phoenix whispered. "I can't believe that any agent—"

"Can't you?" He sat up, jaw set against the pain. "I was taught, like all humans, that Opiri are unfailingly evil. Even dhampires, who work for the Enclave, aren't completely trusted here because of their Nightsider blood. There are agents who are more than happy to torment an Opir prisoner, even if it isn't officially condoned."

"I don't believe it," Phoenix said, turning cold. "I've known a lot of agents. Good agents. Good people. What you're saying—"

"I saw what they did with my own eyes."

"And my father was killed by one of yours!"

"Did they torture him first?"

Phoenix drew her legs up to her chest and hugged them tightly. "They must have wanted information from Julius, even if…if they—"

"I never found out," Drakon said coldly. "Julius was unable to speak at the end. But afterward, I tracked the Enclave agents. I learned who was responsible."

"Aaron Shepherd," she whispered.

"He was on the committee setting and overseeing Aegis policy at the time. I learned from one of the agents I questioned that he had authorized more stringent methods against enemy operatives in the Zone because of certain intelligence he had received about the Citadel's plans."

Phoenix was nearly beyond shock. "I can understand… why he might authorize more stringent methods in the Zone, where agents' lives are at stake," she said, her voice shaking. "But to approve…to approve of torture, and murder—"

She'd still been in love with Aaron when he was on the committee, Phoenix thought, feeling the bile rise in her throat as she remembered how happy she'd been then, thinking—hoping—the two of them might marry one day.

"I didn't know," she said. "I'm so sorry."

"For the death of a Bloodlord, one of the detested enemy, who hasn't been human for thousands of years?"

"Yes," she said. "He was good to you."

"Better than any human I'd ever known except my real parents and my…my own family."

"And so Shepherd has to die. And you'll make Patterson suffer. Was that part of your mission?"

"Vengeance is an emotion Opiri share with humans," he said. "They trusted me all the more because of my personal motives."

"Is that why they chose you?"

He met her gaze, his own almost blank. "I'm an expert marksman. The best there is."

"You learned that in Erebus?"

He didn't answer. Phoenix's mind cleared, and her thoughts began to race.

"What if Shepherd could be brought down another way?" she asked.

"Would you let him be brought down, Phoenix?"

No, she thought. *Not even for you. Not even knowing what he's done.* "I know you plan to try for the mayor during that week I'm supposed to buy from the Enforcers," she said. "But you're not a killer, Drakon, no matter what I thought at first. You'd never have let me get near enough to touch you if you were. I'd be dead." She unfolded her body and rose again. "You can still ruin Patterson. And then you can disappear, until the government is convinced the danger is over."

He sighed and closed his eyes. "Let's stop playing games, Phoenix," he said. "I had a choice, and I made it."

She moved closer, drawn by the torment in his voice. "You don't believe your revenge is more important than the thousands of lives that will be destroyed after Shepherd is dead. If the Opiri succeed in infiltrating the Enclave, every man, woman and child here will lose their freedom."

"The freedom your citizens have now, constantly risking deportation for the slightest infraction?"

"As *you* were," she said, staring at him with all the contempt she could muster. "But I think I understand now. It's not just Shepherd or Patterson or what they did to people you loved. You *do* think the Enclave deserves to fall."

"Maybe all of it does," he said, the grief and anger naked on his burned face. "The Enclave, the Citadel. Maybe none of it should survive."

She clenched her fists. "You're wrong, Drakon."

"There is only one sure solution to your problem. See that I die, or become a real traitor to your people."

"No," she said, unable to comprehend what was happening to her. To *them*. "You said you once believed, like Julius, that we might find a new way of peace."

"I once believed it," he said. "But if it happens at all, it will only be after cleansing by fire and rebirth from the ashes." His eyes grew moist, and somehow she knew he was remembering those he had loved and lost. "Sacrifices must be made."

"And yours will be the most noble of all. Because you can't face the thing that's tearing you apart inside. You don't have the courage to stop what you know is wrong. You're giving in to what you hate, and you want me to save you."

"It will tear *you* apart if you don't stop it."

"Do you hate *me* so much?"

"I only wish I did."

Chapter 14

Phoenix's heart jumped in her chest. She hadn't imagined what she'd heard in Drakon's voice. Or what it meant.

It wasn't only lust, after all, though there was no way to be sure how far his feelings for her extended. And she still didn't understand how she could care so deeply for a creature who could destroy everything she believed in.

What do *you believe in, Phoenix?* she asked herself. *Do you even know anymore?*

"Drakon—" she began.

But sometime during her pause, Drakon had fallen unconscious. Or asleep…she couldn't tell which. She climbed onto the other side of the bed and stretched out beside him. Very, very gently she touched his neck, feeling for his pulse. It was a great irony that, unlike the monsters of legend, Opir *"vampires"* had nearly all the same biological functions as human beings.

And Drakon's seemed fine. His heart beat steadily, and

his breathing was normal. He only needed time to let his body take care of itself.

Until then, he was helpless. He'd let himself go. Had she wanted to, she could kill him in his sleep.

She didn't realize she'd fallen asleep herself until she felt Drakon's chest move under her cheek. Somehow she'd come to rest on one of the burned parts of his body, but she knew at once it was healed by the texture, the firm, warm skin supporting her head.

Before she could pull back, she felt Drakon's hand in her hair, gently twisting the strands around his fingers.

"You slept," he said.

The sound of his voice was slightly drowsy, and yet there was an edge to it. A hungry edge. And her throat was very close to his mouth.

"Why didn't you kill me?" he asked, his chest rising with a deep, slow breath.

"I don't know," she said, making no further attempt to move away. Her thoughts had suddenly fallen into new and disturbing channels. What if she willingly shared her blood with him?

He'd as good as admitted that his feelings for her went beyond what he'd willingly admit. Even if addiction—and all it implied—was virtually impossible, might his taking her blood create a bond between them that would tip him over to her side?

There was always a chance. But she was afraid. Afraid she was making another terrible mistake.

"How long have you gone without blood?" she asked, closing her eyes.

His breath gusted against her hair. "Too long," he said. "Maybe all you have to do is wait me out."

"Take mine," she whispered.

She could feel his stare burning the top of her head. "What?" he asked.

"You heard me," she said, swallowing.

He pushed her away. She rolled onto her side, her own pulse beating so fast that she was sure he must hear it.

"You don't know what you're saying," he said.

"Yes, I do." She met his troubled, hungry gaze. "We have opposing goals, Drakon. We'll always be enemies. But there *is* something between us, and for some crazy reason I want to have at least one good memory, no matter what happens."

He sat up, the sheets she'd tucked up around his chin falling to his waist. "A good memory?" he said hoarsely. "I could convert you into my vassal."

"No. The part of me that's dhampir is one of the forty percent who can't be converted."

"And because you're part dhampir," he said, his expression stony, "you think you can bind me in some way, force me to—"

"No," she said, touching his healed hand. "I know you've been attracted to my blood from the beginning, but you can't become addicted to the blood of someone like me."

"And yet you seem so eager to help me, when you should want just the opposite."

She sat up, ready to get off the bed. "I offered," she said. "Don't forget that, when we're—"

Drakon grabbed her wrist and pulled her back across the bed. "I'm willing to take the risk," he said softly.

Phoenix looked up from her prone position, feeling more vulnerable than she had since she'd first met him. "Something else might happen, Drakon," she said. "Something even you don't expect."

In answer, he pulled her onto his lap. She could feel his cock pushing the sheet into a peak just under her thighs, and in spite of herself she moved until it was between them.

"Watch yourself, Phoenix," he said, "unless you're prepared to give me more than blood."

She half-turned and kissed the side of his mouth. "I said I wanted something to remember," she said. "Can you give me that, Drakon?"

He rolled over on top of her, his lean and graceful body uncovered, holding himself above her with his muscular arms. She thought he would begin by biting her, but instead he kissed her, very gently, as if they had all the time in the world. She pushed her fingers through his hair and returned the kiss with greater urgency, but he pulled back.

"Easy," he said with a warmth that made her catch her breath. "I will survive a few more minutes." He turned slightly away and touched his mouth. When he turned back again, his incisors were clearly visible, no longer covered by the caps that had disguised them. He resumed his former position, and kissed Phoenix again. She sensed the slight change in the feel of his mouth on hers, though his biting teeth never so much as grazed her lips. His tongue slipped inside her mouth, and she opened to accept him.

The kiss was lingering, deep, incredibly arousing. But it didn't give her what she wanted most. She was almost ready to beg him when his tongue made a trail down over her collarbone, above her breasts and suddenly found her nipple. He teased the erect tip with a curl of his tongue, bringing it to almost painful attention. She pulled his head down and his mouth closed over her, taking in as much of her breast as he could. Gradually, he withdrew and began to explore the underside of her breast and below.

It was a slow, fascinating, wonderful thing, how he kissed his way down to the hollow of her ribs and lower to her belly. The way he seemed to remove her pants without her feeling it. The way his tongue was suddenly in just the place she wanted it to be, doing just the things she had imagined.

But so much better. He parted her thighs gently, and his lips settled on the soft curls between them, already damp with arousal. His tongue slid down into the indentation beneath, darted inside, touched her in a place that sent a powerful shock through her entire body.

He didn't linger there, though the torment was exquisite. He began to explore, licking slowly, as if he were savoring a particularly delicious treat. He ran his tongue along every fold, every valley, sometimes skating over the surface, sometimes pushing deep. Phoenix dug her fingers into the sheets and moaned as he slowly circled her entrance and probed inside, making her shudder and gasp. Then, as his tongue darted in and out, he began to rub her clitoris with his thumb.

Bucking helplessly, Phoenix felt herself begin to come. But he withdrew just in time, letting her body relax for a few moments, before returning to her breasts. He slid one, two, three fingers inside her and moved them in rhythm with his eager suckling.

Again she came to the edge, and again he stopped. But this time what she felt between her legs was very hard and large and as hungry to enter her as she was to have Drakon inside her. She wrapped her legs around his hips, and he entered her slowly, an inch at a time, though she could hardly wait to be filled to the brim.

She moaned in relief as he thrust deep, pushing her into the mattress, letting her feel his hardness stretch her before withdrawing and thrusting again. Each movement was deliberate, not desperate, as if he meant to torture her. And each time she gasped as if he were doing it for the first time.

"More," she whispered. And he obliged. He began to move faster, thrusting harder, rocking her, claiming her, kissing her and pushing his tongue between her lips. She was open to him in every way, and still it wasn't enough. She wanted him so deep inside her that he could never leave again.

But that was not to be. He slowed for a minute, taking his time again, and then suddenly was thrusting almost violently, forcing her to cry out not in pain but in ecstasy. She came with a great shudder that sent spikes of pleasure through every nerve, from head to toe, and a few seconds later he came, as well, driving a last time, his chest heaving, his breath coming fast.

Even that was not the end. For as her body throbbed with sated pleasure, he put his lips to her neck and bit her.

There was no pain. She knew there would be none, because no Opir bite was uncomfortable unless the Nightsider wanted it to be.

And this was every bit as wonderful and astonishing as the sex. She felt her blood flowing into his mouth, but it was an incredibly erotic experience, sending new shock waves of orgasm through her body. She came again and again until her senses nearly overloaded, and only then did he draw back, licked the small wounds, healing them with the touch of his mouth.

He lay over her for a while, and she mumbled a soft protest as he withdrew completely and rolled to the side. Still throbbing with pleasure, she maneuvered herself into the crook of his shoulder and laid her hand on his chest, feeling his heartbeat thunder beneath her palm.

They lay together in silence for an indefinite length of time, and eventually Phoenix fell asleep. When she woke, her head was tucked under Drakon's chin, and he had looped his arm around her shoulder. Holding her. Protecting her. Almost making her believe…

"We've still got a problem," she said softly.

His ribs heaved with silent laughter under her stroking hand. "Only one?"

"You gave me a chance to stop you. I didn't take it. Now what happens?"

His faced turned to stone, and his mouth remained firmly closed.

"You can't let me go and make your bargain for you," she said. "Maybe I could never hurt you, but I'll have to tell them who you are. You won't get a chance to try for the mayor."

He stared at the far wall, decorated with a brown photograph in a cracked frame. "And young Patterson?"

"Once I tell them who and what you are, they'll have no choice but to move against you," Phoenix said. "He'll be sacrificed, no matter what outrage it causes or the hell his father will raise. If they have to choose between the consequences of that sacrifice or the far worse problems that will follow the mayor's assassination, it'll be the former." She released her breath. "And unless you stop *me,* they will get you eventually."

His chest rose and fell three times before he spoke. "What if I agree not to take action during the week in question?" he asked. "What if I leave the city the moment Patterson is exposed?"

"Are you—" she began, rising on her elbow to look into his face. "Will you actually—"

"Yes." He turned his head to meet her gaze, and there was absolute sincerity in his eyes.

He meant it. Somehow, she'd convinced him.

Without another word she kissed him, pouring all her passion and gratitude into it, making him feel how deeply he had affected her. He put his arms around her gently, barely returning the kiss, as if he were embarrassed by what he perceived as a terrible weakness in himself.

She drew back, catching his gaze as he tried to look

away. "If you'll have me," she said, "if you want me, I'll come with you."

"Phoenix—"

"Don't tell me now. Think about it. You'll have time while I'm arranging the other things we discussed."

"Then you'll go through with the bargain?"

"To bring Patterson down? Yes. Whatever happens to him and his faction afterward…that I'm willing to risk. He deserves whatever he gets."

Drakon pulled her head down and kissed her brow. "Thank you," he said.

"Are you kidding?" she said, laughing as the tears spilled over her cheeks. "You've made me the happiest woman in the world."

"Then maybe you won't be too upset when I tell you your other part in my plan."

"I don't think I'm going to like this," she muttered.

"It's very simple. When I go to confront the senator with you and his son, I'll have young Patterson read the files while I have a burner trained on both of you. When he's finished, I let him go and hold you as a hostage to make sure they let us leave. Once we're away, we head straight for the passage I'll have arranged for us to use. One just for you and me."

"We have a deal."

"There's only one thing I need you to understand, Phoenix."

She already knew what was coming. "I know you… don't feel the same way about me as I do about you. I never expected you to. You lost people you loved, when you were human. Maybe even if you'd remained human you can't feel that way about anyone again."

"When I was human," he said, his voice thick and heavy, "I believed Opiri couldn't feel the way humans do. In Erebus, I learned it wasn't that simple. Different things are important to them—us—but we can still feel grief, and happiness, and hatred and affection."

"Not love."

"I loved Julius, as a father. He loved me as a son. I saw other examples in the Citadel. But they don't express it the way we… The way humans do."

"I understand," she said quietly.

They lay side by side for a while, legs entangled, until Phoenix began to grow drowsy again. Drakon got up, dressed and left the room on silent feet. She stretched, trying to awaken stiff muscles.

At this very moment, Drakon was probably consulting with Brita, making arrangements, speaking with the other members of his crew, concocting some explanation for why he was sending Phoenix to make a bargain with Matthew Patterson's father when, ignorant of her true purpose as they were, they'd have trouble believing she'd willingly go anywhere near the authorities again.

It would have to be a very good story, Phoenix thought as she gathered up the clothes that had become tangled among the sheets and flung on the floor, but she didn't doubt he could do it. His crew had to trust him, fight him or abandon him. And she didn't think they'd try the last two options. When she left, they wouldn't stop her.

And as for Brita…if they were working together, as Phoenix had always believed, how would she react? She must have known all along that he was the assassin. Would he tell her the truth about his decision not to go through with it, or would he conceal his intentions? Would she consider him a traitor to his own kind, and act accordingly?

Whether he told her or she simply figured it out, she could be a very, very big problem.

Pulling on her shirt and pants, she took stock of all the incredible things that had happened in only four days.

Her clothes felt cold against her skin. All of her felt cold, robbed of Drakon's warmth and of the blood he had taken.

And of the love she knew he could never give her.

There were no windows in this room, not even boarded up. She couldn't see the sky. But she knew it must be after midnight, and she didn't have much time to prepare herself mentally for the task she was about to attempt.

Brita sat on the edge of the table in the meeting room, staring at Drakon. Her dark eyes held neither warmth nor understanding. "You're not going through with it, are you?" she asked. "She's convinced you."

Drakon listened for anyone outside the closed door. Nothing. The others had accepted his story and had gone to bed, except for those assigned as guards at the exits and just outside the Hold.

"I don't know what you're talking about," he said.

"Don't even try, Drakon," Brita said. "I know you told her everything."

"Yes," Drakon said, "I did."

"Elders! And now, because of her, you think—"

"Nothing has changed," he said, holding Brita's gaze as he spoke the lie. "Any feelings I may have for her—"

"Are obviously stronger than the ones you had for Julius. And probably for Cynthia and Mark, as well."

Drakon took a step toward her. "I told you when you first came to me that I didn't want their names spoken in this Hold," he said.

"Except by you, and *her*," Brita said, the corner of her lip lifting in a sneer. "I never thought you could be so weak, brother."

Brother. That was the word that always stopped him when he was angry with her, with her perpetual bitterness—greater even than his own—her easy ability to slide between two worlds without feeling any attachment at all to the humans she was supposed to be serving. Aegis operative on one side, Council agent on the other.

She'd never felt any conflict over her loyalties. She had never been human, though her peculiar genetics allowed her to pass for one. She was considered a quarter human by Aegis, believed to be the peculiar offspring of a male dhampir born before the Awakening and a female Daysider scout from the War, who had come to the Enclave to avoid execution by the Opiri for creating a child of their own. Drakon had once claimed that his own fictional dhampir mother had been seeking the same sanctuary, but his story had been false.

Brita's was not. Not entirely. But her father had not been dhampir. He had been full-blooded Opir, a Bloodlord, whose Daysider mate had fled Erebus near the end of the War out of fear that the father of her infant child could not protect them. She had died at human hands, creating and confessing Brita's half-dhampir heritage and leaving her daughter to be rescued by the very soldiers who had killed her mother. Hardened soldiers who believed Brita had enough human blood to be worth saving.

So she had been brought into what had then been the foundation of the Enclave, just as the Armistice was about to be signed. She had been told her parents had been killed by Opiri. She had become an agent of Aegis at nearly the same time Drakon had become an Enforcer, though they had known nothing of each other then.

"I am not your brother," he said calmly. "You became a double agent the day you learned that your mother had been killed by humans. You returned to Erebus to find your real father. I was—"

"My father's serf, and then his vassal. He set you free."

"And I did love him," Drakon said. "But you didn't even know I existed until two years ago, after you began working for both sides. I didn't know who or what you

were until I *'saved your life,'* so that you could become
Aegis's spy in my Hold. *And* keep watch on me for the
Opiri who sent us."

"Now I know they were right to do it. You've become
a human again...Charlie."

The name sounded like a curse on her lips, but Drakon didn't look away. She slid off the table, her booted
feet rapping against the hard floor.

"Don't lie to me, Drakon. The very fact that you'd trust
Lark—Phoenix—to carry out your instructions by turning against her own people shows you've lost your judgment, if not your sanity. She's very likely to betray you
the moment she arrives at Aegis, and then—"

"She won't. I've convinced *her* that I won't go through
with the assassination, that I only want Patterson. *She's*
the weak one, Brita. She thinks she owes me for making
such a sacrifice."

"Does she know your motive for wanting Shepherd
dead?"

"Yes. But it doesn't matter to her what happens to
Patterson's reputation as long as I leave Shepherd alone
and get out of the Enclave after I'm done with the senator. She won't get a chance to stop me if she believes I've
given up."

"It sounds very neat and tidy. And it all rests on your
judgment of flimsy human emotions."

"Phoenix will return with what I asked for. I'll make
sure it looks as if she was coerced, and she'll be out of
the way when I do my job. Then I'm heading south into
the Zone. I'm not going back to Erebus."

Chapter 15

Folding her arms across her chest, Brita scowled. "You owe your Sire more than—"

"No. I don't love what I am, Brita. I'm not interested in fighting for serfs and a household in the Citadel. I'll make my own life."

"With *her*."

"She won't want me when I'm done. If I survive. But I'll take her, anyway. What would you do if I didn't?"

"I have nothing personal against her."

"Except your fear that she might somehow find out who you are and expose you."

"My *fear*—"

"But you don't really need a reason, do you, Brita?"

"You make me sound like a monster, when the *humans* are the monsters."

"Neither side has a premium on savagery."

Brita didn't answer, but her face was ferocious in its hatred. "When are you going to move?"

"Once Phoenix is gone, I'll start scouting. It'll have to be fast, so I'll need to take some pretty big risks. And that increases the chance of failure."

"You were too cautious before," she said. "If it had been *my* mission—"

"But it isn't. You're too valuable here. Your loss would be catastrophic to Erebus. If I fail, they'll send another assassin."

"That isn't good enough." Brita circled him slowly, ever the predator in a way he had never quite become, even when he'd developed the need for blood.

Phoenix's blood, he thought, his mind drifting. He craved the taste of it, the sweetness of it, as he craved her body. He never wanted anything else, even though he might never taste it again.

Or get the chance to tell her....

"Listen to me!" Brita demanded, swinging him around by his arm. "You *have* to succeed, because something has happened that Erebus didn't anticipate. The humans are making a weapon to use against us. I don't know everything about it yet, but it's definitely biological, probably a pathogenic virus specifically tailored to kill Opiri."

Drakon stared at her. "How did you learn this?"

"I'm trusted in Aegis. I listen to rumors. I've even gotten close to Shepherd from time to time." She waved her hand as if to dismiss Drakon's question as irrelevant. "They've probably been working on it for well over a year, and Shepherd is behind it. I believe that he and Patterson are secretly involved in overseeing the creation of this weapon together, even while they're publicly rivals and enemies. I don't think anyone other than high-ranking members of the government even knows the project exists."

Drakon listened with growing disbelief as she described what she'd recently learned. She would have no reason to lie about such a thing, even to cement his commitment to the assassination.

And he knew what both men were capable of. That they were working together, that Shepherd claimed to want a new peace…there couldn't be a more perfect cover for a secret and illegal act of aggression that the full Senate would never approve, knowing what would be unleashed if such a weapon were discovered by Erebus.

"Is it dangerous to humans?" he asked.

"Not according to what I've learned."

"Are they creating an antidote?"

"I think they've been working on one just in case their research is wrong." She dug her fingers hard into his sleeve until he felt his healing skin protest in agony. "If the mayor is taken out," she said, "the project will be delayed and we'll have time to stop it, or at least find the antidote."

"Doesn't Erebus know about this?"

"I won't be making a report until I have more information. I'm sure that Shepherd and Patterson aren't ready to deploy it yet. You take care of your part in this, and we'll have every advantage."

Drakon closed his eyes. He'd had so many doubts about his mission. He'd even determined to give it up, because of Phoenix, because of his feelings and her influence. And he'd managed to convince Brita that he'd never doubted his loyalty to Erebus.

But everything had changed again. It wasn't only the prospect of the Enclave's ultimate destruction that rode on his success now. How great the irony that his lies to Brita weren't lies anymore, and he was back where he'd started.

He had to go through with it. He had to kill Aaron Shepherd.

"I'm going to help you set things up so there won't be any mistakes," Brita said, breaking into his thoughts.

"I'll find an excuse to return to Aegis near the same time Phoenix does. I'll get Shepherd into his office at noon on the day of the meeting. It's up to you to set up at the right vantage point without being seen or caught."

"You'll have to get the window panels down and the guards out of the way," Drakon said, his chest tight with bitter resignation. "Do you think your acquaintance with Shepherd will be enough to override all his security precautions?"

"I'll make it work. You do what you have to do."

"And Patterson? You may not care about my wife and son, but he has to pay."

"I need him alive for now. He'll pay well enough. Do your job, get out of the city and I'll take care of him."

"How, Brita?"

"I said I'll take care of it. I promise you, brother." She stood on her toes and kissed his cheek, an affectionate gesture that would have been perfectly natural among human siblings but was almost a mockery between Opiri.

The problem was that Drakon could never be sure if she meant such gestures as mockery or not.

"I don't want you killing Matthew Patterson," he said. "Use him, but don't kill him. He doesn't deserve death, unlike his father."

"What makes you believe that?"

"Call it a remnant of honor."

"Very well. But that's it, Drakon. No other promises. If you care about this half-dhampir female, get her out when you leave, or make sure someone else does if you don't survive."

Drakon stared at her until she—daughter of a Bloodlord—looked away. "You *will* leave her alone, Brita, whether I get her out or not." He softened his voice. "For the sake of the Opir we both considered a father."

She nodded sharply without looking at him and walked

toward the door. "Don't fail, Drakon. Our survival may depend on your success."

As she left the room, Drakon walked to the table and leaned on it heavily, staring at the battered wood. He'd been prepared to betray Brita, Erebus, all his kind for Phoenix. She trusted him. And he trusted her absolutely. She couldn't have known about this pathogen, or anything like it. She had guessed at all his weaknesses, seen his vulnerability, and yet she'd never taken advantage of his sincere offer to let her kill him.

To the contrary. She'd given him everything.

No, she'd never betray him. But he would betray her.

He banged his recently healed hand on the tabletop. An hour or two of happiness, of contentment, of something like peace had been granted him. And it would never come again.

Pushing away from the table, he went to find Repo. He couldn't trust Brita with Matthew Patterson's life, but he could count on his most loyal follower. Repo would look after young Patterson, let him go if the assassination succeeded before the deal with the senator went through.

And he'd get Phoenix out if the dragon didn't survive.

"Do you realize what you've done?"

Director Chan stood behind her desk, leaning over it with hand firmly planted on the highly polished surface. Her stare could have knocked the Transamerica Pyramid to the ground—if it still stood—but Phoenix held steady. They'd already been through this once before, and there was nothing Chan could say to her that she hadn't said to herself already.

"It was necessary to tell him something," Phoenix said calmly, standing at parade rest on the other side of the desk. "I had to save Matthew Patterson, and the only way to do that was reveal what I was really out there to do."

"But you told him you'd been sent to expose the Bosses," Chan said, her voice tense with anger. "You could have stuck to your story of wanting revenge, and—"

"No, ma'am," Phoenix said, holding the older woman's gaze. "If I'd hedged then, he'd have had no reason to listen to me at all. I had to hang on to some measure of his trust, and I judged that the risk was worth it. He may still suspect there's more to it than I told him, but—"

"He doesn't realize you're half-dhampir?"

"No, ma'am." Phoenix kept her face expressionless, hoping she could get away with the lies. "I don't think he'd have been willing to let me come back here to make the deal with Aegis and Patterson."

"The deal," Chan said with a snort. "And you think you still might get something out of him regarding Opiri operatives in the Fringe?"

The question was deeply ironic, considering that the director didn't know that the Boss in question was an Opir. "I'm very close," Phoenix said. "I'm fairly certain that one of his crew has some connection to the enemy. If I can get back quickly and spend the rest of the week there, I think I have a good chance. And I can stay close to Matthew."

Chan sat abruptly, picked up a stylus and began tapping the tip rapidly against the desk. "I still don't understand why he'd trust you, given the lies you've already told him, and when you've been with him less than a week."

"You wanted me to use any means at my disposal," Phoenix said, matching Chan's coldness. "It worked. He expects me to return with the information in exchange for Matthew Patterson's life. The mayor doesn't have to be anywhere near the exchange, and the attending senators can bring all the security they want."

"All so the Boss you're working with can publicly expose Patterson's buried secrets and then escape again, this time to disappear completely along with his crew."

"But I'll already be with him. If I can convince him that my loyalty is to him now, then—"

"That's not good enough!" Chan shouted, tossing the stylus down with such force that it flew off the desk.

"You'll just have to trust me to do my job," Phoenix said. "Because if we don't agree to his terms..."

The office door opened almost silently, and a young man entered the room. "I'm sorry to disturb you, Director Chan, but Senator Patterson is here."

"Let him wait," Chan snapped.

"Director," the secretary said, "I don't think—"

The secretary nearly fell over as a tall, burly man shoved past him into the office. Patterson's eyes flickered toward Phoenix with open hostility and returned to Chan, who met his gaze without flinching. Phoenix could barely hide her own loathing for the man responsible for the deaths of innocent women and children.

"Why haven't you authorized the deployment of every available agent to search for my son?" he all but bellowed. He glanced at Phoenix. "You should already have this one under stringent interrogation. The fact that she allowed this to happen—"

"—is not as clear-cut as you seem to think, Senator," Chan said, her voice as even as Patterson's was angry. "Agent Stryker was given latitude to act as she thought best. She almost certainly saved your son from death, considering that he behaved with remarkable stupidity, and she did everything possible to encourage this Sammael to bargain for your son's release. Without her—"

"Without her, none of this would have taken place!" Patterson said, striding into the office and planting his fists on Chan's desk. "I want this woman removed from the case immediately."

"We're not throwing a completely new agent into the mix now," Chan said, holding the senator's stare. "I believe Stryker when she says there is some kind of connection between her and this man Sammael, and to disrupt that now could have unthinkable consequences."

"Consequences!" Patterson shouted, banging his fist on the desk. "*You're* responsible, Chan. You assigned an unproven agent to deal with matters even a decorated commander would have a hard time pulling off. I want you to send every agent in support of my Enforcers, and maybe if your people do their jobs—"

"*Your* Enforcers?" Chan interrupted with a slight smile. "I believe you retired, Senator. You may have some influence, but you do not issue direct commands to us or to the Enforcement Bureau, not without the full committee's backing and the approval of Mayor—"

"Shepherd," Patterson snarled. "Why should he care what happens to my son, as long as he—"

"Your son will be safe if you do as we ask."

"You expect me and my fellow senators to just…show up at the edge of the Fringe and wait for this Boss to return my son. But why should we believe anything he says?"

"I don't see that we have much choice at the moment," Chan said. "Agent Stryker believes she is very close to gaining crucial information about the Opiri spies, which in turn may lead to finding the assas—"

"Believes! May!" He faced Chan with head down and shoulders hunched. "He wants a week! The assassin could make his move anytime before the meeting. If your agent is any good at all, she can set a trap. And if this Boss knows about the bloodsucker spies, we'll get it out of him, even if we have to—"

"We don't use torture," Chan interrupted, "unless it is an immediate matter of life and death."

"It is! My son—"

"Agent Stryker has made it clear that Sammael is no fool, and he will surely be prepared for betrayal," Chan said. "I have no doubt that he will kill your son and escape if we fail to abide by his offer. If you will give us a little time to plan, Senator, we'll find a workable solution that doesn't involve either the death of your son or the failure of our mission. Unless, of course, your objection is to releasing the information Sammael has requested."

Patterson straightened, his nostrils flaring. "I have nothing to hide."

"Perhaps it's simply a matter of Fringe politics, a bet, a challenge to other Bosses that he's willing to take such a risk."

"Or he wants to kill me because I did my job when I was commissioner!"

"Is that the only reason he'd want it?" Phoenix asked. "Maybe you did your job too well."

Chan spoke before Patterson could do more than gape at Phoenix in astonished outrage. "We have no way of knowing, Senator," she said, "but our security measures will be extremely thorough. No one will hurt you. And since, as you said, you have nothing to hide, the only harm you will suffer is to your pride."

"I'll have your job for this, Chan. I'll have you broken. And I'll have *this* one—" he jabbed a finger toward Phoenix "—deported for treason."

"We'll see, Senator Patterson." Chan shuffled files around on her desk as if to indicate how busy she was. "All I can say is that we'll keep you informed of any change in the situation. Now, if you'll excuse us..."

Patterson stared at Chan as if he were unable to comprehend the sheer nerve of anyone daring to address him in such a manner. He took a step back, nearly crashing into Phoenix. "I'm warning you, Director," he said. "If anything happens to my boy…"

"Goodbye, Senator."

He cast Phoenix a final glance and stormed out of the room.

"That wasn't smart, Stryker," Chan said when he was gone. "It's never a good idea to wave a red cape at a charging bull."

"I'm sorry, Director," Phoenix said, standing very straight.

"Normally, I wouldn't be worried. But if we hadn't acted immediately on your request for his records and gained access to certain files that he couldn't manage to destroy in time, he'd already be tearing the Records Department to shreds with his bare hands. He's going to be working on every conceivable way of justifying what we've found or making it appear as if someone's tampered with his files."

"Like the mayor?" Phoenix asked.

"He could make a case for it, at least with his faction and certain senators. This is a highly volatile situation, Stryker, and I think if he could let his son die without turning everyone in the Enclave against him, he'd do it rather than agree to the meeting." She slapped the folders down on the desk. "We could be facing something very ugly. But if it's between possibly ruining Patterson or saving the mayor, Aegis's position is clear."

"Yes, ma'am."

"But you're far from out of the woods, Stryker. You'd better justify my faith in your ability to see this through and find what we're looking for. Quickly. Convince Sammael to let you stay with him. You find that contact in Sammael's Hold and locate at least one of the Opiri spies. When you do, I'm going to advise that we send our people in and take him."

"For interrogation?" Phoenix said, suppressing a shiver. "Even if stringent measures are necessary to make him expose the assassin?"

Chan didn't look at her. *"We don't use torture,"* she'd said, *"unless it is an immediate matter of life and death."*

In this case, it certainly would be.

"Why is that important to you, Stryker?" Chan asked, her chair creaking as she leaned back. "I wonder if you're holding something back."

Phoenix stood absolutely still. "Ma'am?"

"When you speak of this Sammael, you might as well be describing a rock formation. Objectivity is vital, but it's almost as if you're trying too hard." She leaned forward again. "Are you emotionally involved in some way, Agent Stryker?"

"No, ma'am."

The director nodded slowly. "Don't try so hard to prove yourself, Stryker, or you may make a mistake that will destroy this city. I'm not mincing words. It's all on you and the decisions you make now."

"Yes, ma'am. Thank you for giving me this chance to make it right."

"Dismissed."

Phoenix turned to leave, but Chan called after her. "We'll need to go over all the details again," she said, "everything you know about Sammael, everything he's done and everything he's said in your presence. I'll meet you in the debriefing room in one hour. I have a few ducks to line up first."

"Yes, ma'am."

"And get yourself something to eat. It's never good for a dhampir to starve herself. Even a half-breed like you."

Phoenix left the room, trying not to think. Thinking brought doubt. Of herself, of what she had chosen to do. And of Drakon, most of all.

Determined to remain firmly in the present, Phoenix left the office and took the series of corridors and elevators to the agents' mess.

She was only halfway there when she ran smack into the Most Honorable Mayor Aaron Shepherd.

Chapter 16

"Aaron!" Phoenix blurted out without thinking, immediately aware that even a former lover didn't address the mayor by his first name. At least not in public.

But Shepherd only grinned at her, steadying her with his hands on her shoulders as if they were still young and very much in love: she, a ward of Aegis; he, a son of an influential and moderately wealthy citizen with strong ties to the government. She, who wanted to prove herself worthy, in spite of her very mixed heritage; he, always ambitious, urged by his father to climb the political ladder at a speed very few had ever achieved.

They'd still been in love when, at the age of twenty-nine, he had won a place on the government committee overseeing Aegis operations. She was just at the beginning of her career with the Agency.

Now, one of the youngest mayors of the Enclave at thirty-three, Aaron Shepherd was a highly attractive man of great power, charisma and influence, beloved by the citizens, with a higher trust rating than any other member of the government.

Everyone loved him. Everyone, except Patterson's aggressive supporters. And Phoenix.

"Nix!" he said in a delighted voice, dropping his hands. He looked her up and down. "How long has it been? A year? Two? You haven't changed a bit." His voice slowed, grew more serious. "I was hoping to speak with you alone before you return to your duties."

"I'm not permitted to discuss my work, Mr. Mayor," she said, carefully respectful.

"Not even with me?"

He was half joking, but Phoenix saw the harder gleam in his eyes—the gleam she had seen more and more the higher he had risen.

"No, sir," she said, staring at his starched, white collar.

All at once he seemed to relax. "Of course," he said. "But at least come join me for a drink, Nix. I've missed our conversations."

Phoenix didn't believe it. Not for an instant. But one simply didn't turn down the mayor, even if he was a man you never wanted to be in the same room with again.

He gestured her ahead of them, and—trailed by a team of four beefy bodyguards—they went to an empty office on the highest level of Aegis Headquarters, reserved for the use of visiting dignitaries or other special guests. There was a bar, a full-size dining table, a furniture setting with a couch and chairs and a door leading to a bedroom.

Aaron gestured for Phoenix to take a seat and nodded to his bodyguards, who took their places near the doors and huge, heavily paneled picture window. He poured himself a drink and brought another to Phoenix, who stood stiffly near the couch.

"Sit," Shepherd said, handing her a glass. She did as

he commanded, but quickly set the glass down on the coffee table, untouched.

Shepherd clucked. "So formal, Nix. We used to be such good friends." He grew serious. "My name is Aaron," he said softly. "It always sounded best when you said it."

"Until hearing me speak it became inconvenient."

"Nix." He set down his drink and reached toward her in silent plea. "I've missed you."

She wondered how he could possibly say such a thing. Once, in his embrace, she'd felt accepted for who she was. Until Aaron had opened his arms and let her fall.

"I didn't know you hated me so much," he said, reading her face.

"I've never hated you," she said. *Until now.*

"Then just talk to me."

Realizing that she wasn't going to get out without paying the toll, Phoenix moved over so he could sit beside her. He sighed and crossed his legs. "Nix, it's true. I've never stopped missing you."

All that charm, Phoenix thought. It had lost none of its potency since he had become mayor and lavished it on so many. So different from Drakon, though it wasn't just the smell of expensive cologne or the polished urbanity of the Mayor of San Francisco. Drakon had lost people he'd loved to violence and hatred. He'd suffered, had his whole life stolen from him before he'd gone completely over to the other side.

Could Aaron have survived those same trials?

She met his gaze. "Did you bring me here to play games, sir, or is there something you wanted to know?"

He leaned back, swirling his drink in his glass. "Informally, Agent Stryker…how is the mission proceeding?"

"I assume you've had your own private briefings, Your Honor," she said, staring fixedly at the lush white carpet.

"Briefings," he said with a snort, and took a sip of his

drink. "I want your opinion, Nix. It was always sound before."

Before you decided I was more a liability than a help to your ascent, she thought.

"Everything is being done that can be done," she said. "If necessary, I'll give my life to protect our government from the Opiri."

"And for me?" he asked in that seductive voice that could make anyone do whatever he wanted. No force, no command, just the gentlest, most sincere persuasion.

"Yes, Your Honor. You *are* the government."

"I might not be so much longer, if Patterson wins the election." Shepherd finished his drink and set down the glass. "But it seems there may be an impediment to his possible success. Files from his years as captain and commissioner of the Enforcement Bureau. Even I haven't seen all of them. He's not happy about having them revealed to the public, Nix."

"He's made that very clear, sir."

"And you have no idea why this Boss wants the information revealed?"

"No."

He leaned toward her. "It's all right, Nix. You can confide in me."

It was far more difficult to lie to Shepherd's face than Phoenix had imagined. Almost as hard as when she'd lied to Chan.

"I don't know," she said. "I'm sorry, sir."

"I know you are. But what doesn't make sense to me is why any Boss would want Patterson ruined. The people in the Fringe hate the government, and with good reason. Patterson would maintain the status quo. But if I win and deportation ends, they'll have nothing more to fear. We'll integrate them back into society. The Bosses will find it much more difficult to operate so profitably after that."

"That would be the ideal result, sir."

"On the other hand, Patterson may gain something out of this, even if his reputation is put on trial. Many citizens probably agree with Patterson's former actions as commissioner, and he may look better to them because of his willingness to share the files to save his son." He leaned back again. "In any case, this sets a very bad precedent. If any Boss thinks he can kidnap an influential man's loved ones and use threats to expose Enclave secrets…this is obviously something we can't have repeated."

"Of course, sir."

"Then any future attempts will have to be strongly discouraged. And this business of demanding a week… my security is having fits over it." He searched Phoenix's eyes. "Did this Boss of yours think it would take so long to access Patterson's old files?"

"He didn't say, Your Honor."

"But I've been told you've established some kind of rapport with him."

"That's why I think I can get more out of him."

"At the risk of my life?"

"If I suspected you were at immediate risk, sir…"

"I was told it was necessary to instigate these *false sweeps* in the Fringe to allow you to find information that might lead to the assassin. But we've obviously given the Fringers a little too much leeway by leaving them alone to plot. Surely you can find a way to bring this Sammael in before the meeting. I'll see that you get all the help you need."

"Sir…" Phoenix shifted, wondering how she would get out of this one. "Aegis believes it would be unwise to move too quickly."

"Then my advisers may have to take a little more time to explain the situation to Aegis. You understand, don't you, Nix?"

"And if Matthew Patterson suffers because of this?" Phoenix got to her feet, wondering what would happen if she spat on his nice, clean suit. "I have an appointment with the director. If you'll excuse me, Mr. Mayor…"

"Wait." Shepherd waved his hand, and with obvious reluctance his guards left him and Phoenix alone. Suddenly Aaron was very close, gazing into her eyes, his own bright blue and shining with passion she hadn't anticipated.

"We were good together, weren't we?" he asked. "We always understood each other."

"For a while," Phoenix said, turning her face aside. He caught her chin in his hand and forced her to look back at him.

"It took me a few years," he said with a wry twist of his lips, "but I finally realized what a mistake I'd made. I see it more clearly now than I ever have before." He stroked her cheek with his fingertips. "Don't you know, Nix? I'd never let any harm come to you. I still love you."

His words were like Nightsider fangs sinking into her throat, not merely to feed but to kill in the ugliest possible way. They ripped at her flesh and tore at her heart. The heart he had broken.

Phoenix jerked away. "I don't believe you. You want something else from me."

He sighed. "Then let me be completely honest, Nix. You do realize that Patterson would trade my life for his son's in a heartbeat. It would be very convenient for him if I were to meet with an…accident."

"You think he could be working with the Opiri?" she asked, startled by the idea. "Why would they help him?"

"To keep the goods—our human convicts—flowing," Shepherd said. "It has always seemed strange that these rumors of assassination coincide so closely with the approach of the election."

Because it wasn't a coincidence, Phoenix thought. But

the idea that Patterson was involved was ludicrous. Drakon would never work with the man responsible for the death of his family.

"I need you to help me, Phoenix," Shepherd said, cutting across her thoughts. "Whatever he says to Aegis, Patterson will be glad to give the assassin a chance to kill me, even if his son pays the price." Aaron tapped his heel against the carpet in a nervous, staccato beat. "My security won't let me go anywhere but the Capitol building or Aegis. I sleep in the suite next to my office. I don't want to sit around waiting for someone to take a pot-shot at me, high security or not."

"And what would you like me to do about that, sir?" Phoenix asked, disgusted by the self-pity in his voice.

"Work for me, Nix. Not for Aegis, not for the committee. For *me*. Report anything suspicious, no matter how trivial, directly to this office. My Chief of Security will send you to me any time you need me, at any hour."

Immediately, Phoenix understood the very real danger of refusing. Aaron could have her completely removed from the mission if she stood against him. The mayor didn't trust anyone—not Aegis, not the Bureau, not the Senate.

And yet he trusted *her*. That was how sure he was of her loyalty, of her undying love, no matter what she'd said to him.

"I understand, Your Honor," she said, backing toward the door.

"Then you agree?"

"I promise to do my best."

"Of course." He rose. "And I know, Agent Stryker, that you will do whatever is necessary to protect our city from enemies within or without. Take great care." He offered his hand, and she took it as briefly as possible. "I hope to have another, perhaps more intimate discussion with you as soon as your work is complete." He spoke into his wristcom. "Behr, will you escort Agent Stryker to her destination?"

"That won't be necessary," Phoenix said. "I'm very familiar with this building."

She met Behr as she was leaving the room, and he automatically stepped aside to let her pass. She strode through the door and closed it behind her, deliberately repressing her deep sense of betrayal.

Of one thing she was certain: Shepherd had something more up his sleeve than wanting his own private Aegis operative, who happened to be standing in the thick of a very volatile situation.

But she couldn't report this to anyone. Not until it was all clear to her.

Shaking her head, she decided to skip the mess hall and continued to the debriefing room. Chan was already there to meet her. Once Phoenix was inside, Chan spoke to four security personnel outside and made certain all the doors were locked.

"Here are the files," the director said, slapping a locked case of hard copies down on the table between them. "And some new intelligence you'll need when you go back in." Her expression soured, as if she'd tasted something intolerably bitter. "I only just learned myself. There's another Aegis operative deeply embedded in the Fringe, working for one of the Bosses. Even I don't have the clearance to access the details of the operation, but he or she was sent in to monitor Fringe activity long before the assassin showed up. Word's been sent to them through some channel unavailable to me, ordering them to assist you in any way possible without blowing their cover. It'll be up to them whether to risk contact. Be on the lookout."

"I will, ma'am," Phoenix said, working past her shock

at the new information. One image came immediately to mind.

Brita. The trusted lieutenant of one of the most powerful Bosses in the Fringe, so deep undercover that she hadn't been permitted to tell Phoenix who she was.

After they'd first confronted each other at the Hold, Phoenix had assumed that Brita knew what and who Sammael was, and vice versa. That the two were working together to facilitate the assassination.

Now she had reason to believe that everything Brita had told her had been in Aegis's service. If Brita were the undercover agent and was everything Chan claimed, had she always known Sammael was the assassin? Had she deliberately kept that information from Phoenix, either because she hadn't recognized her as a fellow operative or because she didn't want any interference?

Suddenly Phoenix remembered what had happened when she'd tried to take Matthew Patterson to the Enforcers, after she'd escaped from Drakon and the Scrappers. Brita had shown up out of nowhere and helped *rescue* Matthew just as The Preacher's men had arrived. Leaving Phoenix to fight those men by herself.

Maybe Brita, surely knowing who Matthew was, had realized she had to protect him from the Boss's men and felt more capable of doing it than Phoenix. But why had she appeared at exactly the right time? And why hadn't she taken Matthew back to the Enforcers, or tried to get him out since then? Because it would have blown her cover at a crucial moment?

It all seemed too perfect. Maybe she wasn't what Chan claimed. Maybe Phoenix had been right all along. Had Brita been playing such a deep game that even Aegis couldn't detect her real motives?

No matter what Chan had said, Phoenix knew she

could never trust Brita. Not until she was certain where the woman's loyalties lay.

That would be the most dangerous game of all. And she was the only one who could play it.

Phoenix had been ready for The Preacher's men when she returned to the Fringe. She'd been ready for any other Boss who might have heard about her, either from someone in Drakon's crew or by some other method of communication that made secrets so hard to keep in the Fringe.

She was even ready for the possibility that one of Drakon's fellow Opir spies might be watching for her, aware of *"Sammael's"* recent actions and intending to defy his decision to *negotiate* with the enemy.

Even so, she wasn't prepared when Brita stepped from behind an abandoned office building with three of Drakon's crew, including Repo.

Immediately Phoenix was on her guard, but there was no indication that Brita was anything but what she'd always seemed to be, no sign of any special recognition or acknowledgment on the lieutenant's face, no change in her vaguely hostile greeting.

But then again there wouldn't be. Not openly.

"Do you have the files?" Brita asked.

"Yes," Phoenix said, touching the bulge under her jacket.

"Then let's get undercover. I don't like standing out here, even in daylight."

They jogged back into the office building, where the three crew members crouched against the wall and shared a contraband cigarette.

"What's going on?" Phoenix whispered, her neck prickling as if they were being observed by someone she couldn't hear or smell or see. "I thought you were disbanding the crew for safety and moving the Hold. Why are you all together? Where's Sammael?"

"He can't meet you as planned. The Preacher has men watching your rendezvous, so Sammael asked me to take you to the new location."

"Why are The Preacher's men watching?" Phoenix asked, observing Brita's face carefully. "Hoping for revenge?"

"If something else is going on, we won't have time to figure it out now."

"It couldn't have anything to do with your meeting with his rep?" Phoenix said, too softly for the humans to hear.

Brita lifted one eyebrow a fraction of an inch, a signal Aegis operatives used only when they were in close proximity. "It's complicated. Look, we don't have any time to waste."

Unless Brita had learned the signal from a captured agent, she had to be Aegis's operative. Phoenix glanced to the west, where the sun was sinking toward the Pacific. Brita's night vision, like Phoenix's, would enable them to move freely in darkness. Not so the humans with them.

"Why did you bring *them?*" she asked, nodding toward the crew members.

"They'll fall back and keep an eye out behind us," Brita said. "If anyone follows, they'll lead them away."

"That's quite a risk."

"They're willing to take it, for the Boss."

The explanation felt wrong somehow, but Phoenix had no way of knowing if that feeling was because Brita really wasn't the deep-cover agent, or that she had other motives in mind.

There was only one way to find out.

"Lead on," she said.

Brita nodded, signaled to the men and moved as any

Fringer did, darting from cover to cover and gradually working her way south. After about a quarter of a mile she stopped again.

"He's just around that corner, by the Wall," Brita said. "I'll leave you here. I have things I have to take care of for Sammael, and I may be gone a while."

The small hairs on her neck standing erect in warning, Phoenix nodded and waited until Brita was out of sight. The sun was almost down, and Phoenix's night vision was just kicking in as she made her way cautiously in the direction Brita had indicated.

But Brita hadn't misled her. Drakon—dressed in heavy day clothing and standing among the long shadows—was in conference with a small group of humans, looking much as he had the first time Brita had taken Phoenix to witness her Boss performing one of his *"good deeds."*

Now that she knew him so well, Phoenix had no reason to doubt Drakon's purpose. He spoke to each of the people in turn, shook the hands of the adults and helped them pass through a hole in the Wall—new or old, Phoenix couldn't tell—as a couple of tough-looking Fringers kept watch. One of them spotted Phoenix just as dusk gave way to night.

He whistled sharply, and Drakon spun around as the last human disappeared through the passage. He smiled, his capped teeth catching some final reflection of the dying sun, and ran straight for her.

She met him halfway. They crashed together, breathless, Phoenix laughing, Drakon cupping her head between his hands and kissing her hair, her forehead, her lips.

"You wanna get a room?" asked the male observer. "There're plenty around here to choose from."

Chapter 17

Drawing back to search Phoenix's eyes, Drakon waved them away. "Thank you, my friends. If you're still willing to help with the next group—"

"Sure," the woman said. "These're our people. And we can always get out ourselves before the Enforcers come back." She nodded to her companion, who helped her stack up the usual camouflage of boxes, crates, garbage, metal and other detritus in front of the hole. Then they melted into the darkness, leaving Phoenix and Drakon alone.

In seconds he had pulled her into the nearest building and had her up against a wall, urgently working at her zipper. Suddenly, they were both devoid of their pants and shoes, Drakon had lifted her against him with her thighs spread to either side of his hips and he was thrusting into her, hard and fast. It was as if he was trying to make her a part of himself.

Moaning with joy and excitement, Phoenix closed her

eyes as Drakon had his very thorough way with her. She clawed at his back, heedless of the roughness of the wall, as she gripped him more tightly with her legs and gasped as he drove himself even more deeply inside her. She was dimly aware when he removed his caps over his teeth and tossed them aside, but every sensation of pleasure and ecstasy spun to its height as he pierced her neck with his incisors, taking her blood as he took the rest of her.

It wasn't long before she was crying out, and he shuddered with his own release. He withdrew from her neck, and she dropped her face into the hollow of his shoulder. He stayed inside her for some time, and then gradually eased her down to her feet.

She didn't let him go. She kissed the hollow of his neck just above his collar, his chin, his jaw, his lips. He accepted her caresses, eyes closed, and simply held her.

A gust of cool wind blew through the broken door, and Phoenix laughed. "I'm cold," she said. "I think I'd like to put my pants back on now."

He chuckled, though the sound seemed strained to her, almost uneasy. She grabbed her pants from the floor and pulled them on while he did the same. He retrieved his caps, cleaning them with his sleeve, and replaced them. Once they'd put on their shoes, they both sat against the wall side by side, bodies touching. Drakon was very quiet.

"Didn't you feel it?" Phoenix asked, trying to break through his strange mood.

"What, in particular?" he asked, flashing her a brief smile.

She relaxed and pulled the case containing the files from inside her jacket. "I can't believe this wasn't sticking into your chest the whole time."

He glanced at the case almost as if it no longer mattered to him. "You were able to get them?" he asked.

"I wouldn't have come back so soon if I hadn't," she

said. "The plan is set, just as you wanted. Though I wish there was some other way to expose Patterson for what he is."

"I know." He sighed and took her hand, cradling it between his own. "Show me the files."

"Is it safe here?" she asked, glancing toward the door.

"As safe as anywhere. I've got watchers, some of my crew, patrolling and keeping an eye on the entire area."

"Brita had Repo and a couple of the other guys with her."

"Yes," he murmured. "Brita."

His tone seemed completely neutral, Phoenix thought, and yet…

"The Hold has already been moved," he said, "and I'm doing my best to get people out."

"I couldn't help noticing that," she said, squeezing his hand. She put the case on the floor between them, unlocked it and pulled out the contents. "Patterson didn't manage to purge all his files. We have enough here to make him look very bad to anyone who has an objection to the murder of innocents or blatant and horrific miscarriages of justice." Her eyes grew moist. "Nothing can ever change the past. But this may open some eyes, and it will make it pretty hard for Patterson to hold on to his political career, let alone further it."

"And yet nothing will be solved," he said, staring blindly at the littered floor.

Phoenix thought of Aegis, of all the work it had done trying to keep the peace by patrolling the Zone and discouraging any Nightsider attempt to break the Armistice. She'd no longer be a part of that. Aaron Shepherd was determined to make her his own personal operative. She could never let that happen.

"We're only two people," she said softly, touching Drakon's shoulder. "Once we get out, maybe we can locate one of the free colonies, and help them build a new way of life. Maybe that's the only thing that will save all of us, Opiri *and* human. Maybe there's still a way to mend this world without letting it burn to the ground and wait for a better one to be born out of the ashes."

He finally looked at her. "Your wish may not come true, Phoenix."

"But it's all I have. It's what we have to hope and fight for in any small way we can."

She leaned against his shoulder, closing her eyes as she realized that she'd gone without sleep for nearly two full days.

But she was here. With *him*. Everything could fall apart in the next hour, the next day, the next week. But they were together now, and she intended to cherish this moment.

After making love twice more, they went to the half-collapsed market in which Brita, Drakon and one or two others had taken shelter earlier. Matthew Patterson, his hands tied loosely to one of the pylons, seemed strangely relaxed, as if he had become accustomed to his captivity or at least no longer saw any point in struggling.

Repo showed up by midnight, but Brita still hadn't returned by the next day. Drakon didn't seem worried, and Phoenix thought it better not to discuss the subject with him. She needed a chance to get Brita alone before the exchange was made.

But she and Drakon had plenty of work to fill their time. While volunteer Scrappers organized patrols and kept watch throughout the Fringe—ever mindful that the Enclave politicians might yet break their word and send Enforcers in—Drakon, Phoenix and a few of the crew who had refused to leave their Boss arranged to move the other Fringers who wanted to escape the city. They were sent out armed, carrying as much in the way of food as Drakon could dig up, and with spare sets of clothing. After that, their fates were in their own hands.

But they'd chosen possible freedom over the likelihood of eventual serfdom, and Phoenix wouldn't have chosen any differently. She felt more useful, more needed than she ever had in her life, and she had nothing to prove. She and Drakon worked as a perfect team, seldom needing to speak, curling up together at night on ragged blankets and making love—always with a kind of urgency, as if Drakon expected these days to be his last.

Phoenix refused to consider the possibility. She accepted the happiness she'd found, the look in Drakon's eyes, both sad and filled with something very close to love. It was enough for her.

And one night, when they held each other, she told him she loved him.

There was nothing momentous about the occasion. She'd made her feelings clear enough. But he said nothing...only held her close, enfolding her with his arms and gently rocking her as if she were a child in need of comfort.

She thought of his lost wife and child, how he had held them, loved them, and wished with all her heart that she could restore them to him, even if she had to give him up forever.

The day before the scheduled exchange, Drakon spoke privately with Matthew. Though she made no attempt to listen in, Phoenix watched the young man's face. She saw no hostility or resentment, only earnest attention. Afterward, Phoenix asked Drakon what had transpired between them.

"He kept demanding to know why I was so certain his father was...what I claimed him to be," Drakon said, his gaze distant.

"And?"

"It took some time, but I think he believes at least part of what I've told him." He smiled slightly and kissed her lips. "He's been quiet, at least."

"Whatever he may believe, he'll never turn against his father. And what good would it do if he did?"

"No good at all," Drakon said.

"Then why torment him?"

"Why?" Drakon said, meeting her gaze with the same hardness in his eyes she'd seen when they'd first met. "So that the younger Enforcers can understand, even if their elders don't."

"We're not quite elders yet, Drakon," she said, trying to tease him out of his dark mood and herself out of her fear of what tomorrow would bring.

"You'll live longer than any human," Drakon said, his mood changing suddenly to one of profound sadness. "If I survive, I'll live still longer. Can you accept that?"

"Growing old while you don't? It's more a question of the other way around." She cupped his cheek. "Can you live with an old woman?"

"I'll never let you go," he said gently, "unless I die first."

Clenching her fingers around his, she squeezed as hard as she could. "You're leaving your old life behind. We both have too much to live for."

He worked his hand free, turned her palm up and kissed it. "I've found it's possible to go on living when the ones you love have died. If that ever happens to either one of us, we'll survive, because there is much to be done. As you told me, there may still be a way to save this world without letting it burn to the ground. You'll be part of that, Phoenix."

"And so will you."

But he was very quiet after that, and that night they

both fell asleep in each other's arms without making love beforehand.

She woke to find the space beside her cold, and hard hands clutching at her arms. Two men pulled her to her feet, and she recognized Repo's features as well as those of another member of Drakon's crew.

Instantly she began to fight, shouting Drakon's name. But Repo had a stunner, and though it only slowed her down, it was enough for them to force her arms behind her, cuff her and gag her so that she was unable to call out.

When the stunner's effects wore off, she just had time to notice that Matthew was gone and she and her captors were alone in the market. As they dragged her outside, she could see that it was midmorning, only around three hours until the meeting between Drakon and Patterson was to take place.

She continued to struggle, but Repo made it very clear that he'd continue to use the stunner if she tried to break the cuffs or run.

They took her to the Wall, where two Scrappers with military gear were waiting along with several couples and children.

"You know what to do," Repo said, handing the stunner to the woman of the first pair. "Get her out and take her away as fast as you can. If you have to, there's a stronger setting that'll knock her out for an hour or two, but she'll be more of a burden then. You decide what's best." He looked at Phoenix. "Sorry, but this was Sammael's order. Get you out along with the last bunch before the meeting."

Phoenix shook her head wildly, shouting under the gag. Her voice came out muffled and unintelligible.

"He wants you free in case something happens to him," Repo said. "I know you wanted to stay. Most of us would do anything for him. But it ain't in the cards."

Nodding to the pair with the backpacks, Repo passed her over to a large man, who grabbed her and started for the exit. It looked very much as if they would succeed in getting her out.

But desperation was a potent enhancer, and Phoenix was much stronger than they were. Before the woman could apply the stunner, Phoenix kicked out and knocked one of the men down. The other one tripped over the lip of the hole, and Phoenix darted back through.

Repo and his fellow crew member were lying prone on the ground, Brita standing over them with an Enforcer pistol. When the woman with the stunner tried to return through the hole, Brita aimed her gun and shook her head.

"Stay out," she said. "Leave the passage open. These men will be joining you." She glanced down at the outraged faces of the men on the ground. "Get up, Repo. You're both going out."

"What in hell are you doing, Brita?" Repo demanded. "This wasn't part of what Sammael—"

"He changed his mind," she said, waving the gun. "Go. I'm going to seal up this end, so you won't be coming back this way. I'd advise that you take the chance to escape, because it's going to get hairy once the temporary truce is over."

She waited, gun at the ready, while Repo, the other man and the woman—who was still frozen halfway through the Wall—had all gone to the other side. Then she moved to unlock the cuffs around Phoenix's wrists and untied the gag.

"What is going on?" Phoenix demanded, putting a good distance between herself and Brita.

"Just shut up, and stay where you are."

Edging toward the Wall, Brita disappeared behind one of the heavy metal road signs that partly blocked the hole. Before Phoenix could move, the other woman had shoved the sign aside, and a pile of bricks balanced on the top of the Wall shifted and thundered down to completely cover the hole.

Brita stepped back, as expressionless as a mechanic who had just performed the most dull and routine of repairs. She turned to Phoenix.

"Listen up," she said. "I have a lot to tell you, and we haven't got much time."

But Phoenix was already moving, setting off at a sprint away from the Wall. Brita lunged after her, tackled her and threw her to the ground. Phoenix grappled with the other woman, both of them entangled in a melee of arms and legs, fists and boots. Brita was stronger than Phoenix had ever imagined, and she had to fight desperately to keep the other woman from besting her.

In the end, Brita won. As she lay panting with the other woman's foot on her throat, Phoenix knew Brita couldn't possibly be less than at least full dhampir, though she, like Phoenix, lacked a dhampire's catlike pupils.

It was clear now that she really was the deep-cover agent. If Drakon had meant to get Phoenix out and Brita had stopped it from happening, she was acting directly against her Boss's orders. But was it for Aegis?

"Are you a complete idiot?" Brita said in an undertone. "Didn't they tell you to expect me?"

"Let me up!" Phoenix gasped as Brita slowly removed her foot.

"You've nearly ruined everything," Brita said, showing the pointed teeth she'd been so careful to conceal before.

"You mean your mission?" Phoenix asked. "Because I was told—"

"That I was supposed to help you. *If* my own mission wouldn't be compromised. I've believed you were an Aegis operative from the moment we made that agreement, and I had my suspicions the first time we met."

"But you didn't bother to tell me?"

"I wasn't supposed to make contact with any other operatives they sent out. Not until I'd found as many Opir spies as I could."

"You mean you were sent by Aegis on the same job I was?"

"Not quite. They really didn't tell you anything, did they?"

"The director didn't have clearance, and she didn't tell me what she knew until I was about to return."

"Stupid. I would have sacrificed you without a thought if I believed you'd endanger what I've already achieved."

"Then why did they send me at all?"

Brita shrugged. "I have no idea. When you went back to Aegis, you didn't tell them he was the assassin, did you?"

So Brita *did* know, Phoenix thought. And she rightly assumed Phoenix did, as well.

"No," she said slowly.

"That was smart. It could have complicated things even more on this end."

"How did you know I'd found out?"

"As close as you and Drakon had become, I figured you'd learn the truth sooner or later." She grimaced. "All the time I worked for him, starting around the time he became a Boss, I never guessed he was the assassin. I didn't know his real name. I was ready to expose the other spies I'd found...until you arrived, and I learned the truth about him."

"How?"

"It doesn't matter now. But I realized soon after you slept with him that he was going to make mistakes. And that would be to my advantage."

Phoenix swallowed. "So you really aren't in love with him?"

Brita laughed. "Not at all."

"But you went out of your way to show me the good in him. Why?"

"I needed to see how you'd respond. Just like all those tests and traps I set for you, telling you your story had already checked out. I still didn't know how you'd fit in, or what I should do with you if you became a problem. And Drakon *did* save my life once. For a while, I thought I could—" She shook her head. "When he took Matthew Patterson, I had to change my plans."

"So why didn't *you* take Patterson back to the Enforcers?"

"I wasn't ready to expose myself, and I'd realized your connection with Drakon was the best way to stop him."

Phoenix let the obvious question pass. "You're dhampir, aren't you?" she asked.

Brita stepped back, letting Phoenix climb to her feet. "Not quite," she said. "My father was a Bloodlord. My Daysider mother sought refuge in the city when the Enclave needed accurate intelligence about the Nightsiders. I was born here."

"You mean Opiri can produce children?" Phoenix asked, stunned by the revelation. "Does Aegis know—"

"You think even Aegis knows everything?" She laughed again. "I'm a freak, you see. I have my mother's immunity to sunlight, and my father's ability to see at night. And I look human. All very handy for an agent."

"Where do you get your blood?"

"The same way Drakon does, though I wouldn't mind taking it by more direct means."

"Why does Drakon look human, too?" Phoenix asked, testing Brita as *she* had been tested.

"No time for more questions now," Brita said. "The only reason I've told you so much was to make sure you know I'm on your side. I have a vital task for you. One only you can carry out."

"I wasn't told you were to give the orders."

"I got you back, didn't I?" Her eyes narrowed. "Or are you really willing to turn traitor because you love someone who could destroy our civilization?"

"But he's not going through with the assassination."

Brita laughed contemptuously. "Did you think he'd turn against his own kind just for your sake?"

She's lying, Phoenix thought. *She has to be.* Drakon wouldn't do that. Not now. Not after all the things he'd said.

"He's been lying to me," Phoenix said bitterly, hoping she sounded convincing. "I thought I was seducing *him,* but he must have guessed who I really was all along."

"Oh," Brita said, "I'm not denying that there's something between you, on both sides. It's just not what you think it is."

"You said he'd make mistakes because of me."

"You're a distraction. That's enough."

"But he must have a reason for wanting me out of the city."

"And you don't know what that is?"

"I have no idea. He said he was going to let Matthew go after the files were read and then pretend to hold me hostage until we got out of the city. He was supposed to have everything prepared."

"Drakon isn't going to meet the senator now," Brita said. "Matthew Patterson is already gone, off to expose his own father."

"I don't believe you," Phoenix said, backing away. "Matthew would never—"

"You'd be surprised," Brita said. "But that's not at issue here. I'm going to need you to use the bond between you and Drakon, and hope it's enough."

"To stop him from killing Shepherd? After all you've said, you think I can do that?"

"I said he wasn't going to betray his own people. But his plans have changed." Brita squinted up at the sun. "Right now he's on a certain rooftop at a perfect vantage point overlooking the meeting, armed with a high-powered sniper's rifle.

"He doesn't plan to ruin Senator Patterson. He plans to kill him."

Chapter 18

Drakon had taken cover on the roof of a tall apartment building just to the south of Old Market Street, crouched in the shadow of the stairwell bulkhead. From here he could see across the city as far as the rough borderland of the Fringe, where the exchange was to take place.

He had checked the rifle over a dozen times, taken it apart and put it back together, cleaned every last speck of dust from every surface and component, made certain that there could be no question of optimum performance.

Even at this distance, he might have taken Patterson out. Only the finest marksmen in the world could possibly manage it, and there would be a high risk of failure.

But it wasn't Patterson he was focusing on. He was situated on the *"right"* side of Market, in the better part of the Mids just below the Nobs, where Cits were going about their daily business. There was a definite edge of nervous excitement in the air, a sense of something momentous about to happen.

That was how he had made it this far into the Mids before dawn. Nearly all the city's security, its common police and Enforcers and Aegis, were concentrated in two locations: the mayor's Capitol apartments, and the place where fully a quarter of the senators would be waiting to see Matthew Patterson returned to his father.

And quite possibly witness Senator Patterson's downfall.

Drakon had done all he could to ensure the success of that venture. Matthew had proven to be quite a surprise, reacting with horror to what he'd seen in the files. He'd expressed a desire to seek some way to find peace by different means than had been tried so far, and, in spite of his previous behavior, he had proven to be both reasonable and mature for his age and occupation.

But Drakon couldn't be sure that the young man would go through with the plan to confront his father and urge him to face the consequences of his former heinous acts. It was still quite possible that Matthew had deceived Drakon all along, or would be *"rescued"* before he could read the pertinent records, though the young Enforcer had agreed to let his father believe there were snipers ready to kill him if he failed.

Holding the rifle as close as he would an infant, Drakon closed his eyes and breathed deeply, in and out and in and out, as he had learned during his specialist training in the Force. But as much as he tried to keep his mind clear, it wouldn't stay that way. Phoenix's face was always before his eyes, smiling at him, kissing him, trusting him. Loving him.

By now Repo would have taken her out of the city. If Brita had managed to do her part, she would have arranged to leave the mayor vulnerable for a few precious minutes, though how she would achieve such a miracle Drakon couldn't imagine. Once she had raised the panels and managed to get the mayor into position, not even the supposedly bulletproof glass could save Shepherd. The Enforcers had a handful of prototype firearms the senators didn't even know about, and one of them was in Drakon's hands.

Whether she succeeded or not, Drakon had already prepared himself for what would follow. He had told Brita he wouldn't be returning to Erebus. He'd told Phoenix that they would find some way to live outside the Enclave, facing the dangers of the Zone together.

But he wouldn't be leaving this city. If he was unable to kill the mayor today, he'd try to hide long enough to get to Shepherd another way. Or, if not him, then Patterson. Brita planned to focus all her efforts on learning the location of the laboratory creating the biological weapon, but *his* odds of getting anywhere near the source were virtually nil.

Leaning back, he waited. The minutes ticked by with agonizing slowness. By 11:00 a.m., he knew the reception committee would be gathering at the appointed place. He tried again not to think of what would happen there, or the fact that Patterson might find himself spared the airing of his flagrant repudiation of the very law he claimed to serve.

It would be only a temporary reprieve.

Sweat trickling over his forehead, Drakon wiped at his face with his sleeve. He'd put on his heaviest clothing, knowing he'd be exposed to the sun for anywhere from twenty seconds to several minutes. He should survive the burns, though the previous ones had just healed.

But the shadow cast by the bulkhead was growing thin. The timing had to be perfect in every way.

As noon approached, he turned his attention to the Capitol building. He knew exactly what to look for—the precise moment when Brita gave the signal. A brief flash of reflection. A second for her to drop to the ground.

The sound of someone climbing the stairs inside the bulkhead sent him spinning to face the door. It opened, and he caught a scent so familiar and beloved that he was momentarily too stunned to move.

"Drakon?" Phoenix called softly.

Running at a crouch, he reached the door, grabbed her and yanked her down to the concrete beside him. He pulled her back into the scant shade around the corner and held her arm in a desperate grip.

"How did you get here?" he asked. "You were supposed to—"

"Be outside the Wall," she said, her breath coming short. "I know that was what you planned." She didn't try to break free of his hold but scanned the area around them, taking in the vantage point and the meeting place a little over a half-mile away.

"Brita was right," she said.

Drakon pulled Phoenix around to face him. "What do you mean, Brita was right?" he asked.

"She knows you're the assassin, Drakon," Phoenix said.

He was too stunned by her presence to pretend to be surprised. "And she *told* you I was here?"

"She told me where to find you after she helped me get away from Repo and the others you ordered to take me out of the city." She met his gaze without anger or reproach, only with deep sadness. "You didn't trust me."

Fury burned through Drakon's body like the sunlight. "Damn it, I wanted you safe!"

"Because you always intended to do this."

He shook his head, fighting a wave of dizziness. The sunlight, reflecting off the metal and windows of surrounding buildings, was beginning to affect him. He pulled her closer still, catching her face between his hands.

"Yes," he said, "Brita has been working with me. But she always expected me to go through with it. I was going to quit, but then she told me—"

"Drakon, you can't do this."

Brita had sent Pheonix here, Drakon thought, even as she was setting up the mayor's assassination. She'd deliberately put Phoenix in terrible danger.

"I found out she was a double agent, Drakon," Phoenix said. "I just didn't know which side she was really on. But when she told me where you'd gone, I chose to believe that she really was on our side."

Our side, Drakon thought, shaking his head. Brita, his *"sister,"* a double agent.

Eyes moist with anguish, Phoenix touched his cheek with her fingertip. "She was never your loyal lieutenant, Drakon. She's been an Aegis operative since long before she joined you. She was hunting for Opiri spies before we even knew there might be an assassin planning to kill the mayor."

Drakon burst into choked laughter. "You *knew* this?"

"Not until I returned from talking to the director. She told me to watch out for a deep-cover agent in the Fringe who might be able to help me. Brita revealed herself to me and said she had been about to expose the others just before I—"

"Stop." He looked away, sick with heat and rage and despair. "I don't know what Brita thought she had to gain by sending you here. But you're wrong." He met her gaze again. "Phoenix, she's more than my lieutenant. Her Opir father was my Sire. She's been working alongside me from the beginning, pretending to serve your side while gathering information for ours. We discussed the need to take Shepherd out...yes, even after I promised you I wouldn't do it. And I wasn't planning to. But we discovered something that changed those plans. And I had to keep you safe, no matter—"

"So you're saying she was only half lying to me," Phoenix said. "Telling me what I wanted to hear. If so, she must have done very well in deceiving my superiors." She glanced around again, scanning the skies as if she expected a sudden onslaught of black Enforcer helicopters, and looked back at Drakon. "I don't think you're lying about your relationship with her. I've known almost from the beginning that she wasn't human."

"You knew that, too?" Drakon asked bitterly. "And yet you—"

"I discovered Brita wasn't human when she met with one of The Preacher's men just outside the Hold."

"She what?" Drakon snapped.

"She turned down his offer to join The Preacher's crew. But when I confronted her, she claimed I was a spy for Aegis, and not quite human myself. We promised that neither of us would expose the other."

Drakon leaned back against the bulkhead again and closed his eyes. He should have been shocked, but he felt nothing. He knew where Brita's real loyalties lay.

But why hadn't she told him? Why hadn't she shared what she'd learned with him, so that they could take full advantage of the enemy's intelligence?

If he had been deceived so easily, how could he fault Phoenix for believing Brita?

Drakon inhaled sharply. Was it possible that she really didn't want the mayor dead after all? Had she only pretended all along, never intending Drakon to go through with the assassination?

It wasn't possible, Drakon thought. If she'd wanted to stop Drakon, she could have done it a hundred different ways before he'd reached this rooftop.

He blinked sweat out of his eyes. Brita hadn't told Phoenix about the pathogen, or Phoenix would have mentioned it. Whatever her former loyalties, she'd have been horrified.

Unaware of his racing thoughts, Phoenix pulled his hands away from her face. "You lied to me, Drakon," she said softly, squeezing his fingers. "But it's not too late. No revenge is worth what this will do to you even if you get away afterward."

"Phoenix—" Drakon began, barely able to speak.

"We need to leave, now, and get you to shelter. Then we're getting out of the city, just as we planned."

He checked his watch. Eleven-thirty. Almost no time left.

"I didn't come to kill Patterson," he said. "I've come to remove a man who's helping to create a biological weapon that could kill every Opir who comes in contact with it."

Phoenix stared at him, a look of blank incomprehension in her eyes. "A weapon?" she said. "The mayor?"

Resisting the urge to shake her as he wished someone would shake him, he gripped her shoulders. "Brita didn't tell you, did she?"

"No," Phoenix said slowly. "Everyone has been lying. You, me, Brita, Shepherd, Patterson. Everyone." She pushed Drakon away. "Shepherd would never be a party to something like that, whatever he's done in the past. But I don't understand why she would tell you to—" Understanding swept across her face. "Drakon, she's set you up. Maybe she thought I could succeed, but if I don't, she's going to send people up here after you."

"I don't know why she said I was after Patterson or told you to come here," he said, "but you have to go. If you leave immediately, you can return to the Fringe. You can make up some story about trying to save Matthew and being incapacitated while I escaped before the meeting."

"You should know by now," Phoenix said gravely, "that no matter what Brita said, I'm not leaving here without you."

"Patterson is working with your mayor. Would you stand by while they create an illegal and devastating weapon?"

Phoenix shivered, looking genuinely shaken. "Do you have any proof but Brita's word? If Shepherd and Patterson are actually working together on something like that, killing either or both of them won't stop it. Others must be involved."

Her sensible words were convincing, but Drakon knew far better than she what they were facing. "Once news of this gets out of the Enclave," he said, "Erebus will—"

"Attack first? And then we'll have the new war so many on both sides seem to want." Her voice thickened with tears. "Don't you see? You wanted Patterson's sins aired in public. Maybe they will be, maybe they won't. But Aegis doesn't know I'm any kind of *traitor* yet. I can go back and look for evidence of this weapon. There will be ways to expose it to the public, bring it to the attention of other senators—"

"Many of whom will support it." He looked into her eyes, hardening his heart against everything he had ever felt for her. "And since Brita is still apparently trusted by Aegis and has already lied to you, she could turn on you in a heartbeat if she thought it would serve her—our—cause."

"Neither of us can trust her, Drakon," she said.

Drakon set his jaw. "There is nothing you can do, and nothing more to discuss." He glanced around the bulkhead at the Capitol building. "If you ever felt anything for me, find Repo and tell him my orders stand. He'll get you out."

But he knew, as soon as she'd finished speaking, that she'd never go.

"Phoenix," he said.

She looked at him, weary and bewildered.

"Come here," he said gently.

She edged closer to him, a wariness in her eyes that cut him to the quick. He opened his arms, and she fell into them, holding on to him so hard that his ribs protested and he grunted with surprise. He kissed her, and she responded desperately. So many times it happened this way—in desperation, in haste, in fear of some terrible, inevitable loss.

"No one's watching this building," she whispered into his neck. "We still have time to leave without being caught." She pulled back, her eyes dry but filled with the ferocity he knew burned beneath the facade of calm composure. "I choose to trust you, Drakon, over everyone else in this world, no matter what you've done. Will you trust me the same way?"

They gazed at each other as Drakon felt his heart slowly tear itself apart. His watch pinged. Five minutes left. He laid down the rifle and, still crouching, led her to the bulkhead door. She smiled at him, believing he had given up, and preceded him through the door to the landing.

Careful to make sure she wasn't watching, he removed two capsules from a tiny inner pocket in his jacket. He popped them into his mouth, holding them on his tongue, and pulled Phoenix around to kiss her again.

She struggled when she felt the pills pass over her tongue and into her mouth. She tried to spit them out, but he covered her lips with his hand and massaged her throat with deliberate, carefully calculated strokes.

"Don't fight it," he said, resting his cheek against her hair. "If they find me, I'll tell them I drugged you. You'll only be out for an hour or less, depending on how the drug works on your metabolism."

Phoenix tried to shake her head. She was weeping, but she couldn't keep fighting him. She swallowed, and after a minute her eyes drifted shut. Drakon carefully laid her out on the landing, stroked her hair one last time and ran back out onto the roof. He retrieved the rifle and set up facing the Capitol building, the sun already beginning to burn through his clothes.

One minute passed. Two. And then it was noon, and there was no flash, no signal, nothing to suggest that Brita had succeeded. He waited another several minutes until he could feel his skin begin to blister, and then withdrew halfway inside the bulkhead.

It was over.

Letting his head drop back against the inner wall, he pulled Phoenix into his arms, wondering how he could get her down the stairs and to safety when she couldn't walk. Carrying an unconscious woman over his shoulder would be too conspicuous. If he could just—

"Drakon!"

Brita was running up the stairs, her expression tight with anger and urgency.

"I couldn't make it work!" she said, stopping just below the landing as her gaze flickered from his face to Phoenix's. "I had no way to communicate, but at least she found you." Brita crouched. "What's wrong with her?"

"What's *wrong* with her?" Drakon asked, dragging Phoenix's limp body behind him. "You sent her up with some story about my intending to kill Patterson, telling her to stop me! Elders, Brita, what were you thinking?"

"I sent her here to stop you and get you away because I had to try to make sure no one else found you here," Brita said. "I never told her you meant to kill Patterson."

Drakon didn't believe her. Her voice was strained, lacking its usual confidence. She was too earnest, almost pleading with him to understand. To accept.

"I had to knock her out in case someone found me here and believed she was helping me," he said, holding Brita's eyes. "You told her you were working for Aegis, and I told her you're with me. Whatever the truth is, she knows that much. Are you planning to kill her for that?"

"We can't let her go back to Aegis."

"She's still going outside the Wall. Once I know she's safe, you and I will do whatever we have to."

Brita looked out the half-open door to the roof. "The meeting's happening right now. Matthew Patterson is out there, standing in front of the assembled reporters and politicians and Enforcers. If you ever wanted revenge, you've lost it now. Matthew will never talk."

"You convinced me that killing the mayor was necessary," he said. "More vital than any revenge."

"But now we're here, and you've got nothing to lose. You can take Patterson now, and that makes their pact to destroy us almost as unstable as if you'd killed Shepherd. We can still use it."

Drakon looked down into Phoenix's face. It was almost peaceful. As if even now she trusted him.

"No," he said. "I'm getting her out of here."

"I expected you to say that," Brita said. Without warning, she half-jumped, half-ran over Drakon, snatched up the rifle and ran out onto the roof. Drakon had barely rolled Phoenix off his lap when he heard the shot. Ten seconds later Brita was back through the door and on the landing, perched on her toes and ready to run. She dropped the rifle at Drakon's feet.

"Congratulations," she said. "You have your revenge. And so do I."

Drakon moved, but not soon enough. Brita jammed a gun under his jaw, and he heard the wail of sirens on the streets surrounding the building.

Brita had set him up, exactly as Phoenix had said.

She'd never intended for him to kill the mayor. Whether she'd really wanted Patterson dead or only wanted to make it look as if Drakon had killed a major political figure in the Enclave didn't matter now.

For some incomprehensible reason, she had betrayed her so-called *"brother."* He no longer had any understanding of her loyalties. All he could do now was maintain a plausible story that Phoenix had in no way been involved. A story plausible enough to counter anything Brita might claim to her masters at Aegis.

"Down," Brita said, her voice utterly unfamiliar. "On your belly. If you fight, you know what happens to *her.*"

Drakon knelt and lay down as best he could in the small space beside Phoenix's body. He turned his head, resting his cheek on the concrete to look at her quiet face. Her hair had fallen over her eyes, and all he wanted to do was tuck that errant strand behind her ear.

Planting her knee on Drakon's back, Brita cuffed him forcefully enough that she would have broken a human's wrist. Then she chained him to the banister. Drakon could hear the Enforcers starting up the stairs from the first floor.

"Why?" he rasped. "Why, Brita?"

She didn't even look at him. She knelt beside Phoenix, pulled something out of her pocket—a small vial of blue liquid—and forced Phoenix's lips open. Drakon kicked at her desperately, just managing to jar her arm before she'd poured more than half the contents into Phoenix's mouth. The vial went flying and smashed against the wall, leaving a spatter of sapphire streaks on the graffitied concrete.

Swearing in the Fringer way, Brita kicked Drakon in the head. By the time he was able to see and think again, the Enforcers were on him. One spoke with Brita, one of them called for an ambulance, and three others hauled Drakon to his feet.

"She was right," a woman's voice said into her com. "We have him, and the weapon. There's a woman here with him, but she's unconscious. We're bringing them in."

Moving with all his carefully hoarded strength, Drakon spat out his caps, flung himself at Brita and snapped at her neck. A baton connected with his skull, and everything went black.

Chapter 19

The first thing Phoenix smelled was the acidic stench of antiseptic grotesquely mingled with the fragrance of a bouquet of flowers on the table beside her bed.

Or, more precisely, the medical cot with its uncomfortable pillows and a stiff, white sheet pulled up to her waist, covering her bare legs under the hem of her gown. The infirmary was very quiet, the walls very white, the amenities sparse. Phoenix was alone in the room. A black-and-white picture of the original Golden Gate Bridge hung on the opposite wall.

Memories came back in bits and snatches: Drakon's grim face, the black rifle in his hand, her own voice pleading, bitter pills being forced into her mouth, sorrowful eyes.

Drakon had drugged her. But she'd heard the shot. She'd heard someone speak the word *revenge*.

She swung her legs over the side of the cot, yanking the IV out of her arm, and searched the room for her clothes. She didn't get very far. The door opened, and a nurse walked in, his white uniform untouched by a single stain or discoloration.

"Up already, I see," he said, scribbling something on his tab. "Good to see you doing so much better, Agent Stryker. But I'm afraid I'm going to have to insist that you lie down."

Phoenix strongly considered resisting him, but she soon found she was too dizzy to stand. The nurse tucked her in, replaced the IV tube into the access port in her arm and studied the monitor over the bed.

"Vitals good," he said, making another notation. "They'd be better if you hadn't tried to get up. It was touch-and-go there for a while, you know."

"I've been unconscious?"

"On and off for two days." He frowned at her over the tab. "Do you remember anything from during that time?"

"No." She realized she had an agonizing headache, but it was the last thing in the world that mattered to her now.

Drakon. The last she'd seen of him was when he'd given her the drugs. She'd heard a little of his voice after, and another woman's. Then...the shot. Drakon had killed someone. Patterson? Had Drakon left her there and gotten away, knowing she wouldn't be considered an accomplice if she'd been unable to participate?

"You were drugged, almost fatally," the nurse said. "Fortunately, your system was strong enough to fight it off. I'll send the doctor in to speak to you. You'll have to follow a—"

"Tell me what happened," she said, sitting up.

"Easy." He pushed her down gently with a big hand on her shoulder. "You were found on the roof of an apartment building with the man who tried to poison you and the woman who brought him down. She's an operative, like you. She said you knew where this Drakon was headed and went to stop him, but he overpowered you and killed Patterson. She was able to stop him from escaping before the Enforcers arrived."

There was only one *"she"* the nurse could be talking about.

"Drakon," she said. "He—"

"The mayor has given you and Agent Ward commendations for your work in bringing the assassin in. Congratulations."

The monitor above the bed began to beep as Phoenix's heartbeat shot up to almost dangerous levels. Moving efficiently, the nurse checked her IV and made an adjustment.

"You need more rest," he said. "Your entire system has been through a bad shock, and you're naturally experiencing some trauma after being held hostage and nearly killed by an Opir assassin. The more you cooperate, the sooner we can let you out of here." He checked her vitals again. "I'm going to speak to the doctor. Try to sleep, and he should be around in about an hour."

With an encouraging smile, the nurse left the room. As soon as she knew he was away from the door, Phoenix got off the bed.

All at once various monitors began to beep and complain loudly, and she knew she wouldn't be able to get out of the room simply with determination and brute strength. She lay back down, and the monitors went silent again.

They'd all come running if she set off the alarms. Especially since she'd received a *"commendation"* from Mayor Shepherd.

As had Brita. Brita, who'd betrayed both her and Drakon. Whatever Drakon had given Phoenix, he hadn't meant to kill her. Something must have gone wrong.

Brita had brought him down. If she'd made Drakon helpless somehow, she could have done anything she wanted to Phoenix.

And no one would believe a top agent like Brita would attempt to kill a fellow operative. But if she'd meant to, why wouldn't she just accuse Phoenix of being a traitor and let Aegis take care of her?

I should have convinced him, she thought. *I should have made him see that Brita was his enemy.*

The *why* didn't matter now. She had to find a way out of this place. She had to find out what had become of him.

Two days. He was probably under interrogation in one of the cells built for Opiri. Two days.

And since he'd never tell them anything…

Reaching back to her most basic training, Phoenix breathed deeply and relaxed all of her muscles one by one. When she was calm again, she let herself drift, convinced her body that it was well and whole, that any distress was long past. She heard the monitors humming contentedly. Maybe, if she could use a form of biofeedback to keep her vitals level…

It wasn't the doctor who entered the room as she was preparing to get up again. Only the most rigid discipline kept her from leaping out of the bed and attempting to strangle the woman in Aegis casuals standing several feet away.

"I wouldn't advise it," Brita said. "You might relapse, and that wouldn't be good for anyone."

"Where is Drakon?" she demanded.

"Incarcerated, as you might expect." Brita wandered around the room, pausing before the photograph of the bridge. "We're not being watched or recorded, so we can speak freely here. As far as I know, he's still alive. As for his condition…" She shrugged. "That I can't tell you. But torture, of course, isn't condoned by Aegis or any part of our government. So I suppose he's uncomfortable, but not badly hurt."

Even if they did hurt him, Phoenix knew Drakon would

never break. He'd say nothing of his fellow operatives or the Citadel's plans. He'd never tell them why he had a personal reason to hate Aaron Shepherd and John Patterson.

And he wouldn't beg to live. He knew none of it would make any difference.

"If any harm comes to him," Phoenix said, "I'll—"

"You do realize he tried to kill you?" Brita said, coming to stand beside the bed again.

"No. I don't know what happened, but he didn't want me to have any part of what he was going to do. And I know you set him up. You wanted Patterson dead, but you didn't want to take the risk of getting caught."

"An accurate assessment," Brita said, her voice as cool as ever and yet with a completely different cadence than the one she'd used in the Fringe. "But everything I told both him and you is true…there is a deadly biological weapon in production. And Drakon is expendable."

"Expendable? He said you two had—"

"Come from the same father?" She laughed, revealing teeth as neatly capped as Drakon's had been. "Drakon was only *made* by my father. Maybe families don't mean the same thing to us as they do to you, but we have our loyalties. And our knowledge of what a man or woman is worth."

"And he's worth nothing."

"Except as a tool. That was all he ever was, a tool with his own agenda, one that also suited Erebus. But he lost any usefulness when he began to have feelings for you. He could no longer be trusted."

So his feelings for me brought him to this, Phoenix thought. Would it have been better if he'd never felt anything at all?

"So now Patterson's dead," Phoenix said. "How will that help you?"

"I don't plan to share all my secrets."

"I can tell them everything you told me. I'll—"

"Sound a little crazy, given the drugs you've just recovered from. And I'm by far the senior operative. I've given them results. Whatever you did to help, I brought the assassin in. And saved your life."

"Why didn't you kill me, when you knew I might give you away?"

"Who says I didn't try?"

"The drugs—"

"I…shall we say, attempted to enhance their effects. But Drakon interrupted, and I had to hope what I'd given you was enough. Evidently, it wasn't."

Phoenix clenched her fists. "You made a big mistake, leaving me alive."

"That can be remedied, if you cause me any trouble. But I may still find a use for you. That is, if you want to save Drakon."

Phoenix's heart set the monitor to buzzing again. "How?"

"I don't know yet." She sighed and glanced toward the window, where the sun cast stripes of golden light across the floor through the blinds. "It might interest you to know that something good came of all this. Matthew Patterson actually stood before the assembly and his father and read off those secret files. He seemed to take some satisfaction in doing it, I hear, though he was naturally horrified when his father was shot." She shrugged, as if none of this mattered to her at all. "The mayor has already issued a statement proposing strict new anti-brutality measures to the Senate. And I've heard Shepherd blames himself for Patterson's death. He assumes the assassin received faulty intelligence and believed *he* was to be with the group going to meet Matthew."

"I want to see Drakon," Phoenix said.

"I'm sure Aegis will want to discuss your experiences with him as soon as you're fit."

"I want to see him. Now."

"Maybe that can be arranged. I have some influence, as you might imagine. But I can also arrange that you never see him again...if you make the mistake of sharing what we've discussed in this room."

"I won't betray my own people again."

"We'll see." Brita bent to sniff the flowers on the bedside table. "I hope you liked my little get-well gift. I think I'd better leave you to your rest now, or the doctor will come charging in, demanding to know why I'm taxing your strength."

"Physical strength isn't everything," Phoenix said through clenched teeth.

"I might worry if you had more of the other kinds of strength," Brita said as she walked to the door. "But you aren't particularly clever, and you suffer from the worst weakness of all. Sleep well."

Phoenix lay still for a long while after, mastering her emotions, thinking carefully. Brita could attempt to expose her as a traitor, if she chose to. And she claimed to have influence over Drakon's fate, as improbable as that sounded. She was still extremely dangerous to the Enclave.

But if the part about the biological weapon was true, then Brita couldn't be blamed for wanting to stop it. Phoenix wouldn't hesitate to do whatever was necessary to bring such a horror to light.

Could Shepherd possibly be involved? The man she'd once loved? The one who wanted a peace that could never be broken? *Had* he been working with Patterson, who claimed to want to maintain the current Armistice with its brutal deportation laws?

Killing the majority of Opiri would achieve a *"lasting peace."*

Hardly able to bear the wait, Phoenix composed herself again and was ready to be at her most cooperative when the doctor arrived. She did such a good job that the doctor agreed to let her dress and take a walk—a short one—through the medical center. She gave Phoenix a pair of loose hospital pants and slippers, as well as a less flimsy top that pulled on over the head. Then the doctor left and resumed her rounds.

Phoenix found her ID badge in the side table drawer and was out of her room and into the corridor in minutes. She located an unlocked office and a closet containing a pair of neatly pressed women's pants and casual shirt, a size too large, which she threw on over her hospital clothes. Then she left the medical center, concealing her dizziness with a bold front of authority, and made her way to her quarters. She exchanged the borrowed clothing for her casual fatigues and went straight to the underground detention facility.

Guards stopped her at the first gate, but she managed to get past them by flashing her ID and telling them who she was. The second set of guards were not so easy to convince. They were more sympathetic when she explained that she wanted to see the bloodsucker who had nearly killed her, even if it was only through the observation window.

The third set of guards turned her away with a brusque apology and a recitation of orders that could not under any circumstances be disobeyed. Phoenix spun around and strode back the way she had come, knowing that she'd have to go straight to the top.

Chan would see reason. Phoenix just had to think of the right approach. She had to find out how much, if anything, Drakon had told his interrogators, and then make a case that she might get more out of him because of their *relationship,* which Brita might or might not already have reported.

She was almost to Chan's office when a familiar man intercepted her: Behr, one of Mayor Shepherd's top security men. He made it very clear that the mayor was very anxious to see how she was doing, and that he would be happy to request the doctor's permission for her to visit him in his Capitol apartments.

Phoenix had no interest in waiting a second longer than necessary. Behr escorted her to a side entrance, where three other security men and women were waiting. Outside, where the trees were leafing out and birds were singing, it might have seemed as if nothing at all was wrong—except for the complete absence of civilians on the normally busy streets and the scores of Enforcers, police, Aegis and military personnel patrolling the area and guarding the complex of government buildings around the Capitol building. Phoenix had to pass through unusually strict and thorough security measures to enter the building, amounting to virtually a strip search. Only her status as an Aegis operative spared her a cavity search as well.

She followed Behr and his colleagues to the heavily guarded elevator bank and up to the top floor, where dozens of security personnel lined the hall leading to the mayoral suite. After further identity checks, she and her escorts continued past a quartet of heavily armed guards outside the door and entered the mayor's reception room. Another eight guards ranged around the room. The security panel had been closed over the reinforced window overlooking the square.

"Nix," Aaron said, embracing her under the hard eyes of his security team. "When I heard you'd nearly died…"

Forcing her body to relax in spite of her urge to spit in his face, Phoenix smiled. "As you see," she said, "I'm fine." She pulled away and met his troubled gaze. "I only wish I'd been able to stop the assassination."

With a low mutter, Shepherd walked a little unsteadily to a teak sideboard. "If you don't mind," he said, and poured himself a measure of rare whiskey. He downed it in one swallow and turned abruptly to face her again. "You know it wasn't Patterson they wanted. The assassin thought *I'd* be there."

Phoenix took a deep breath and looked around, noting the expressionless faces that watched her as intently as they did their employer. As if they expected her to attack the mayor right in front of them.

But his would-be assassin was already in custody. He might have some reason to fear a second attempt by one of Drakon's allies. But how could any of them be so stupid as to try now?

Drakon, she thought. *Focus on Drakon.*

Feeling unsteady herself, Phoenix took a seat on the couch. Aaron fiddled with an empty glass as if he was considering a refill. But he set it aside and glanced around the room at his army of protectors.

"I want all of you to step outside," he said.

"That won't be possible, sir," said the woman who was obviously the head of the team.

"There is no other entrance or exit from this suite except that one," Aaron said, nodding at the door. "And no one's getting through that window. I want to speak to Agent Stryker alone."

At first it seemed that the team leader would refuse, but at last she signaled to the others, including Phoenix's escort, and they all filed out of the room.

"We'll have to leave the door partly open, sir," the woman said as she stood in the doorway.

"Fine," Shepherd said. "But don't interfere unless I call."

"Understood, sir," the woman said with a short nod. She closed the door halfway and stepped outside.

Phoenix got to her feet, unable to bear sitting still. "Are you all right, Aaron? I know this has been a terrible shock...."

He smiled as he joined her, though his expression was more than merely strained. It concealed the kind of suppressed fury that only comes with the frustration of some grand ambition.

The ambition of a man who wanted to make a name for himself that would never be forgotten.

Chapter 20

"You've decided to use my name again," he said to Phoenix. "Maybe coming so close to death has made you see things a little differently than you did before."

His words truly startled her. They were almost malicious in tone, as if he felt he'd won some kind of victory. Over her.

"Sit," he said, almost pushing her down onto the couch. He sat beside her. "Agent Ward gave me a personal report when you returned," he said. "She told me how courageous you were, following the assassin up to the roof." He stretched his arm along the back of the couch, his hand inches from her shoulder. "She also told me what a remarkable job you did in gaining his trust, in spite of your ultimate failure to stop him."

That Brita had given such a glowing report was only another cause for alarm, Phoenix thought. She remembered her last conversation with Shepherd, how he had expected her to bring *"Sammael"* in before the meeting to exchange Matthew Patterson. How he'd implied that Patterson wanted him dead. How he'd asked her to work for *him*, not Aegis, and report any suspicions she might have about Patterson directly to his office.

Instead, Patterson had died. And somehow Shepherd still believed *he* had been the target. Wouldn't his rival's death have changed all his theories about Patterson's possible part in an assassination attempt?

But if Brita's claims were true, and Patterson was working with Shepherd in the creation of the unknown weapon…what did his reaction mean?

"I fully acknowledge my failure," she said, lowering her head. "I let you down, after you trusted me."

He turned toward her and tilted her chin up with his fingertips. "Don't be so hard on yourself, Nix. I know you did your best. Though I admit I'm a little puzzled about how it took you so long to realize he was a Nightsider, let alone the assassin."

Taking care to breathe normally, Phoenix waited for the other shoe to drop. Had Brita told him that she and Drakon had been lovers, and that she'd deliberately failed to report any suspicions she might have had? Could Brita have told him she and Drakon had planned to leave the city together?

No, she thought. If Shepherd really believed that, she'd be in a detention cell herself. He was probing, trying to extract more information than he'd already been given. She didn't plan to let him have any more than she had to, and she'd have to be extremely careful about asking to see Drakon. Or asking any questions about him at all.

"You're right," she said, meeting Aaron's gaze. "I wasn't prepared for how far I'd have to go to get the information I was sent to retrieve. I suspected he had some connection to the Opiri almost from the beginning, or that someone in his Hold did. I had to earn his trust, and

I was eventually put in a position where I had to admit that I had been sent to locate and expose Bosses in the Fringe. After that, I had to win his trust all over again."

"By becoming his lover?"

Phoenix knew she was walking on the edge of the Wall, in danger of cutting her feet to ribbons even if she didn't fall.

"I was told to use any and all means at my disposal," she said. "But I'm sure you know that."

He pulled his hand back and clenched his fist against his thigh. "And you finally discovered what he was *after* you left Aegis with our response to his offer for Matthew Patterson's life."

"Yes. I did what I could to protect Lieutenant Patterson. And until the end, Drakon wouldn't let me out of his sight. He had a personal grudge against Patterson, but that was from before he was converted. I was only able to get through to him as much as I did because he was still attached to his human past."

"But not enough to refuse to kill the leader of his own former people."

"No." She looked down again. "I'm sorry, Aaron. Sorry I didn't do a better job. Sorry I had to go so far with him, and ended up with so little."

"Are you?" The harshness in his voice compelled her to meet his gaze. "You didn't develop any feelings for this monster?"

She widened her eyes as if she were genuinely shocked. "For a bloodsucker? The kind who killed my father and caused my mother's suicide?"

"But you're part of them, too, aren't you?"

She held his gaze, refusing to give ground even if it might have been the wiser thing to do. "So was my father," she said, "and he died a hero. So are the best Aegis operatives, and the Enclave couldn't survive without them to patrol the Zone. That doesn't mean we have to *be* like them."

He seemed to relax a little, as if she'd just passed some kind of test. "I'm glad to hear you say that, Nix," he said, running his hand through his perfectly groomed hair. "We've picked up three other Opir spies in the Fringe, exposed by an anonymous informant. We hope to get more information out of them, as well as this Drakon."

Anonymous informant? Phoenix thought with a deeper sense of dread. "It's possible Drakon intended to kill Patterson all along," she said, testing the waters to see how Shepherd would respond to the suggestion…especially when it was very close to the truth. "When Drakon was human and Patterson was Commissioner of the Enforcement Bureau, he was responsible for killing Drakon's wife and son. Maybe it wasn't enough for him, holding Patterson's son hostage and forcing the senator to hear his private records read aloud in front of his peers."

"Yes," Shepherd murmured, as if he'd never considered the idea at all, so intent had he been on the idea that the assassin's bullet had been meant for him. "I'm sure the prisoner will tell us very soon."

"I know how important it is to get the intelligence," she said cautiously, "but I came to understand Drakon well enough to know he's not likely to give up any information that might in any way reveal the details of his mission."

"He has courage," Shepherd said, rising and moving toward the window as if he could see through the panels. "It has required stringent measures to even begin to break down his resistance."

It was one of the most difficult things she had ever done, but Phoenix managed to conceal her rage. "You mean torture."

"That's forbidden by Treaty," he said. "Though of course we know the Opiri use it against our people."

"But you're considering the possibility that Drakon really was trying to kill Patterson?"

"You always managed to make me see things more clearly, Nix," he said, turning back to her with what seemed a genuine smile. "Perhaps I was too hasty. But if Patterson was the intended target all along, we still have to be sure of the motive. Revenge seems the obvious reason, but if it wasn't…"

"Could someone inside the Enclave have hired Drakon to do it?"

"What?" He stared at her as if she'd gone crazy. "Hire an Opir spy?"

"Drakon used to live in the Enclave. He knew people here, had family. There might have been others who hated Patterson as much as he did."

"Highly unlikely."

She decided to step straight off the cliff, hoping she wouldn't end up broken at the bottom along with Drakon. "I knew you and Patterson weren't friends. You even said he wouldn't mind seeing you dead. But *you* didn't hate him, did you?"

"No," he said, a harsh note entering his voice.

"Still, if someone—one of Patterson's more fanatical supporters, for instance—were to get hold of that idea, no matter how unlikely it seems," she said, "someone could possibly think one of *your* supporters had it done."

All at once Shepherd was striding toward her, his eyes filled with irrational fury. "Shut up!" he yelled. "Don't you dare—"

The security chief appeared in the doorway, her weapon halfway drawn. "Your Honor?" she said, staring at Phoenix. "Do you need assistance?"

"No," he snarled, standing over Phoenix with clenched fists. "Get out." He breathed sharply through his nose, obviously struggling to gain command of himself.

"Why would you even say something like that?" he demanded, his voice raw with anger. "None of my people—*none* of them—"

"I'm sorry," she said, injecting a plea into the words. "I was only considering every possibility, especially the ones that might hurt you and what you're trying to achieve."

The tension went out of his clenched jaw, but there was no lessening of the ferocity in his eyes. He almost looked like a Nightsider out for blood.

"You know I would never allow that to happen," he said softly.

"Of course not."

"But you're right. It isn't impossible that someone might come up with such a fantastic scenario. That's why we have to get a full confession out of Drakon."

Phoenix's stomach knotted. She'd managed to make it worse. He'd do anything it took....

"I see how much that disturbs you, though you've done an excellent job trying to hide it," Shepherd said. "I guessed at our last meeting, but I kept telling myself I was wrong."

"I don't know what you're talking about."

"Don't bother, Nix." He sighed, returned to the sideboard and poured himself another two fingers of whiskey. "There are a few things I need to tell you, things I'd never confide to someone who didn't have as much riding on this as I have." He swallowed the whiskey and set it down very carefully, as if he was afraid another loud noise would arouse his security to stronger action. "I want you to understand something very clearly. Patterson and I were not enemies. We were allies. Almost no one knew about this, but we shared the same goals. Defeat the bloodsuckers once and for all."

Rigidly still, Phoenix waited. Waited for him to admit his part in creating the biological weapon, trusting her with a secret that literally meant life or death for thousands, perhaps hundreds of thousands.

"We know they're planning something," Shepherd said, apparently unaware of her horror. "Something big. We needed to get them panicking over the prospect of a mayor who wanted to stop deportation, and let Patterson take the heat in the Enclave for continuing to support it. We wanted the Nightsiders confused, off balance. We wanted their war party to make a premature move, without the backing of the entire Erebusian Council. And when we heard about the assassin, we knew it was paying off."

Phoenix released her breath. "I...I don't understand. You *wanted* them to make an attempt on your life?"

"We deliberately set things up so that there would be opportunities for a clever Opiri operative," he said. "We let it get out with our agents in the Zone that our government was weakening because of the battles between me and Patterson. Obviously, we succeeded in provoking a response."

"From the Expansionist Party," Phoenix said slowly, remembering what Drakon had said. "But you were taking a huge risk. A successful assassination attempt would give that party power enough to gain support for a more direct attack."

"But if they failed, and word of the failure got to the Council, there would be political upheaval in Erebus. We'd have more time to...deal with the unstable situation between our nations."

More time, Phoenix thought. But not merely to *"deal with the unstable situation,"* as he'd suggested.

"But Patterson is dead," she said.

Shepherd picked up a pack of cigarettes and tapped it against the sideboard. "Because you weren't the only agent who failed. Brita was one of the first. She discovered the plot in the first place, but we still didn't know who the assassin was, who he'd be targeting, or if there was more than one. She was supposed to carry out the same assignment you were, but not to break cover until she was certain she could identify and expose the assassin or assassins. We sent out more than a dozen other operatives to support her. We were lucky; only three of them died, apparently in ordinary altercations with Fringe crews. The rest of them got back before they were exposed."

Phoenix got to her feet. "Why wasn't I told any of this?"

"We didn't want any future operatives to be…influenced by what had happened before."

"And you sent *me* in…why?"

"Because you were an unknown quantity, and that was exactly what we seemed to need. Not human, not full dhampir. And I knew you were motivated. You wanted to prove yourself. We decided to take a chance."

She laughed. "Phoenix Stryker, the only agent capable of finding and defeating the evil assassin you wanted to show up."

"We didn't know what would happen," Aaron said, removing a cigarette from the pack. "We hoped Brita would be able to make contact with you and pass on information, in which case she'd have instructed you to return immediately. Which was, I believe, what you were originally ordered to do."

Phoenix ignored his chiding, knowing it was just another way Shepherd was trying to throw her off balance. "Brita didn't contact me or tell me who she was until she knew Drakon was going to make the assassination attempt."

She expected disbelief, but Shepherd only pushed the cigarette between his lips and pulled a gold lighter from an inner pocket of his jacket. He lit the cigarette.

"I'm aware of Brita's…shortcomings," he said in a flat voice. "More than you can imagine. And that's why I've got a proposition for you." He inhaled and blew the smoke in Phoenix's direction. "Maybe your lover won't have to suffer quite as much if you help me out now. I'll let you speak to him alone, with no cameras or recorders."

Black dread fogged Phoenix's vision. He wouldn't believe any more denials now. He knew *her* too well. And what he was about to ask must be terrible, indeed.

Aaron stared toward the door a long time. "When I told you I still loved you," he said, "I meant it. I would have done a great deal to win you back."

"What do you want me to do?" she asked.

He smiled absently. "If you could get him to admit that he'd been sent by the Expansionists to kill me and taken out Patterson by mistake, I could stop the interrogation and get him transferred to a more comfortable cell. But I'm afraid nothing less than execution will satisfy Congress or the people."

"What else do you want to get him out of the city?"

Smashing his cigarette into a crystal tray on the sideboard, he gestured for her to sit again and joined her on the couch. "You weren't so far off the mark, Nix. Someone has actually threatened to release supposed *'evidence'* that I had this Drakon kill Patterson because of my political ambitions."

And Phoenix knew. She didn't yet understand the reason, but she *knew.*

"I'm being blackmailed," he said, as if she hadn't understood the first time. "All lies, of course. Ridiculous. But it *could* cause difficulties, a temporary scandal until the matter is sorted out. It won't help this city or the Enclave. I have to make sure the blame is fully placed on those it should be."

"Who's doing this?" Phoenix asked. "Who would dare try to blackmail the mayor of the Enclave?"

"The operative who was supposed to help protect me. Who was so slow to tell you she'd found the assassin. Brita Ward."

Phoenix closed her eyes. "And what can I do about it?"

"It's very simple." He got up, walked to an antique rolltop desk and tapped a complex series of numbers and letters onto the keypad that locked the top in place. He pushed it back and entered a code on one of the small drawers underneath. Then he moved something around inside the drawer, finally withdrawing a narrow, opaque tube about the length of Phoenix's hand.

"This," he said. Once again he glanced toward the door and sat on the couch, so close that his shoulder touched hers. "Inside this tube is a syringe. It contains a drug that will insure that she never gets a chance to destroy me or the Enclave with her lies."

The biological weapon, Phoenix thought. The means of destroying the entire Opir species.

"What is it?" she whispered, pretending ignorance.

"Painless death," he said. "It'll seem as if she has a common virus, with flu-like symptoms. Slightly uncomfortable, no more. Then she'll just drift off to sleep."

"You're talking about murder."

"Not murder. Political necessity. I believe she's a double agent, Nix…working for the other side as well as ours. But if that gets out, it could cause as much chaos as if I were assassinated or charged with Patterson's murder."

"How did you find out what she was?"

"I don't have hard proof. But given her attempt to blackmail me, I can't take any chances. *We* can't."

"If this drug… If it's so deadly, how can you use it where it might—"

"It can't harm anyone else," he said. His voice hardened. "You'll have to take my word for it. If you do as I tell you, and make absolutely sure no one ever knows what happened, I'll get your precious Drakon out of the city, and you can go with him. If you fail or word of this gets out, he'll be executed, and I'll have you exposed as a traitor." He pushed the tube into her hand. "Hide this, and go see your lover. You'll have fifteen minutes with him. If you don't get your chance to take Brita out in the next few hours, I'll arrange to have the two of you meet in a convenient location."

She stared at the weapon in her hand. He wasn't worried that it might hurt someone else, because it only worked on Opiri. If it worked on dhampires, he'd never risk it.

And that meant he knew Brita was more than half-Opir.

"Remember what I've told you," Shepherd said, rising. "I'll speak to Chan personally. It might take an hour or two to arrange, but you'll be able to see the prisoner within the next few hours. No one will interfere."

"I can return to my quarters, then?" she asked.

"Of course. By all means, rest until my men come to get you." He smiled. "Don't disappoint me this time, Nix."

Without bothering to answer, Phoenix pocketed the tube and strode toward the door. The security people parted to let her pass, and the four who'd brought her fell in around her again.

As they set off for Aegis headquarters, Phoenix nearly trembled with rage. Whatever Brita had done to her and Drakon, whatever plans her Citadel might have for the Enclave, Phoenix couldn't commit cold-blooded murder. Especially not with a biological weapon meant for genocide.

But she *could* do something so dangerous that it could lead to devastation of everything she held dear, as well as the destruction of the enemy. Unless she was very wrong, she had a precious sample that might have some use in the hands of an expert who could study it, break it down to its components, learn how it was made and perhaps...

It was only a desperate hope. But it was all she had. And Brita had better be reasonable enough to see it.

Or everything they both valued would end.

Chapter 21

Phoenix.

She was there when Drakon returned to consciousness as, suddenly and painfully, someone plunged a needle into his arm.

But as the room swam into focus around him—bare, brightly lit, with only a table between him and the interrogator's chair—he knew it couldn't be true. Phoenix...

Phoenix was dead. They had told him so. Brita had killed her, after he'd left her helpless. They had used that against him, as if they'd known what it would do to him.

Somehow, they had known.

"Awake, are we?" the woman's voice said from across the table.

He blinked to clear his vision. The room was too bright for his Opir eyes, but he knew it was meant to be. He had fed from Phoenix—how long ago?—so there was little danger yet that he would starve. Not yet. But he had no doubt that they'd try that measure along with many others in order to obtain his secrets.

They must also realize he was prepared to die before he told them anything.

Phoenix.

"In case you're wondering, it's a new drug, recently developed in our labs," the woman said. She had graying black hair in a short, practical style, a lined but handsome face, and wore a conservative dark suit. It was clear she was high up the chain of command, and Drakon was vaguely surprised that she would have been assigned to the second round of interrogations.

"Very effective," Drakon said, his speech still a little slurred. He lifted his head. It felt as heavy as one of the pylons in the market where he, Phoenix and some of his crew had taken temporary shelter.

Was this the biological weapon meant to wipe out the Opiri, or some variation of it? If the former, he was probably already dying, though the mechanism of the pathogen remained a mystery. Perhaps they were still testing it, knowing he'd be executed, anyway.

It would be very good if he were to die, preferably as quickly as possible.

"Have you devised a method for delivering it as a projectile?" he asked.

The woman leaned back. "I believe we're here to question *you,* Drakon."

He pulled his arms against the restraints that held his hands bound together and fixed to a chain set into the floor, too weakened by the drug to make more than a token effort. "I've told your interrogators everything I know," he said.

She tapped her tablet with a square fingernail, bringing up a screen he couldn't see. "My name is Director Chan. I will be conducting the second phase of this interrogation.

If you cooperate, we can finish this matter quickly, and you'll be remanded to a reasonably comfortable cell—"

"I'll be executed," Drakon said.

"—or," Chan went on, as if he hadn't interrupted, "if you are stubborn, I'll be sending some of my experts to deal with you."

"Experts whose usual methods of questioning include daylight or simulators with the same effect, starvation and of course the conventional forms of torture, which cause pain to Opiri even if we're somewhat more durable than humans," Drakon said.

"So you are." Chan pursed her lips. "It sounds as if you are familiar with our procedures, Drakon."

"Every Opir knows about human techniques."

"Especially every Opir agent. Or assassin." She leaned forward again, pushing her tab to one side. "Where shall we begin?"

Six hours later, near what Drakon estimated as dawn, they left Drakon alone to *"think over"* what he and Chan had discussed. Chan had expressed her deep disappointment in Drakon's refusal to be reasonable, and profound regret at what would follow as a result.

After two more hours of enduring the blinding light, he began to feel the first stirrings of hunger. He could go several days without blood, but he suspected the drug they had given him was somehow affecting his metabolism, weakening him and insuring that he wouldn't recover too quickly from any torture the interrogators might inflict.

He knew his brief respite was about to end when the lights brightened still more, taking on the heat and brilliance of a simulated sun. It was not yet hot enough to burn, but he felt his skin tighten and the first pain begin. The two men who entered the room were expressionless, professional, prepared to do whatever it took.

But so was Drakon. He smiled at them, showing his teeth.

"Good morning, gentlemen," he said.

As one of the men closed the door behind him, the other approached Drakon with his right fist tightened. There was a loud clang from the corridor as another door closed.

And then it began.

"Drakon."

The voice cut through the fog of constant pain as neatly as Opir incisors through the softest human flesh. He knew it wasn't real; he'd been in a nearly constant state of delirium, his vision blurred by the bombardment of bright light, his nose filled with noxious odors meant to offend the keen Opiri sense of smell, his skin icy from the bitterly cold temperature. The heat and light of the sun could destroy a Nightsider, but Opir bodies functioned at a much lower temperature than humans'.

In every way, they had made the place *"uncomfortable"* for him…after beating him thoroughly, though only with fists. That had been unpleasant enough, though far from sufficient to make him break. Or die.

"It's all right, Drakon. I'm here."

He tried to shake the phantom voice out of his head, wondering how they'd managed to devise this new form of torture. Recordings? More simulations?

The woman, who might have looked something like Phoenix if Drakon had been able to see properly, entered the room carrying a tray with a pitcher of water and a glass. With one hand she closed the door behind her, and looked around as if she were assessing the small, featureless space. Suddenly, the temperature warmed, the lights dimmed and the hideous stench diminished.

The illusion approached the table, set the tray down

and made a slow circuit of the room. It seemed she was looking for something; she glanced up at the cameras, examining them closely.

"They've been turned off," the vision said, as if to the air. "And so have the recorders and listening devices. We're alone."

"Is that important?" he asked, trying without success to focus on her face. "Do they think this is going to work better than the other methods?"

She turned to him, her expression suddenly dark with rage and anguish. "I'm so sorry, Drakon."

He leaned back as much as he could, his body afire with pain, and smiled. "I'm sure you are," he said. "Who are you? A projection? Or did they just find someone who looked like her and dressed her up nice and pretty?"

"This is Phoenix, Drakon. I'm alive. I'm here to help." Moving like an old woman, she took the chair on the other side of the table and poured water into the glass. "Please try to believe me."

"I believe you," he said, his head rolling on the back of the hard chair. "Why shouldn't I?"

Without warning, she pulled something from the inside of her jacket pocket. She got up and moved toward him slowly. He braced himself as she knelt behind him.

There was a low, brief buzz, and Drakon felt the bonds give way. Immediately, he freed his hands, turned in his chair and reached for the woman. She remained kneeling where she was, looking up into his face. He grabbed her shoulders and slid his hands toward her neck. He still had just enough strength....

"I know they haven't given you any blood," she said. "You can have mine, or you can kill me. My stupidity brought you to this."

He withdrew his hands. They were shaking so hard that he couldn't have hurt her if he'd tried.

"Who are you?" he rasped.

Taking him gently by the arms, she kissed him. The thought came to him that only one person in the world had ever kissed him that way. It wasn't something anyone could fake.

"Phoenix?" he said.

"Yes. It's me. I'm alive."

He took her face between his hands, examining every feature, every tiny imperfection that made her so beautiful.

"Alive," he said.

This time he kissed *her,* and it went on for a very long time. Then he enfolded her in his arms and held her fast, his cheek resting on her hair. When he pulled back, she was smiling and weeping at the same time.

"We're both alive," she said. "And we're going to stay that way."

He rested his forehead against hers. "Will it do any good…if I tell you that the only thing that matters is that you're alive and safe?"

"None whatsoever."

"If you're wrong about the monitors—" He gripped her shoulders. "Phoenix, you've signed your own death warrant."

"I have reason to believe they did as I asked," she said.

He stiffened. "What reason? Because you can convince me to tell them what they want to hear?"

She got up and moved around to the table. "Please," she said. "Drink some water."

Slowly he turned in the chair and took the glass. He stared into the clear liquid for a moment and then, holding Phoenix's gaze, drank it all.

Nothing happened. He felt no different. If it was drugged, it was very slow-acting. Which it very well might be.

But Phoenix would never do that to him. Never. *"I love you,"* she'd said. And he'd believed it then. He wanted to believe it now.

"They said they caught my fellow agents," he said. "Were they lying?"

"No."

"How did they find them?"

"With the help of an *'anonymous source,'*" she said.

"Are they still alive?"

"Yes. But you can't help them now, Drakon. Neither can I." She reached across the table to take his hand. "I didn't come to trick you. I came to tell you that there is hope."

"Hope…of what?" he asked, gazing into her eyes with a strange feeling of contentment.

"Just believe me. Please, Drakon." She poured him another glass of water. "Drink."

"Where is Brita?" he asked, ignoring the glass.

She must have heard the fury in his voice, though he never raised it above a near-whisper. "She spoke out for me," Phoenix said. "Gave me part of the credit from stopping you and bringing you in. I don't know why."

Once again Drakon glanced at the cameras and recorders set into the walls. Phoenix followed his gaze.

"If anyone's listening," she said, "they won't report what they're hearing to anyone except the person who's arranged this meeting."

He didn't ask her who she meant. He knew he'd find out soon enough.

"I believed Brita," he said, his emotions overcoming his determination not to let her see him falter. "I had no idea—"

"I know what she is," Phoenix said evenly. "I know why she turned against you. She always regarded you as a tool to be thrown away when you weren't useful anymore."

"When she saw me…as too weak," he said, perfectly understanding why she had come to that conclusion.

"She's brilliant, Drakon," Phoenix said. "But no one here is going to believe me if I try to tell them. She's been with Aegis a long time. She's highly trusted. And she captured the assassin who killed John Patterson."

"She tried to kill you."

"I know. But only one person realizes who she really is. And he's the one who's going to help us."

Drakon clenched his fist. "The mayor."

The mayor. One of the men responsible for the pathogen that might be killing him even now. And Phoenix said he wanted to *help* them.

"Don't trust him," Drakon said, swinging around to face her again. "Whatever he's told you to do—"

The door opened again. Phoenix shot to her feet, falling automatically into a defensive crouch. Weak as he was, Drakon did the same.

But the young man who entered raised his hands above his head and stopped just inside the closed door. "You don't have to worry about me," he said. "I'm the one who made sure the monitors really were turned off. It helps to be a hero who wants to give the bloodsucker who killed his father the beating of his life."

Matthew Patterson didn't smile. He glanced from Phoenix to Drakon and walked into the room, slowly lowering his hands.

"Drakon," he said. "Phoenix."

"I didn't kill your father," Drakon said, approaching the younger man slowly.

"I know." The Enforcer's brown eyes were glazed with tears, and Phoenix's heart ached for him. She'd thought him incredibly foolish at first, this young man who had so valiantly tried to help maintain Phoenix's cover in the Hold, and then become Drakon's hostage to expose his father's crimes against justice. Just as Brita had told Phoenix before she'd sent her into the trap, John Patterson's son had done what Drakon had apparently asked of him.

And then his father had been shot right in front of him.

"I don't know what to say," Phoenix said, genuinely at a loss.

"You don't have to say anything," Matthew said. "I know neither one of you had anything to do with it."

"How?" Phoenix asked, wondering what he had heard since Patterson's death. What he had been told.

"Because I spent two days talking to Drakon while you were gone from the Hold," he said. "I learned a lot about him, what he thought and believed. And he told me about you." He almost smiled. "What a guy says about a woman gives you a good idea about who he is."

Phoenix swallowed. What *had* passed between them during her absence? Had Drakon seen something of his long-lost son in the younger man, or what he might have become had he lived? Opiri aged almost imperceptibly, over centuries rather than years.

But Drakon looked to be only in his late twenties, and his own son would have been considerably younger than Matthew. Some kind of bond had grown between them—one, Phoenix thought, that she might never understand.

"I didn't know why you'd agreed to go through with… what Drakon asked you to do after he let you go," she said to Matthew.

"Once I read through those files, I knew my father deserved to be exposed. I admit I didn't expect…" He blinked rapidly. "Sometimes even enemies can gain a little respect for each other. Drakon didn't kill me. And even if he used me, he had reason." He sighed. "You look sick," he said, meeting Drakon's gaze. "I know what they've been doing to you. I would have stopped it if I could. You'd better sit down."

When Drakon didn't move, Matthew looked at Phoenix. Feeling dazed for what seemed like the hundredth time since she'd woken in the hospital bed, Phoenix grabbed Drakon's arm and steered him back to the chair. He didn't fight her. She offered him the water again, and he drank.

"Maybe you'd better fill me in," she said to Matthew, "and tell me why you're here. If you want to sit…"

He remained where he was and gazed at the stained concrete under his feet. "I haven't forgotten what Sammael—Drakon—said when you and he brought me to the Hold. That my father was the most brutal captain and commissioner the Department of Deportation had ever seen. I thought it was all just part of Drakon's interrogation. To break me down. I was proud of my father for keeping the peace, helping to keep the city alive, but I didn't know…"

"It wasn't your fault," Phoenix said quietly.

He looked up again. "I should have known. There were…signs, the way he acted, even at home. And I've been an Enforcer for three years. I heard talk sometimes, when people thought I couldn't hear. And then I really saw the Fringe, what goes on there, how those people suffer. I still didn't want to believe, because when I joined, I just wanted to make him—"

Matthew broke off, flushing, but Phoenix knew exactly what he'd been about to say. How much had *he* been trying to prove, when his father, for good or ill, was such a legend in the city. Was that why he'd tackled her and *"Sammael"* alone that night?

"Lieutenant Patterson—" she began.

"Chavez," he said. "My mother's name. That's what

I'm using now." He lifted his head. "I'm sorry about what I said to you in the Hold."

"You were trying to protect my cover."

"They didn't tell us that you were after spies," he said. "Only that your real purpose was to find the Bosses." He looked at Drakon. "You're the real victim in all this."

"You know that's not true," Drakon said, a grim set to his mouth.

Something Phoenix couldn't interpret passed between the two men. "I understand why you thought you had to kill the mayor," Matthew said. "You were a soldier, doing your duty. But you had another reason, too. I didn't have any idea when I left the Hold with the files. But since I got back, I've had access to things I know my father didn't want anyone else to see. I have a pretty good idea of what my father was doing besides trying to become mayor of the Enclave."

Glancing quickly at Drakon, Phoenix took a deep breath.

"It's okay," Matthew said. "No one can hear us, even though someone should be shouting this from the rooftops." He dragged his hand over his face. "You knew about this…thing, didn't you?"

"Not until very recently," Drakon said.

"So Erebus doesn't know yet?"

"Not unless…" He trailed off, and Phoenix knew he wasn't ready to tell Matthew about Brita. It could set off a whole avalanche that no one might be able to stop. "Not when I left. Do you have proof?"

"Not yet. But I'll find it." Matthew managed another very faint smile. "The thing about my generation…most of us don't hold with the idea of going through another war. We don't want to put our asses out there to be killed because we're all too stupid to make it work. So I guess we have to find a way to stop it, if no one else will."

"What will you do when you have the information you're looking for?" Phoenix asked, feeling a fresh stirring of hope.

"First I plan to resign from the Force, as soon as the investigation into my father's death is finished. Then we'll have to figure out a way—"

"You," Drakon said. "*You'll* have to figure it out. It's unlikely I'll still be here."

Phoenix turned on Drakon. "I told you—"

"We don't lie to each other," Matthew said. "Maybe what we do isn't right sometimes. Maybe most of the time. But we've always stood together. I trusted what Drakon said before. I believe him now."

"What do you mean *we?*" Phoenix asked. "Who doesn't lie to each other?"

"Phoenix," Drakon said, pulling her toward him. She knelt beside his chair, looking up into his pain-racked face. He touched her cheek. "I told you I was deported because I was a dissenter. I told you my wife and child died in a clash between the Enforcers and protesters."

"But you weren't there when it happened," she said, the words thick in her throat.

"No. But I was never a dissident. I was an Enforcer."

Chapter 22

An Enforcer.

Hardly able to make sense of his words, Phoenix tried to rise and listed to one side. Immediately Drakon was up, helping her to the other chair. Matthew was beside her in an instant.

"It's the drug she gave you," Drakon said, standing over her protectively as if he expected Brita to come charging in and force more of the stuff down her gullet. "You left the infirmary too soon."

"Drug?" Matthew said, alarm crossing his face. "What—"

"I'm all right," she said, waving the men off. She was both shocked and furious—again—and she was sick and tired of being both. She'd been nothing but an utter idiot from the moment the mission had begun.

"You were an Enforcer?" she whispered.

"Yes," he said, crouching beside her. "Beginning when Patterson was still a captain and through his appointment as commissioner. I was young and determined to protect the Enclave. I never noticed the abuses, or believed I was contributing to them. I married the year after I joined up, and my son..." He paused, as if to catch his breath. "Mark was born the year after that. But Patterson got worse as time went on, actively searching for ways to tempt or even force people into committing crimes."

"And no one had any idea," Phoenix said quietly.

"Everyone in the Force did, whether they wanted to admit it or not. And someone outside had to have known. Until a few years ago, most people thought the Enforcers were doing the right thing, ridding the Enclave of crime while keeping the Opiri from attacking. And I was one of them. I did exactly as I was ordered."

The pain in his voice was almost more than Phoenix could bear. "You arrested innocent people?"

"I stood by even when I suspected that many were being pushed into committing proscribed acts and participated in arrests of men and women who should never have been considered offenders," he said. "It was all quotas, meant to enhance Patterson's political ambitions." He met her gaze, and she could see him struggling with his shame and overwhelming grief. "But a time came when we were rounding up an entire family because they had raided a Dumpster behind a restaurant frequented by the elite. That was when I understood it was wrong."

Phoenix reached out for him. "Drakon—"

"Charles, remember?" he said bitterly. "But then Charlie went rogue. He started looking for chances to read the rosters before the days' sweeps started, for names of people to be *'investigated.'* That almost always meant arrested. I'd find those people—usually only a few—and warn them. Some fled into the Fringe. Others were still arrested and deported."

"And you were always in danger of being caught yourself."

"That didn't matter. I began to see that I still wasn't doing enough. My wife—" He seemed to choke, and then found his voice again. "Cynthia encouraged me. When I said I wanted to help people find ways out of the city, she went along with me all the way. So I started contacting some of the Fringe Bosses and learning where the secret passages were. Sometimes I used blackmail, threatening to expose them. After a while I knew enough that I was able to gather allies, some dissidents and some people from the Fringe, to help me with a kind of Underground Railroad."

"But they caught you," she said, guessing the rest of the terrible story. "You were arrested and condemned and deported."

"The men and women I thought of as friends tricked me," he said. "Even the ones I thought might be sympathetic. They set a trap and I walked into it. Cynthia and my son—Mark, who was five years old then—were caught in the wrong place at the *right* time. The day after I was sentenced, the so-called dissidents attacked the Enforcers, in the park where Cynthia and Mark usually spent the afternoon after he got out of school. But it wasn't the dissidents who were killed."

Rising from her chair on unsteady legs, Phoenix put her arms around him. "I'm sorry," she said, her tears wetting his torn shirt. "I'm sorry."

He hardly reacted. "It wasn't coincidence, or bad luck," he said in a dull voice. "*They* wanted to set an example. And they made sure I knew about it before I actually left the city with the other new convicts. When I got to Erebus…I was treated better than among my own people. I had a lot of time to think about what they'd done."

And that was when he'd turned against the Enclave,

Phoenix thought. Against its corruption, against a way of life he had come to hate.

Yet he still wanted to help the people of the Fringe, the desperate and disenfranchised, knowing that what he planned to do…

"You told me," she said, "that some dissenters on the Council in Erebus had been considering other ways of creating a new peace by tearing down the old and re-building."

"But they weren't the ones who sent me," he said. "Do you know where I learned my marksmanship? I was a sniper for the Force. I only took out *dangerous* criminals. According to Patterson."

My God, she thought. The guilt. The terrible, wrenching guilt.

"Why hasn't anyone recognized you?" she asked.

"For the same reason they didn't know I was Opir. I don't look exactly the way I did before. Geneticists in Erebus altered my appearance. It would have been pointless to send me into the Enclave otherwise."

So much made sense now, Phoenix thought. Terrible sense. But whatever had been done to Drakon and his family, even if he could prove it, he could never be pardoned. She had to go on just as she'd planned.

Without telling Drakon.

"You see why I had to help him," Matthew said. "I owed him. For what my father did to help destroy his life."

"You owe me nothing," Drakon said, moving Phoenix gently aside and getting to his feet again. He swayed a little, and Phoenix braced him. They held on to each other, as if together they made one strong, invulnerable whole.

"It's so clear now, why I had such a hard time understanding how you could be a good man, an Opir, and an assassin all at once," she said, resting her cheek against his. "You found out that the life you'd devoted yourself to was wrong. You tried to help, and your family was murdered. You were a serf, a vassal and a Freeblood who lost a beloved mentor. And then a spy for Erebus in this Enclave, posing as a Fringe Boss. It got to the point where you didn't know who or what you were anymore."

"It's no excuse. Hundreds have been through worse. Matthew," he said, looking at the young Enforcer, "do whatever you can to find proof of the weapon, and where it's being produced. Phoenix, it'll be up to you and anyone you trust to find a way to get word out to people who would be against it." He hesitated. "Lieutenant Chavez, will you give us a moment alone?"

The young man flushed. "Yeah." He glanced at his watch. "And I don't think they'll let us stay in here much longer, anyway. Not with the monitors off. But there's something I have to do first."

Drakon nodded, and Matthew advanced on him, fist raised. Before Phoenix could intervene, he punched Drakon in the face with his full weight behind it. Drakon staggered but didn't fall. Dark, thin blood gushed from his nose. He smiled wryly.

"Thank you," he said.

"No problem," Matthew said. "I'll buy you another five minutes." He ducked his head and quickly retreated, buzzed the door open and almost ran out of the room.

"Was that really necessary?" Phoenix asked, vainly searching for something to stanch the bleeding. But the flow had already lessened to a trickle, and Drakon showed no additional signs of pain.

She moved toward him to take him in her arms, but he stepped back as if he had just seen something terrible enough to rob him of speech. He touched his nose and whispered an unrecognizable curse.

"The drug," he rasped.

"I told you…I'm all right," Phoenix said, reaching toward him.

"They drugged *me*," he said, focusing on her face. "It… knocked me out, weakened me. The woman—Chan—said it was recently developed in their labs. I thought then…"

"Chan?" Phoenix asked, shaking her head in helpless denial. "No. I can't…"

Drakon stared at the blood on his fingertips. "It could be the pathogen or something like it. They could have been…testing it. And I…"

Phoenix's heart forgot to beat. "You think they've infected you?"

"I don't know. But we don't know how it's spread. I *kissed* you."

She tried to make her brain work again. If this was the same pathogen Shepherd had given her to use on Brita, Drakon would be experiencing flu-like symptoms. Shepherd hadn't said how long it would take to kill, but he hadn't indicated that it would be a protracted illness. And though he was weak, Drakon didn't seem to be suffering serious effects.

"I think you'd be dead by now," she said, desperate to believe it. "And we have to assume it doesn't work on dhampires, or the Enclave would never dare risk developing it. They might accidentally kill their own agents, or have it used against them by the enemy."

"You have to stay away from me," he said. "Go, now."

"If I were going to get it through a kiss, I already have it," she said, as calmly as she could manage. "We don't have much time left."

It was as if she were talking to the Wall. He drifted away.

"Drakon!" She ran up behind him, grabbed his arm and pulled him around to face her. Then she slapped him as hard as she could.

He snapped out of his detached state with a snarl and

a lunge, as if he'd forgotten who he was. Then the savagery and confusion slid from his face, and he recognized her again.

"I'm sorry," she said, "but we're going to have to operate as if we're both going to survive this. We need to talk about Brita, before we—"

"Brita is dangerous, but I know she's still looking for the source of the weapon," Drakon said, fully rational again. "She's unlikely to return to Erebus without hard proof or a sample of the drug itself, but if she feels threatened, there's no telling what she might do."

Phoenix detested the fact that she had to keep lying to him. "We're looking for the same thing she is," she said. "And if the mayor can help, we'll have to trust him in this. I think I know what to do about Brita, and you're going to have to believe I can do it." She gripped his shoulders. "I've made a lot of mistakes. But please, believe in me, Drakon. Don't try to protect me. This is my job."

Careful to use only his clean hand, Drakon stroked a long strand of hair out of her face. "I believe in you. When I…" He closed his eyes. "When have I ever protected you, Phoenix? When have I ever protected anyone?"

"People are free and safe because of you," she said, rubbing his chest gently. "You want to protect me because of the ones you lost before. But I'm ready, Drakon. I'm ready."

She stood on her toes and kissed him. He tried to break free, but in a moment instinct took over. And perhaps the knowledge that it was too late to go back. It was a kiss of tenderness, not passion. Of hope, not despair.

And of love. *Her* love, if not his.

A sharp buzz interrupted them, and they separated quickly, Drakon moving to the chair, Phoenix to the other side of the table.

"Visiting time's over," the guard said as he walked

through the door. His expression was blank, and Phoenix had no idea what he was thinking, if he was permitted to think at all. If at any time the monitors had been on, Shepherd would know everything that had passed in this room.

But she believed that Matthew had managed to shut them off, even if Shepherd had been lying to Phoenix about leaving her and Drakon alone. The mayor would have no reason to believe that she wasn't fully prepared to go through with what he had demanded of her.

She strode to the door without looking back.

Phoenix didn't have to look for Brita. The Nightsider was stationed in front of Phoenix's quarters, leaning casually against the wall as if she had been waiting to share coffee and a bit of Agency gossip with a good friend. Phoenix thought of the syringe hidden among the uniforms hung in her small closet, deliberately left there because she couldn't abide the thought of carrying such a lethal and hideous weapon when she'd gone to visit Drakon. As long as Brita didn't suspect, Phoenix could get to it if she had to. If there was no other choice.

But she hoped Brita would give her a choice.

"Why don't we go into your room?" Brita asked as Phoenix approached cautiously. "Don't worry, I won't bite."

Phoenix brushed past her and unlocked the door. "I didn't think you would," she said coldly. "Come in."

Brita shut the door behind her and glanced around the small room. "Maybe now, having helped bring down the bad guys, you'll rate an upgrade."

"I'm not interested in upgrades," Phoenix said. "And if you're still concerned about the matters we've discussed before, you'll shut up and listen."

Arching an eyebrow, Brita turned the desk chair

around and sat, seemingly all polite attention. But her eyes burned with hatred and the promise of death.

"Before you tell me your news," she said, "I want to know what you were discussing with our beloved mayor."

"A finger in every pie?" Phoenix asked, walking casually to her closet and pretending to look through her uniforms. "Or did you know he'd want to see me?"

Brita laughed. "There isn't a single man or woman in this Agency who doesn't know about you and Shepherd. But he didn't want to see you because of your past relationship or out of concern for your health, did he?"

"Since you already seem to know," Phoenix said, finding the tube and slipping it into her jacket pocket, "let's get down to brass tacks, shall we?" She sat on the bed facing Brita. "Shepherd told me that he and Patterson were working together to find a way to stop the Opiri once and for all, and they were convinced that the Council was planning some kind of attack very soon. He said they'd deliberately heightened the appearance of political conflict in the Enclave to goad the Expansionist Party into making a premature move, hoping to encourage conflict within the ruling Council. The rumors of an assassin in the Fringe confirmed that they'd taken the bait."

The look on Brita's face told Phoenix that something she'd said *was* news to the double agent.

The part about egging on the Expansionists? Phoenix thought. Did Brita just now realize that she and her people had fallen into a trap deliberately set by their enemies?

"He told me how Aegis had sent several agents, including you, to dig out the assassin," Phoenix continued. "Most of the operatives failed, and they didn't want you breaking cover, so they sent me in to stir the pot, though Shepherd made it seem as if they wanted me because I was different from every other agent in Aegis."

Brita laughed with a sharp, vicious edge. "You made a little trouble for me, I'll admit."

"Very generous of you," Phoenix said. "He said you held off telling me that you knew who the assassin was, or reporting it to Aegis. He said he was sure you were a double agent, and had been all along. And then he told me you were blackmailing him by threatening to release information proving that he had a hand in Patterson's death."

Leaning back, Brita feigned an indifference she obviously didn't feel. "Did he say why I was doing it?"

"No. And he didn't mention his and Patterson's secret weapon."

"So there are limits to what he'll tell you," she said, "even though he regards you as his puppet."

"I've given him no reason to believe that," Phoenix said.

"But it's clearly what *he* believes. What did he tell you to do?"

"He offered me another one of those *'bargains'* we've all been making lately," Phoenix said. "Freedom for Drakon in return for your death."

"My *death?*" Brita's lips curved up into a smile of genuine amusement. "And how were you to kill me? With your superior strength and wit?"

"No," Phoenix said. "With this." She withdrew the tube from her pocket. Brita nearly leaped from her chair.

"Stand down, Agent," Phoenix said. "I'm not armed. Not unless I take the syringe out of this tube and stick you with it. Shepherd didn't say what this was, or where it came from. He told me it would be painless. You'd have the flu for a while, and then…drift away."

"The pathogen," Brita said. "Give it to me."

Phoenix handed the tube to the Opir, who unscrewed it and peered inside.

"It's empty!" she snarled, throwing the tube to the ground. "Where is it?"

"In a safe place. And I *will* give it to you…eventually, if we reach an agreement." She leaned forward, holding Brita's furious gaze. "I don't want to kill you, Brita, let alone use that abomination against you or any Opir. But Shepherd made it very clear that Drakon would die and I'd be exposed as a traitor if I didn't go through with this. So you and I are going to have to come up with a plan that takes care of Shepherd and his threats, frees Drakon and enables us to find the source of this pathogen."

"You may want Drakon free," Brita said, "but you don't give a damn about the Opir race."

"Even if I didn't care about Drakon, I'd give a damn about genocide. I think most people in the Enclave do, too. But we have to have proof, and we have to make sure this stuff isn't released before we get it."

Brita wasn't stupid. Phoenix could see the thoughts racing behind her eyes, scheming, weighing, reaching a decision all in a matter of a few tense minutes.

"I was blackmailing him because I'm trying to find out where the lab is, and he's strangely reluctant to tell me," Brita said. "Drakon had already been sent to assassinate the mayor before I found out about the pathogen. I thought Patterson was the major player then. I was going to help Drakon kill the mayor and blackmail Patterson afterward. But then I realized the mayor was the brains behind the deal. Drakon was too involved with you to be trusted, and I wanted you both out of the way. So I set Drakon up to kill Shepherd, knowing he wouldn't have access."

"And though you made it look as if Drakon killed Patterson, Shepherd knows he didn't," Phoenix said. "His entire career is on the line." Phoenix held Brita's gaze. "Are you going to work with me on this, or do something stupid? Aaron Shepherd has turned unpredictable. He was always ambitious, but it's more than that now. He's gone too far, and he knows it."

"He'll give me the information," Brita said.

"But not in the way you think, because you're not handling this alone. We work together, or I'll risk everything to expose you for what you are."

She could see that Brita was beginning to accept her conviction and consider the possibility that Phoenix would go through with what she promised. "What can *you* possibly do?" she asked.

"Shepherd thinks he has me over a barrel because of Drakon. We're going to make you vanish, and I'm going to distract Shepherd by telling him you're dead and I've disposed of your body. He probably won't believe me without seeing it, but since he's sure I'll do anything to save Drakon, he'll hear me out.

"When you disappear, you're going to arrange some kind of major distraction that will get most of Shepherd's security team focused on something else. And then you're going to take out the rest of the guards outside Shepherd's suite. Without killing them. You'll hide their *living* bodies, and I'll force Shepherd to say he dismissed all but a few of his security to see to the emergency. If you do a good enough job, no one will notice a few missing security personnel."

"I never knew you had such faith in me," Brita said with a sarcastic laugh.

"You managed to convince everyone you were a loyal Enclave citizen and agent," Phoenix said. "Can you do it? Tell me now if you can't, because we have to come up with something else fast."

"I can do it," Brita said, in a tone of complete confidence. "And what will you be doing, while I'm handling all the work and betraying myself to the entire Agency?"

"Once most of his security are involved elsewhere, I'll

be telling the mayor that you and I are working together, and between us we can destroy him in a heartbeat. He's going to get Drakon out, along with those other Opiri, and show us where they make this pathogen. He'll make sure nothing is to be said about his *'secret'* departure from the city."

"What makes you think you can force Shepherd to agree?"

"Because I don't think even the prospect of destroying all the Opiri on the West Coast is enough to make him give up his position or his life. His confidence is already badly shaken, and he'll be thrown even more off balance by my defiance…since, as you said, he obviously doesn't think too highly of my ability to resist him or his threats."

"And the syringe? I can make you show me where it is."

"And I'll scream bloody murder. That'll cause you some inconvenience, even if no one believes what I say about you. Once we've found the lab, you can have it. Because by then it won't matter. We'll be able to destroy it all." She got up. "We've got to move fast and use the element of surprise, because once Shepherd realizes I didn't go through with killing you, he's likely to do something drastic."

Chapter 23

They removed the blindfold and cuffs when Drakon and his escorts of two dhampires and two human operatives were through the Wall. They'd exited just outside the small, seldom-used side gate in the north Embarcadero Wall. Rotting piers jutted out into black water, and the night was utterly silent.

It had all happened with swift efficiency, and Drakon had been too weak to resist even if he'd seen the point in doing so. There had been some great emergency in Aegis headquarters while he had lain in a half-delirious huddle on the floor in the corner of his cell, the wail of distant alarms and raised voices echoing from all directions.

He'd never found out what it was. The operatives had come, and he'd known when they'd taken him from his cell and escorted him outside that they were either a part of Phoenix's unexplained plan, or he was about to be executed and his body dumped into the frigid waters of the Bay.

He had been prepared for death since the moment of his capture. Since well before that. But he scanned the darkness, searching for the one thing he wanted and feared to see before he learned his fate.

When the black-clad figures appeared from the north, he knew. He whispered a half-forgotten prayer and watched Phoenix walk toward him, her gaze fixed on his. She was followed by the Daysiders and Freebloods who had been Drakon's fellow operatives in the Fringe. They were bound and surrounded by several heavily armed guards, one of them carrying a highly valuable weapon knows as a Vampire Slayer—a weapon that could actually kill an Opir quickly and quite thoroughly without a precise shot to the heart or brain. Aaron Shepherd walked off to the side with his own team of three Enforcers.

What kind of bargain had Phoenix made?

She embraced him, resting her cheek against his chest without any regard for their audience. "It's okay, Drakon," she murmured. "It's all worked out. We're going to the hidden laboratory. We're going to get that pathogen and destroy it."

He pushed her away gently and looked into her eyes. "Why is Shepherd here?" he asked, getting to the heart of the matter. "Where is Brita?"

"I said I'd take care of it," she said. "You and I and Brita are on the same team at the moment. I didn't want to tell you what I planned because I didn't want you worrying."

"You made a truce with Brita?" he said, holding tightly to her arms as he searched the area again.

"It's in her best interest as well as ours. You see, Shepherd wanted me to kill her with the pathogen, and—"

"He *gave* it to you?" Drakon asked in disbelief.

"A syringe full of it. She was blackmailing him for the location of the lab. He didn't know I guessed what it was, because he didn't realize I knew anything about the weapon. But he also told me it wouldn't work on dhampires. I couldn't tell you that, either. I'm sorry." She searched his eyes with obvious anxiety. "Are you all right? No more symptoms?"

Drakon smiled and touched her hair. "None."

She obviously didn't see the lie in his eyes. He was growing progressively weaker. Something was wrong with his gut, but it was far worse than influenza. The operatives and guards who'd come for him hadn't seemed to notice the dark, almost grainy stuff he'd expelled onto the cell floor several times since Phoenix had left him.

Or they simply hadn't cared.

But that didn't matter now. Drakon measured his remaining strength against the number of Enclave personnel and his former colleagues, wondering how many he could take down if he had to. He wanted to trust Phoenix. He believed in her courage, her conviction, her loyalty, her compassion. But she'd never been made for treachery, no matter how often she'd expressed guilt for deceiving him.

The Enforcers led Shepherd to Drakon and Phoenix and backed away, one of them nodding to Drakon. He couldn't see the man's face through the infrared visor, but he recognized the shape and movements of the body and its scent.

Matthew Patterson. He wasn't there to protect Shepherd. He and his two companions were escorting a prisoner. Shepherd stared at Drakon, flexing his hands in the prisoner's cuffs as if he were prepared to attack his enemy like a wild beast.

"Do you think you've won, you and your bitch?" the mayor said quietly. "Do you think it's so easy?"

"If you weren't bound," Drakon said, "I'd kill you for speaking of her like that."

"You'd kill me, anyway," Shepherd said with a wry

smile. "I'm supposed to take you to the lab, and that's it for me."

"I promised to let you go," Phoenix said. "Just as soon as the lab is—"

"You'll leave us helpless!" he shouted. "You half-breed slut…"

Drakon grabbed the mayor by his throat and bared his teeth.

"I'm hungry," he said. "Very hungry. And while I wouldn't kill you if I fed from you, I don't think you'd find it a pleasant experience."

Paling, Shepherd backed out of Drakon's reach, stumbled and was hauled upright by Matthew, who kept a firm grip on him.

"Who are the other guards?" Drakon asked as soon as they were alone again.

"More of Matthew's friends, fellow Enforcers who share his views. No one questioned us when we left with the mayor. He was very…persuasive."

"Where is Brita?" Drakon repeated more urgently.

"She's coming," Phoenix said, though a crease appeared between her brows. "We've got to get moving, and let her catch up."

Drakon knew he didn't have to tell her that Brita might already be working against them in some way, even if they did supposedly share a common goal. He also didn't have to tell her that he was ready to give his life to stop his *"sister"* from carrying out whatever scheme she was undoubtedly planning.

"What about my fellow agents?" he asked.

She glanced behind her, where the captive Opiri were looking around them with wary disbelief. "We're going to leave them somewhere, tied up, until we've taken care of the rest. Then we'll let them go."

"They're still your enemies."

"And I'm not a murderer, even for Aegis," she said.

"No," he said softly. "Where are we going?"

"Across the Bay, to the Marin Peninsula," she said. "There's a patrol boat waiting a quarter mile southwest of here, docked at one of the old piers. We'll disembark at the old Larkspur Ferry Terminal." She looked him over again as if he were an ancient, fragile sculpture on the verge of disintegration. "You should take my blood now, before we go."

"I can hold off until we get across the Bay," he said.

"If you're lying to me, I'll kill you."

He mustered up a smile and cupped her face in his hands. "And I'll let you," he said.

With one final, dubious glance at his face, Phoenix signaled the others. She turned west along the waterfront, running at a half-crouch, the others right behind her.

The boat was waiting as promised, large enough to hold a few more than the fourteen of them. Brita still hadn't shown up when they'd all boarded.

"We can't wait," Phoenix said, swearing under her breath.

"We can't trust her," Drakon said, staring across the pier. "You go on, and I'll look for her."

"No," Phoenix said. "Only Aaron knows where to find this lab. Even if Brita has betrayed us in some way, that won't matter if we accomplish this one thing. It's worth our lives, isn't it?"

"Without a doubt." They exchanged a lingering look, and then Phoenix moved away to speak softly with one of Matthew's colleagues.

A moment later the patrol boat's almost silent engine kicked in, and they began gliding north across the dark, choppy water.

There were always other patrol boats on the Bay, day and night, but Phoenix, Drakon and their party were extraordinarily lucky. Drakon assumed it was Shepherd who had arranged their safe passage. Unwillingly, of course.

Drakon leaned against the port side of the boat near the stern, dividing his attention between the receding city, the Bay around them and Phoenix, who was still talking with Matthew and one of his companions. He didn't try to listen in. He focused instead on being prepared to move at an instant's notice, first to protect Phoenix and then to take down whoever might threaten her.

And he remained alert to any sight or sound of a smaller boat slipping across the water. Phoenix was obviously on her guard as well, in spite of her firm air of confidence. The confidence of one who knew herself to be in the right.

As she was. Everything about her, Drakon thought, was right. And so much about *him* was…

"We're coming in," a male voice announced. The boat glided up to the dock, and two of the guards hopped out to secure it. Drakon moved close to Shepherd when he was briefly alone and bent to whisper in the mayor's ear.

"I was prepared to kill you once," he said. "And I'll do it without hesitation if any harm comes to Phoenix."

"Even though you're a dying man…I mean, bloodsucker?" Shepherd whispered with a faint smile.

Confirmed, Drakon thought. He returned the smile. "Your life may mean more to you than your people do," he said, "but I don't overestimate the value of mine."

"The way you didn't overestimate the value of the lives you ruined when you arrested innocent people and sent them to Erebus?" Shepherd clucked reprovingly. "Oh, I know about your past, Lieutenant Charles Cruise. There's enough of your human DNA left to identify you."

The mayor's words struck true. *I'm no better than he is,* Drakon thought. *I never have been.*

"If Phoenix has promised you your life," he said, "I'll

hold to her agreement. But because I was such an amoral bastard even before I was converted, I would take great personal pleasure in tearing your throat out."

"But you will keep to her agreement, won't you?" Shepherd said. "Because you love her."

"Once you're converted, you lose that particular weakness," Drakon said.

"Are you trying to convince me or yourself?" Shepherd chuckled. "Don't mistake sex for love. I kept her as long as I did because she was so good in bed. But she was always tainted. In every way."

Drakon ground his teeth and stood to the side as the guards escorted the mayor off the boat. Phoenix joined him, and they disembarked together.

"No Brita," she said.

He was still trembling with rage and weakness, but he quickly brought both body and mind under control. "You should wait here with a few Enforcers," he said. "Let me go ahead."

"I've got plenty of protection," she said, gesturing to the woman with the Vampire Slayer. "If something goes wrong…"

"I have the keenest senses," he said. "I'll take the rear. It's just as likely that if we're going to be attacked, they'll come from behind us."

"Whoever *they* might be," she said. "Please don't take any stupid risks."

"I'll take no risks with your life."

She stared at him a moment longer, squeezed his hand and moved ahead to join the others. They fell into a wedge formation with Phoenix, the woman with the VS—Sergeant Trembley—and Matthew in the lead. Drakon followed—listening, smelling, watching.

The Enforcers had been trained to move quietly, if not as silently as a dhampir agent, and they'd obviously *encouraged* Shepherd to take equal care. Hardly a leaf rustled as they made their way through the underbrush near the landing and found a path parallel to one of the crumbling roads leading into the north Peninsular Zone.

Though Drakon had been given heavy clothing, Phoenix had told him that the location of the laboratory complex wasn't more than a three-hour walk from the landing. Once again they met no opposition, no sign of any hostile presence.

After an hour, they reached the edge of one of the many towns that made up the vast sprawl of interconnected urban and suburban communities stretching south from the former Santa Rosa. As in most of the Zone, the streets were filled with the scraps and skeletons of rusted appliances, stone fallen from the abandoned buildings and near-jungles of trees that had burst up through the cracked concrete.

Approximately a mile from their goal, they left the bound Opir spies covered with fallen branches and hidden in a wildly overgrown park. Drakon heard one of them curse him as he and the others moved on.

After making their way through a literal maze of streets, they reached a block of industrial structures and wide parking lots. There was a distinct smell in the air, one Drakon recognized as the complex chemical combination of scents typical of a medical facility. A compound of several interconnected buildings was surrounded by a high wire fence topped with barbed coils, almost certainly electrified.

Shepherd indicated that they'd reached their destination, and everyone found concealment among the nearest buildings, Drakon with Phoenix and Shepherd, the others scattered to various strategic positions.

But there wasn't so much as a single guard patrolling the fence, nor anywhere visible in or around the compound. The gate was open.

"This can't be right," Drakon said to Phoenix.

"We expected to meet guards," Phoenix said, her body coiled with tension. "Shepherd was to get us through."

"Then he's betrayed you."

"I didn't do this," Shepherd said as Drakon turned on him. "For God's sake, I didn't warn anyone!"

Grabbing the mayor by his soiled collar, Drakon dragged him to his feet. "You go ahead," he said, "and we'll find out."

"Drakon!" Phoenix said. "Wait!"

But he was already force-marching Shepherd ahead of them, and by the time they reached the gate it was evident that there would be no immediate response.

Phoenix caught up to him, followed by Matthew and his companions, all combat-ready and on edge. They walked through the gate. Still no one met them, and there was neither sound nor movement anywhere around the partially camouflaged laboratory buildings. The rank, chemical odor was almost overpowering.

"Go back," Drakon said to Phoenix, who walked at Shepherd's other side. "All of you, go. This is a trap."

"If it is, I'm responsible," Phoenix said. She turned to Matthew. "I want you to keep watch outside."

"You're kidding, right?" Matthew said from under his visor. "I've already instructed six of my men to keep watch outside the gate, but the rest of us are coming. And we're not leaving until this is finished."

Phoenix flashed a glance at Drakon. He nodded, and the eight of them—he, Shepherd, Phoenix and Matthew with the four remaining Enforcers—moved on. The main door of the largest building was half-open, like the gate. Drakon came to a sudden halt, and Shepherd cursed as his collar nearly strangled him.

A woman walked out the door. Brita, dusty and alone, her expression weary and lined with defeat.

"It's all gone," she said. "Every last vial."

* * *

"What are you doing here?" Phoenix asked, moving in front of Drakon and Aaron. Drakon grabbed her to pull her away, but she stepped out of his reach, painfully aware that he was so much slower and weaker than he should have been.

But he refused to stay back. He moved to stand beside her. The Enforcers' weapons locked on Brita.

"Brita," Drakon growled. "What is this?"

"I apologize," Brita said, running her hand through her cropped hair. "I was expecting more treachery from Shepherd, so after we separated I came alone to make sure there wasn't some kind of trap set up." She looked at the mayor with contempt. "He's not always as stupid as he looks."

Shepherd didn't so much as sputter. He was so pale that he almost glowed like a beacon in the early-morning darkness.

He didn't know, Phoenix thought. *This wasn't what he expected.*

"They've evacuated," Brita went on. "It was done very quickly, but they took everything important. They can't have gone too far." She clenched a fist. "Give Shepherd to me. He'll tell *me* where they've gone."

"No," Drakon said, before Phoenix could speak. "He'll stay with us."

"Don't trust me, brother?" Brita said with an ugly smile.

"If I were anything like you," Phoenix said, "you'd be choking on the virus." She pulled the tube, complete with syringe, out of her inner pocket. "But I'm not, and neither is Drakon. So you can move ahead of us, and we'll find out where they've gone."

"Not until we check inside," Drakon said. "She could

be lying. She could have found a way to get rid of the guards."

"Me? Alone?" Brita said. "I'm flattered, Drakon, but I'm hardly that powerful."

Phoenix met Drakon's eyes. They both knew nothing was as it seemed.

"We're going inside," Phoenix said, sealing the tube inside her pocket again. Without further communication amongst them, Drakon moved ahead with Shepherd while Matthew and his comrades spread out, approaching the building from both sides as well as the front. Tremblay kept the Vampire Slayer trained on Brita.

The interior was what anyone would have expected of a medical clinic: sterile walls painted a neutral shade, a very small waiting room with simple chairs, long corridors opening onto offices and, deeper inside the apparently empty building, examination rooms, storage areas and laboratories.

All were empty, though they showed signs of very recent evacuation. A short walkway led to another smaller building.

Phoenix knew at once that this was the primary research area. The chemical stench was stronger than ever, mingled with the odor of many human bodies.

And bodies that weren't human. Bodies that lay in rows of cots, covered with sheets, surrounded by gleaming metal tables and machinery and monitors.

Pushing Shepherd into the arms of one of the Enforcers, Drakon pulled back the sheet of the body nearest the door. The woman had the pale skin and white, flowing hair of a full Opir. She was emaciated, and there was a dark crust around her mouth.

Drakon replaced the sheet and turned to stare at Shepherd, his breathing harsh and his eyes wild.

"Where are they?" Phoenix shouted, snatching Shepherd and shaking him until his head snapped back and forth like a puppet's. "Where are the people who did this?"

But the mayor's eyes had glazed over, as if the situation had finally become too much for him. Phoenix looked at Drakon, allowing her attention to wane for a few seconds, and Shepherd burst into sudden motion.

Abruptly Brita slipped away from her own guard and grabbed Shepherd, holding him as a shield in front of her. She tore at his pants. His belt snapped, and Brita reached around to the front and ripped open his fly.

"You didn't search him very well, did you?" she asked, lifting her hand. She was holding a syringe tube exactly like Phoenix's, and the mayor was making a vain, pathetic grab at his crotch.

Phoenix cursed her carelessness. She hadn't been the one to search Shepherd, but she should have taken care of it herself. The damage was done. Whatever Shepherd— and Brita—intended that damage to be. Tremblay took careful aim at Brita, but Drakon waved her down.

"How did you know he had the drug, Brita?" he asked as the Opir woman dropped Shepherd and kicked him aside.

"We had an arrangement, he and I," she said. "A deal within a deal, you might say. I convinced him that you were going to kill him no matter what Phoenix promised him. If he got me another sample of the pathogen, I'd make sure he got away once we were across the Bay. But, as you see, he was holding out on me."

"He made the wrong decision," Phoenix said, wondering how many times she could make the same mistakes and not destroy everything she cared about. "You weren't really surprised to find the place evacuated, were you?"

"I have no idea what happened."

Phoenix knew she was lying. "You aren't going anywhere with that, you know," she said. "Not until we have the truth from you."

"I need to find the antidote," Brita said, her voice almost pleading. "I know there's one being tested. Probably on *them*," she said, jerking her head toward the bodies. "Do you know how they planned to introduce this virus into our population? Through infected serfs. The pathogen doesn't affect humans, only those who take their blood." She looked at Drakon. "It detroys an Opir's ability to derive any nourishment from blood, until the body starts to devour itself. I think even the most peace-loving members of the Council will regard this as an open and vicious act of war."

"Like sending an assassin to kill our leader?" Phoenix asked.

"You mean *that* one?" Brita said, nudging Shepherd with her boot. "One leader down, the other ruined. Who will save you now?"

Chapter 24

"**W**ho will save *you?*" Phoenix asked, gesturing behind her at the Enforcer with the Vampire Slayer. "Right now, we still want the same thing, and Shepherd's our only way to get it." She helped the mayor to his feet. All his casual elegance was gone, leaving a shell of the man he'd been when she'd loved him.

The man he'd never been at all.

"You still have a chance," Phoenix told him. "If you don't take us where we have to go, there will be war. I imagine you'll die in a pretty terrible way when Opiri get hold of you. And they will."

Shepherd's throat bobbed. "Phoenix. If we ever meant anything to each other…"

"Drakon may want to kill you," she said, "and Brita, and every Opir on the West Coast. But I'd be fighting them for the privilege."

"I told you, I didn't warn them," he whispered. "I didn't

betray you. If they're not here, she—" he pointed at Brita "—knows where they are."

"He's right," Drakon said. "I can smell his fear. He'd tell us if he knew."

Brita gripped the tube tightly in her left hand and stared at Drakon. "That's too bad," she said. "I'd very much enjoy seeing you pay for his betrayal of our people and for causing the torture and death of my father, but I'd prefer to spare you the kind of death you're facing now."

Drakon rested his hand on Phoenix's shoulder and squeezed. His fingers spasmed, and she flinched.

"Haven't you noticed, Phoenix?" Brita asked. "Drakon's been exposed to the pathogen. They were testing a new strain on him while he was being interrogated."

"We know that," Phoenix said as calmly as she could. "You already know where to find the pathogen and antidote, don't you?" She moved toward Brita. "Why would you hide it from us? Is that syringe holding the antidote, not the pathogen?"

"Yes," Shepherd said. "She—"

"Shut him up," Phoenix snapped.

Drakon grabbed the mayor and wrenched his arm behind his back, though his face went a little gray as he did it. Phoenix swallowed a cry of protest.

"Again," she said to Brita, "why keep the location from us? What could you possibly have to gain?"

Brita refused to answer. Phoenix signaled to one of the Enforcers.

"Shoot her," she said. "Not to kill, of course. Just remind her that even Opiri can feel pain."

"I'll drop this," Brita said, lifting the tube, "and then there'll be no hope for your lover."

"If she's willing to drop it, she has access to another supply," Drakon said. "We'll find it sooner or later, Brita."

"And when I do," Phoenix said, "I'll destroy the antidote, every last drop of it. What will Erebus do then?"

"You wouldn't do that," Brita said softly. "You wouldn't allow an entire species to be slaughtered."

"If you take Drakon from me, I will."

"No," Drakon said, his breath coming short. "We must destroy the pathogen. That's something you can't do alone, Brita. And once we take that syringe from you, you'll have nothing. If the pathogen is being produced anywhere else…"

"I'll give Drakon the antidote if you get out," Brita said. "All of you."

"Don't listen to her," Drakon said. "None of this makes sense."

Phoenix was desperately tempted. But when she looked at Drakon, looked into his eyes, she could see it would never work. He would never forgive her.

And they couldn't leave Brita alone here. If others were inside somewhere…

"Shoot the vial, Matthew," Phoenix said.

"I'll show you where they are," Brita said, her shoulders dropping in defeat.

Matthew grabbed the tube and secured it in one of his uniform pockets. Glancing contemptuously at the Enforcers who surrounded her, Brita pointed toward the end of the corridor, which ended in a bank of elevators. "They're all underground, in the bunker," she said. "The pathogen, the antidote and the staff."

"How did they get there?" Phoenix demanded.

"I made them think an army of Opiri was on its way," Brita said.

"To trap them," Drakon said. "Why? How would that serve your purpose?"

"I blocked all the exits to this building," Brita said with a hard smile. "Easier to get to them when they aren't scattered all over the compound and might escape. I didn't know they'd go underground."

"Can you get in?" Phoenix asked.

"There's a key to getting down there," Brita said, "and I persuaded one of the guards to share it with me before I—" She broke off, but Phoenix understood perfectly. "I'm the only one who knows it now."

"Phoenix," Drakon said with an ominous shiver, "I believe she *has* summoned Opiri. She's stalling for time. We must go down now if we want to save the lives of the people here and get what we came to find." He glanced at Matthew. "You'll need to come with us, as will the mayor. You'll have to play hostage again."

"I figured," Matthew said with a crooked smile.

"We'll also require weapons. One of your men should stay with us. The rest of your comrades can stand guard outside."

Matthew looked at Phoenix, who nodded. "If Opiri are coming," she said, "we have to have warning."

The young Enforcer instructed the others, who reluctantly returned the way they had come. A short and stocky young woman called Yeshevsky remained behind, clearly ready to fight.

"I hope they don't have too many guards down there," Matthew said.

"Less than there were," Brita said.

Phoenix clenched her teeth and took one of the submachine guns the Enforcers had left behind. Matthew readied his own weapon, and Drakon took another with his free hand while he held on to Shepherd with the other.

"We can't kill you with these," Phoenix said to Brita, "but we can incapacitate you. Keep that in mind." She nodded to Yeshevsky, who pointed her weapon at Brita. "Go." When they reached the elevator, Phoenix tapped Brita in the back with the butt of her rifle. Brita's fingers danced over the keypad that locked the elevator, and the doors slid open.

"Drakon," Phoenix whispered. "This may be…"

He smiled warmly, though he was unable to touch her. "I know," he said. "Let me go first, with the mayor. That may be enough to persuade them to cooperate. If we don't return in twenty minutes, come down with Matthew and Brita."

"Out of the question," she said, hovering on the verge of panic.

"You asked me to believe in you before," he said. "I did. I still do. Now you have to believe in me."

"Then there's something you have to do for me first," she said, barely keeping her trembling in check.

"Whatever is within my power."

"Take my blood." She shook her head at his expression of alarm. "You know you can't infect me. You have to do it, Drakon, or you might not make it another ten feet."

"It may do no good," he said. "The virus prevents—"

"I know. But we have to try it."

Closing his eyes, Drakon nodded and set his weapon down. While Shepherd slumped to the ground, his collar still gripped in Drakon's fist, Phoenix offered her neck. Quickly and efficiently and without any trace of emotion, Drakon brought her close and bit her. He finished in a minute and pulled back.

Resting her forehead against his chest, Phoenix swallowed thickly. *No tears,* she thought. *Not now. We're fellow soldiers. We always knew the risks.*

"You're coming back," she said, smiling up at him.

"I'll come back," he said.

He pulled her against him with one arm and kissed her, hard and fast. And then he and the mayor, staggering with exhaustion, were inside the elevator. Drakon released Shepherd just long enough to punch the door button.

No one expected Shepherd to move as fast as he did. He darted out of the elevator, caught Brita in the face with his left elbow and snatched the tube from her hand with the other. He ran, and Brita bolted after him. Phoenix caught up and grabbed her.

Brita whirled about and struck hard at Phoenix's face. Phoenix ducked, and Shepherd's head appeared behind Brita's shoulder. A bare needle plunged into the Opir woman's neck.

The color bled from Brita's face. She slapped at the back of her neck, spun around and sent Shepherd flying. He hit the wall, slid down and lay still.

Drakon came running, rifle in hand. He glanced at Brita's face and smiled grimly.

"It seems we both have a personal stake in this now," he said. "That syringe didn't hold the antidote after all."

"Give me a gun," Brita said, holding out a shaking hand.

"Stay where you are," Drakon said as Yeshevsky pointed her rifle at Brita's head. Phoenix ran to Shepherd and knelt beside him. She had expected to find him dead of a broken neck or spine, but he was still breathing. She knew that moving him now might kill him, but she had no other choice.

"I am at fault," Drakon said grimly. "Obviously, I can't trust my own judgment." He coughed, turning his head aside.

"Then we'll have to go together," Phoenix said, carefully lifting the mayor over her shoulder. "Don't even try to argue with me."

This time, he didn't.

Chapter 25

The underground room was as white and sterile as nearly every other part of the building, outfitted with dozens of what seemed to be cold storage units, glass-doored shelves, shining steel tables and other equipment Phoenix didn't recognize. Nearly three dozen people—scientists, technicians, administrators and support staff—were crowded inside, filling the entire rear half of the room and almost hiding the rear exit, presumably blocked by Brita like all the others. Five technicians in full protective suits stood near the largest storage unit, where a half-dozen armed soldiers and their captain had formed a protective cordon around them.

Phoenix entered the room first. "Everyone remain calm," she said, easing the mayor to the ground at her feet. "Don't get in our way and we won't hurt you."

The captain of the guard raised his rifle. "You won't hurt anyone," he said.

She nudged at Shepherd with the muzzle of her gun. "Do you know who this man is?" she asked.

The captain looked down and signaled for his men to lower their weapons.

"Who are you?" stammered a man in a white coat, whose name tag read Dr. William Svengaard, Director.

"Someone you don't want to mess with," Phoenix said. Drakon moved up behind her, gripping Matthew by the shoulder while Sato nudged Brita into the room.

"This man is the son of Senator Patterson," Drakon said, pushing Matthew forward. "If anyone here opens fire, both he and the mayor will suffer."

"But you are… Surely you are with the Enclave?" Svengaard asked. He pointed at Brita. "This woman forced us to—"

"I know." Phoenix glanced back at Drakon, who looked increasingly ill. "She's not in control anymore."

The director shuddered. "What do you want? What is your purpose here?"

"Not everyone in the Enclave agrees with what you're doing here," Phoenix said. "There are a lot of people who would like to shut this place down. We're here to get the antidote and destroy the pathogen."

"By whose authority?" the captain of the guards demanded.

Phoenix ignored him. Svengaard's face wrinkled up as if he had smelled something noxious. "It isn't so easy," he said. "The antidote is experimental. We haven't—"

"Why the suits?" Phoenix asked sharply.

"The virus is inert in the human body," Svengaard said, almost as if he were proud of his work. "The suits are merely standard protocol for anyone who handles the—"

"Murder weapon?" Phoenix said.

"No," Svengaard protested. "No, you don't understand."

"We understand," Drakon said. He forced Matthew to his knees. "Give us the antidote, or everyone dies."

He sounded, Phoenix thought, extremely convincing, though the men and women in the bunker wouldn't recognize him as an Opir or know that he was slowly dying. The director scurried away to consult with the suited technicians.

Brita moved to follow him, and Phoenix nodded permission to the Enforcer who guarded her. Brita wouldn't do anything stupid now. She needed that antidote, experimental or otherwise.

And Drakon needed it far more urgently. He could barely stay on his feet, his breathing had become labored and his grip on Matthew's shoulder was so weak that it would soon be obvious to everyone that the young Enforcer would have no real difficulty in escaping.

And yet Drakon smiled at Phoenix, even knowing whatever they gave him could fail. All the hours they had spent together—good and bad, as friends and enemies, as haters and lovers—flashed through her mind.

It wasn't enough. It would never be enough.

They held each other's eyes until Brita hissed and pulled their attention back to the technician's work. They had pulled a small, heavy box, wreathed in condensation, from within the unit and set it down on one of the polished steel tables.

"There are…seven strains," Svengaard said, "three for the pathogen and four for the antidote. I insisted we create such an antidote because—"

"I'm not interested in your reasons," Phoenix said. "Get on with it."

"Only two of the antidotes have been tested," Svengaard said, wringing his hands, "and both failed. We have not tested the last two. Their efficacy is unknown."

"But you've been testing them on those Opiri in the sickrooms," Phoenix said.

Svengaard didn't answer. The technicians had put another case on the table beside the first.

"The pathogen," Svengaard said, his voice very faint. "Both these cases have been designed to keep the contents intact for up to twelve hours. They will degrade after that."

"Prepare syringes for the two untested antidotes," Brita said.

The technicians exchanged glances. "Why?" Svengaard asked. Then he looked at Brita more closely.

"You're infected," he said. "You have to be Opir." He glanced at Drakon. "And so are you."

"Get them ready," Brita snapped.

"Why are you aiding Opiri?" the captain said, beginning to raise his weapon again.

Yeshevsky pointed her rifle at the captain, and Phoenix aimed her own gun at Shepherd's head. "Lay down your weapons."

At a curt nod from the captain, the other guards did as Phoenix commanded. Svengaard jerked his head at the technicians, instructing them to proceed. Phoenix turned back to Drakon. There was nothing to say, but she couldn't bear the silence.

"Whatever happens," she said, "I'll be at your side. You won't go alone."

Alarm and anger erased the exhaustion on his face. "If you mean to...take your own life—"

"I mean I won't leave you until this is over," she said, "one way or another."

Abruptly, Drakon fell to his knees, losing his grip on Matthew. Matthew remained where he was, pretending to be dazed and unable to move.

"The antidote!" Phoenix shouted, striding toward Brita and Svengaard.

"Which one do you want?" Svengaard asked, touching the tray bearing the two syringes.

"Both," Brita said.

"If you take both, the interaction will almost certainly kill you!" Svengaard said.

"Brita—" Phoenix began.

But the Opir was already stabbing the first needle into her arm. Before Phoenix could intervene, she'd used and discarded the second.

"Fill two more," Phoenix said, snatching up the other weapon and pointing it at Svengaard. "Fast."

The director and technicians worked quickly to prepare two more syringes. Aware that the compound's soldiers were still waiting for their chance and that Matthew would appear to be unguarded, Phoenix shouted to the young Enforcer and tossed her rifle to him. He caught it deftly and stood over Shepherd, ready to shoot. When the technicians were finished, they gingerly handed a second tray of syringes to Phoenix.

She knelt beside Drakon, whose heart had slowed to the point that she could count ten seconds between beats.

"Which one?" Matthew asked.

Phoenix looked up at him, her hands trembling so badly that she was afraid she might drop the syringes. "I don't know," she said. She glanced back at Brita, who seemed to be listing to one side. Svengaard had warned her not to take both antidotes. He'd be more apt to want Brita dead than save her, so he'd have no reason to lie.

If she were to give Drakon both untested cures…

"It doesn't matter," Drakon whispered. He smiled at Phoenix and felt for her hand. "I can't see. You choose."

Praying as she never had in her life, Phoenix chose one of the syringes. She pressed the needle against Drakon's skin. The flesh felt stiff and hard, and she had to use some force to get the needle to penetrate it. When she was done, she bowed her head and rested her hand on Drakon's forehead. He closed his eyes.

And stopped breathing.

No, Phoenix thought. *No, no, no...*

But she had no time to grieve. Brita was writhing on the floor, gasping for air, reaching inside her jacket for something Phoenix couldn't see. As her last convulsion ended, she wheezed out a laugh.

"There are no Opiri waiting for you out there," she said, turning her head toward Svengaard. "It was all... me, and *them*." With a spasming hand, Brita rolled something across the room toward Phoenix. Instinct alone made Phoenix pick it up.

She glanced down at the thing in her hand. After a long moment she recognized it for what it was.

A bomb. Set to go off in ten minutes.

"Enjoy your revenge," Brita rasped. And died.

There was a span of shocked silence, and then the soldiers dove for their weapons. Yeshevsky fired a warning shot, blasting a hole in the floor beside the captain. Matthew pressed the muzzle of his gun to Shepherd's head.

"I don't know why you're doing this, Lieutenant Patterson," the captain said, "but you're no traitor. Whatever they have on you won't help them now. These Opiri are dying, and this one—" he jerked his head toward Phoenix "—is obviously working for *them*."

Phoenix got to her feet. "Matthew," she said, "get these people out." She opened her hand to reveal the tiny bomb. "I'm going to destroy this place," she said, "and I'd hate to see any of you die here, in spite of the evil you've done. You've got exactly nine minutes to leave and clear the area."

"Lieutenant Patterson," the captain said. "We can still work this out, disable the device. None of this has to happen."

"I'm afraid it does," Phoenix said, deadly calm in the face of her grief. "I've never had to kill in the course of my work. But I'll gladly die now. Whatever any of us may feel about our enemies, they don't deserve to be wiped out by a deadly virus. That's genocide, and only the evil commit it."

"She's right," Matthew said. "I read the reports my father and Shepherd didn't want anyone else to see. They developed the pathogen a year and a half ago and put it into fast-track production." He looked down at Drakon, anger and sorrow in his eyes. "Did you know what they've been doing here, Captain? Stockpiling the pathogen so they can infect convicts being sent to Erebus without their knowledge."

"Do you hear him, Captain?" Phoenix asked. "Did you know what was going on?"

The man stared at her, sweat gathering along his hairline. "I follow orders," he said.

"But you knew, didn't you? You, and all the others who worked here. And you all went along with it."

No one answered, though a handful of the staff had the grace to look ashamed.

"Maybe everyone in this room should die for crimes against humanity," Phoenix said, wanting so badly to return to Drakon, to lie down beside him and hold him one last time.

"Humanity!" one of the techs shouted. "It's our enemies we—"

"Crimes against what we value in our species," Phoenix said. "The things we think make us better than the Nightsiders, even though we lump all of them together as if every one of them is a monster. As if *we* aren't as fully capable of those same heinous acts." Her gaze swept the room. "When we destroy this, we'll be saving ourselves."

"Listen to her!" Matthew shouted. "My own father did this! My father and Aaron Shepherd, pretending to be enemies." He nudged the still-dazed mayor with the toe of his boot. "My father's already paid for his sins. And once word of this gets out, the mayor will lose everything."

Phoenix met the captain's gaze. "You can try to shoot us, and let this continue. Or maybe you can redeem yourselves by working toward peace instead of murder."

For a moment it seemed as if the captain understood. But then, moving with almost inhuman speed, he snatched up his rifle and prepared to shoot Phoenix, clearly indifferent to his own fate. Neither Matthew nor Yeshevsky had time to react. Something moved at Phoenix's feet, sprang up and shot past her like a stone from a slingshot, slamming into the captain. Bones snapped, and three other soldiers, who had managed to grab their own weapons, went down before any of them got off a shot.

Phoenix's brain caught up with her senses. Drakon was *alive,* and moving like a demon out of legend. Phoenix pocketed the bomb and dove for a dropped rifle, while Matthew took careful aim and shot two more soldiers in rapid succession, bringing them down without killing them.

When he, Phoenix and Drakon were finished, every soldier in the room was disabled, and those civilians who'd considered joining in were cowering on the ground. Drakon stood over the captain, teeth bared, breathing fast from sudden exertion but very far from death. He looked at Phoenix and grinned.

That was all she needed, that smile. The fact that they were both alive in this moment, no matter how long it lasted.

"Matthew," she said, "get everyone out."

"Give me the bomb," Drakon said.

"Forget it," Phoenix said. "You've just recovered."

But he was too fast, and in seconds he had the bomb out of her pocket and in his hand. He sprinted for the elevator.

"Drakon!" Phoenix cried. "We have to destroy this place! If you take the bomb—"

He spun around, panting. His eyes lost their wildness.

"Everyone out!" he commanded. He shoved the bomb in his own pocket, ran to the mayor and lifted him over his shoulder. "Anyone who has the strength, take the wounded. You have less than five minutes."

Without hesitation, Phoenix grabbed one of the wounded soldiers, who wasn't stupid enough to struggle. Matthew and Yeshevsky carried two more while other staff members crowded into the elevator.

It took nearly the entire five minutes for everyone to get out of the building. As Phoenix passed the last of the wounded on to one of the stronger staff members, she turned to find Drakon speaking urgently to Matthew. The young man nodded, signaled to Yeshevsky and jogged after the fleeing employees.

Phoenix started for Drakon, but he was already running back into the building. She ran as hard and fast as she ever had, catching him just as he stepped into the elevator.

"No!" she said, grabbing him. "Not alone!"

"I won't have you die," he said, reaching for the door button.

"And I said I wouldn't leave you."

She squeezed her way into the elevator just as the door closed. The bomb in Drakon's pocket began to beep a warning.

And then Phoenix was alone with the man she loved.

He took her in his arms and kissed her, burying his hands in her hair.

"Phoenix," he said when they finally separated. "You had so much to live for, so much you could have done to rebuild your Enclave."

"It isn't my Enclave now," she said, pressing her fingers over his lips. "And I said I'd never leave you." She smiled. "There's nothing you could have done to keep me away, Drakon." She laid her cheek against his chest, hearing his heart beat strongly beneath his ribs.

"What was it like to die?" she asked.

"After all the things I've done," he said, stroking her hair, "even though I didn't want to leave you, I was ready. But something called me back. It didn't feel like anything foreign in my body. It felt…like a part of me." He kissed her forehead. "Maybe it was."

Phoenix closed her eyes and felt for the bomb in his pocket. The elevator reached the bunker, and together they walked in.

Brita was sprawled on the floor, her body still. Phoenix swallowed and placed the small device on the table next to the container holding the vials of pathogen. Drakon stood beside her, his arm locked tightly around her waist.

"Maybe you can still get away," she said suddenly, breaking free. "I've failed at so many things, but you can go back to Erebus and tell them what we've done. Make them understand. You may be—"

"There's a stairwell…in the back—" Brita gasped, her eyes half opening. "Save her, brother."

Then her head rolled to the side, and suddenly Drakon was lifting Phoenix off her feet and carrying her toward the rear of the bunker. The door was unlocked, as if someone had already planned to escape by the stairs. Drakon raced up them three at a time and didn't slow until they were outside the building. There was no sign of the others, but he kept running until he turned a corner of the nearest building outside the fence and the shock wave of the explosion nearly knocked him off his feet. He stumbled, pushed Phoenix to the ground and curled his body around her until the noise subsided.

Phoenix squirmed out from under him and staggered to the front of the building. The laboratory complex had collapsed, and rubble filled the depression where the bunker had been.

Dropping her face into her hands, Phoenix shuddered. Warmth closed in around her, strong arms, firm lips against her cheek.

"It's over," she whispered, barely able to speak the words.

"This part is," he said into her hair. "The rest…"

She turned in his arms and pressed her face into his shoulder. "I know. So much left to do. So much anger, and hatred and prejudice."

"And yet here we are," he said. "Alive. Opir and half-dhampir."

A helpless laugh burbled out of her throat. "I've never been so confused in my life."

"Neither have I." He kissed her gently on both eyelids. "But we'll work it out."

She met his gaze. "If we hadn't made it…"

"We would still have been together. But we both have responsibilities we can't ignore."

Phoenix tried very hard not to hear what she couldn't accept. "What if they have more of the pathogen hidden away somewhere?" she asked. "The antidote is gone."

"I believe it was your blood, not the supposed antidote, that saved me."

"I don't understand," she said, gazing into his eyes. "You think that something in my blood—"

"What if a cure could be in part derived from some property in your DNA? What if something in you holds the key to combating any future strain of this pathogen?"

She laughed wryly. "At least I'd have a real way to help, considering how badly I've handled everything else."

"Is that really what you still believe?" Drakon asked, nuzzling her cheek.

Phoenix was quiet for a moment, thinking back over the past two weeks. She'd made a mess of so many things, and yet she'd at least in part convinced Drakon not to hurt Matthew, stopped an attempted assassination, helped bring down a would-be mass murderer and destroy a deadly, genocidal weapon....

"You were willing to die for the sake of an enemy," Drakon said. "You gave me a new life. You helped me find something greater than my grief and need for revenge. And you've touched and saved the lives of people you'll never know." He gazed into her eyes. "*I'm* no hero, Phoenix. Maybe you aren't, either. But it's not always heroes who make the difference."

Phoenix remembered what Shepherd had said to her when she'd asked why Aegis sent her out into the Fringe. *"You were an unknown quantity, and that was exactly what we seemed to need. Not human, not full dhampir. And I knew you were motivated. You wanted to prove yourself. We decided to take a chance."*

He'd definitely been right about her need to prove herself. But she was done with that. Done with trying to show that she was as good, as capable, as confident as every other operative in the Enclave.

She was herself. She did the best she could. And sometimes that was good enough.

"No," she said slowly. "It's not always heroes." She kissed Drakon, and they were lost to the world for several minutes. Phoenix came back to herself when she smelled the subtle change in the air, felt the temperature begin to warm ever so slightly. She looked up at the sky.

"It's nearly dawn," she said. "We have to get you to shelter."

"I have my shelter," he murmured, refusing to let her go.

"This isn't a joke, Drakon. You have to get out of the sun, and then we have to find the others and help figure out—"

"Do you want a life with me, Phoenix?" he asked, searching her eyes.

"More than anything in the world. Haven't I made that clear?" She squeezed her eyes shut to keep the tears from spilling over. "But you can't go back to the Enclave. You'll return to Erebus, and I—"

"Together," he said stroking her lips with his fingertip. "Wherever we go, we'll go together. There are the new colonies…"

"Where we can spend our lives in hiding?" She shook her head. "Maybe for a while. But once the first political upheaval in the Enclave has settled, I need to return to San Francisco. I'll have to stay away for a while, until Matthew can testify as to what happened. But I can't leave him and those who think like him alone to handle the changes that are coming."

"I know," Drakon said, smiling at her with fondness and affection and pride. "That's why I'll go back with you, to prove that even an Opir can change and become an ally."

"No!" she gasped, turning to grab his arms. "They'll kill you!"

"Are you willing to let me take that risk?"

How could she refuse, when she'd asked him to let her do the same? If there was any hope for them, any chance of happiness, it had to be won openly. No disguises, no hidden identities. Only two people in—

Drakon had never said the words. He'd proven that Opiri could truly experience human feelings: compassion, shame, guilt, self-sacrifice. But that…

It was enough that he wanted to stay with her. It had to be.

"We'd better go find the others," she said, beginning to rise.

Drakon pulled her back down. "There's one more complication we have to work out," he said.

"We can talk about that later," she said, refusing to look at him.

"What about love, Phoenix?" he asked softly. "Can you, mostly human as you are, live without it?"

"I will never ask anything of you that you can't freely give," she said, trying to break away. "You know I love you. That's enough."

"No, it isn't," he said softly. "Not for me. Or for you. You deserve to be loved. And you are." He took her hand between his and kissed her knuckles. "And I love you, Phoenix."

There was only time for one final kiss. But it was a very, very good one. And Phoenix knew something new and better would arise from the ashes, as both of them had dreamed.

* * * * *

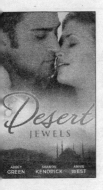

Discover more romance at

www.millsandboon.co.uk

- ❤ WIN great prizes in our exclusive competitions
- ❤ BUY new titles before they hit the shops
- ❤ BROWSE new books and REVIEW your favourites
- ❤ SAVE on new books with the Mills & Boon® Bookclub™
- ❤ DISCOVER new authors

PLUS, to chat about your favourite reads, get the latest news and find special offers:

- 🟦 Find us on facebook.com/millsandboon
- 🐦 Follow us on twitter.com/millsandboonuk
- ❤ Sign up to our newsletter at millsandboon.co.uk

B_WEB